DRAGON'S DESTINY

BOOK SIX OF THE WESTWOOD PACK

F.D. FAIR

Foundations Book Publishing
4209 Lakeland Drive, #398, Flowood, MS 39232
www.FoundationsBooks.net

Dragon's Destiny
Book 6
The Westwood Pack

ISBN: 978-1-64583-115-0

Published in the United States of America
Worldwide Electronic & Digital Rights
Worldwide English Language Print Rights

Prologue

The Prophecy

Ethina sat on her bed with her eyes closed and her breaths coming in a shallow, halting rhythm. She could feel the vision approaching. That was nothing new. She had seen visions for as long as she could remember. Even for an oracle, though, the visions become harder as time goes on. Her health had faded fast after the death of her mate, and she was no longer certain she had the strength to leave the vision unscathed. She had a feeling—somehow both terrible and peaceful—that this vision would be her last.

She did not resent the fact that death was rushing to meet her after all these years. It was only right. She had lived longer than any witch ought to because her fated mate was a dragon. He had shared his life force with her during their mating, granting her life-times far beyond her own. After his death, those years caught up with her, and they caught up quickly. She knew her children would be devastated when she was gone, but that is the inheritance all parents leave. Every child is born knowing there is a final farewell that they will—gods willing—be the ones to say. If that day came sooner than they had expected, she believed her children —Andres and Andrea—would forgive her.

The vision overtook her. Her body shook, and her eyes fluttered behind closed lids. She followed the images—the possible futures—as they sped past her, their edges blurring in their rush. There were many paths, but they all led to the same place.

There was only one ending, and it was total and utter destruction. Of everything. Of the earth. Of all the creatures living upon it. They were only awaiting retribution from a sleeping goddess who was prepared, finally, to cleanse the world of the parasite that is humanity. The Mother was frustrated and exhausted. She no longer worried about her children—the supernatural beings—who would not be spared from the extent of her vengeance.

Ethina sank into her straw mattress, her body and mind feeling weaker than they ever had before. She had hoped her final vision would be a happy one. She had hoped to catch a glimpse of the lives her children and grandchildren would lead once she was gone. Instead, she received certainty that the future is bleak—not only for her children but also for the entire world.

Although her heart is broken by this future, she has been an oracle long enough to know she has little chance of altering it. Even if she had the energy or strength to act, there are consequences for altering the flow of time. An oracle is bound to give the warnings the gods allow. Nothing more. Nothing less.

As her eyes drift closed, she wonders if they are closing for the last time. Before sleep and grief can take her, a final scene flits through her mind. This possible future rushes toward her as if it had been left behind by the others and is fearful of being forgotten altogether.

There is hope in that future. Ethina can recognize, from long experience, that this is the important scene—the only future that matters. This future holds the opportunity to save this world—to save her children and future grandchildren as well. She will not be there with them; she knows that. She will not be there to aid or comfort them, but she knows who needs to be there. She knows the only one who will do what needs to be done.

Ethina has been an oracle all her long life, and she knows now there is a final prophecy for her to deliver.

Chapter One

Andres—1000 years ago

I stare at the glassy lake as the sun begins to rise over it. The pale pinks and reds turn to oranges and more vibrant crimsons as they rise. I close my eyes, soak in the warmth of the first morning rays, and pray to the gods as I do every morning. It seems to be working for the most part...The world is at peace, and supernaturals and humans live in harmony. Shifters run, jump, and fly without prejudice. Vampires revel all night long with no worry of being hunted. They are all free as long as they obey the cardinal rule—do not feed upon anyone without their consent. Most of the sky, however, belongs to the dragons, and being the oldest and strongest of the supernatural races, we have been tasked with keeping peace on earth.

It should be a time to celebrate life. Perhaps others are doing just that, but not me. My mother is dying, and there is nothing I can do about it. I lift a smooth rock, running my thumb along the surface, and throw it across the lake, watching as it skips over a dozen times before it finally sinks beneath the surface.

"Andres, Mother wishes to speak with you," my sister calls

from the hill above me, breaking my peaceful morning routine. I turn toward her.

"It can't be happening already," I tell her, turning back toward the lake. I pick up another smooth rock, cocking back my arm and throwing. Instead of gliding along the surface of the water, however, the rock hits once and sinks. "I won't go."

"Avoiding her isn't going to stop this, Andres. You know that," she says. She approaches me with an apology in her blue eyes and places a graceful hand on my forearm.

"Surely she must hang on if I refuse," I plead. I'm not ready for her to leave this world. Perhaps I should be after almost three hundred years on this earth, but I'm not.

"She's been asking you to speak with her for days now. I'm afraid this will be your last chance. Please." Andrea sighs, and I know she is carrying just as much grief and pain as I am. "It's going to happen whether or not you are ready."

Reluctantly, I nod and briskly walk back toward our modest home. It's little more than a hut in the middle of nowhere, but it has always suited our purposes. It has four walls, a roof, and is always filled with love and laughter. At least, it was.

"Andres? Is that you?" my mother calls from her bed as the door squeaks open and then shut behind me.

"Yes, Mother. It's me," I respond sullenly and make my way to the chair beside her bed.

"Come now, Andres. Stop your pouting. I've lived a long life. Longer than any witch ought to. I had the love of a good man who gave me two beautiful children. I'm not afraid to die. It's the natural order of things," she says, her eyes filled with compassion and patience.

"Andrea and I—we will live such long lives. Why must you grow old and leave us? It's not fair. Why would the gods punish us like this?"

She's right; I am pouting. It is easier and less dangerous to succumb to pettiness instead of grief. As a dragon shifter, I will live thousands of years before age even touches me. My mother, a witch, is resigned to wither in her bed, dying of old age. Being mated to a dragon allowed her extra time and strength, but my father's death has stolen it all from her again.

"Andres," my mother scolds. "I raised you better than that. My mating with your father extended my life exponentially. No other witch on this earth is as old as I am. All this time has been a gift; the end of it cannot be a curse. Your father is waiting for me in the next life, and I'm ready to start anew with him." There is a tired smile on her thin lips, and her hand—so much thinner than I remember—is laying placidly atop my own. "You have distracted me, my dear. This is not what I need to tell you," she says. Her shaky breath dissolves into a cough.

Her breathing has become more labored with each visit, so I know her time is nearing. This is also why I have been avoiding coming to sit with her for several days. It is senseless, but I had hoped that her decline would not be so sharp if I was not here to witness it. I thought if I put off coming to her side, she would have no choice but to cling to life. I feel helpless having to watch her suffer while unable to do a thing about it.

When she first fell ill, I scoured the earth for a cure to this ailment or anything that would prolong her life. Short of attempting the transition to vampirism, I found nothing. Most supernaturals who undergo that transition don't survive. Although we live in peace, our different magics conflict so that there are few hybrids in this world. My sister and I are among them, but we were lucky that our mother's magic has never sought dominance over our dragons.

"I have one last vision to share with you," she tells me, looking tired and worn. Her normally bright green eyes and shiny silver hair seem dull. Even her skin has a yellow tinge that makes me uneasy and seems to be hanging from her bones.

"But you've always shared your visions with Andrea. Not me," I say in surprise.

"This one is not meant for Andrea. It's meant for you and you alone. You have a great destiny, my son. A destiny you cannot outrun, though I fear you will try. I need you to be strong. There is much I must tell you, and we seem to be nearly out of time," she struggles to sit upright, so I gently lift and adjust her. I pause for a moment, my arms wrapped gently around her frail body, and soak in the scent that is my mother. She smells like sunshine and lavender, a scent that is uniquely hers. As I release her and sit back in the small chair beside the bed, she nods, knowing that I was committing her scent to memory.

"Years from now," she begins, and I recognize the shift in her voice that signals she is speaking as an oracle and not just my mother, "the world will turn to darkness. Humans will rise, and the supernatural world will hide in the shadows."

"When?" I ask. I know better than to ask *how* or *why*. Her vision will come to pass regardless of what we do to stop it. It may rush toward us even faster if we attempt to change it.

"Hush now. Just listen. When the tides of the war begin to turn, you must take my granddaughter to the far north and place her in a deep sleep."

"But you don't..." I begin to tell her she doesn't have a granddaughter, but I am familiar with the impatient look she gives me and immediately quiet.

"Your sister will have a daughter. As I said, when the tides turn, you—and only you—must take her to slumber in the north. She is not to slumber with her parents. On that, the vision is very clear. Neither her parents nor you can join her. All will be unraveled if she does not rest alone."

"How will I know when and where?" I ask.

"You will know when it's time. Trust me. It will be a fight with your sister to allow this, but you and she must accept your roles to keep the future safe. Along with this, I've been given one last prophecy."

"*When the daughter of the storm and the son of the moon become one;*
A hunter and her prey put aside their differences;
The lost daughter of air mates the first son born of magic and fire;
A son and daughter of fire join together.
The dual-natured son and the dawn cement their bond.
A new age will arrive where supernatural beings will need to come out of the shadows as a new enemy awakens."

"But what do I have to do with that?" I ask. "There is no mention of me at all."

"You will need to guide them. If not, all hope of survival will be lost. On this path, you will also meet your mate. She will need time and understanding, on this I am certain, but yours will be a love to last the ages. A reward from the gods for your assistance," she says.

"What if I should fail or if these pairings do not come to be?" I try to not sound as fearful as I am. I am too caught up in the grief of her impending loss, and I cannot imagine bearing the weight of the future along with that grief. She closes her eyes and takes a deep, weary breath.

"I am afraid that the vision is very clear on that point as well.

Should the pairings not come to fruition, the world will fall into a darkness from which there is no return."

"A darkness? What do you mean?"

"Andres, if this prophecy fails, the saviors of the earth will not exist. It's not necessarily these pairings that will save the world, but their offspring. These mates and their children will be some of the most powerful beings the world has ever known. They are the future you must protect."

"But Mother, surely this can't all depend on me?" I plead.

"Andres, my son. You are the strongest of our kind and blessed by the gods yourself. You are the best chance we have. There is only one future in which we succeed," she tells me. Her hand reaches up to cup my cheek, and I cover it with my own. "I love you, son. Please remember that. In your darkest days, know that I will be with you always."

I watch as she takes her last breaths. Her eyes flutter shut, and her hand slips from my cheek.

"No. Please come back," I weep. I allow myself to crumple on her bed, my hands clutching at her hands. Sobs wrack my body. I have lost my mother and my dearest friend. After my father was taken from us last year, my mother became the one person I could turn to in a time of need. Without my mother, I alone hold the weight of our family and the politics of the supernatural community on my shoulders.

As the king of dragons, my father ruled with an iron fist, ensuring that everyone under our protection was kept in line in order to keep them safe. With him gone, the duty fell to me though I was unprepared and ill-suited for it. Now, with my mother gone, I have no choice. She can't cover for me any longer.

* * *

Five hundred years go by before my mother's prophecy shows signs of coming true. I have taken my rightful place as the king of dragons and head of the supernatural council with ease. Some would say that I'm not much of a leader and—given the fact that I try to stay out of most issues—they would be right. I'm not my father and never will be. If people want to quarrel amongst themselves, I let them. There's no use trying to stop nature. I do not ignore my duties, but I also do not make everyone's business my own. My mother taught me long ago that sometimes trying to fix a thing can only make it worse.

Even when you know something is coming, there's not much you can do to stop it. I wasn't cut out to be a leader, but I did what I could with my mother's warning. I tried telling them. They simply didn't believe me.

Now, though, they are starting to realize their error. With humans across the globe rising up against supernaturals, it seems clear that my mother's predictions of war are coming to fruition. Of course, supernaturals are faster and stronger than humans, but the amount of bloodshed makes my stomach churn. If something isn't done soon, there will be no humans left.

That is why I agree when someone on the council suggests that the supernatural factions go into hiding until things calm down instead of continuing the bloodshed. When it comes to a vote, I say yes. After days of deliberation and arguing, we come to an agreement and leave to make our arrangements. For the foreseeable future, we will no longer be able to shift in the open. Instead, we will need to blend in. If the humans do not know who to fight, the fighting may stop.

Time passes, and most of us adjust to the change. The transition isn't easy. In fact, some don't even try. I admit that going into the shadows isn't what I wanted either. There is something inherently unjust in having to inconvenience yourself just to back out of a fight you didn't start but could easily win. However, when my sister met her mate and gave birth to my niece soon after, everything changed. The importance of my family—its next generation so young and small—took precedence easily over my pride.

River, my niece, is beautiful and so full of life. Her dragon's scales are the color of the ocean. When she's flying, she looks like a wave crashing into the shore. I wish I could offer her a different world to live in. Because we must keep our existence a secret from the humans and hunters, she does not have the freedom to explore the skies that is her right.

It is not long until, just as my mother predicted, the tide in the war between humans and supernaturals turns with the arrival of the hunters from across the ocean. They claim to be descended from the gods themselves and are tasked with eradicating all supernatural species from the planet. At the first rumor of their landing, I waited. At the first widespread threat they issued without hesitation, I began to listen. As the first village burned to the ground, I worried I had waited too long already.

The ground is not yet cold under that village when I walk into my sister's house without knocking or greeting.

"Andrea, I need to talk to you."

"Yes," she says, looking at me skeptically.

"Alone," I tell her, looking at both River and her father before turning my gaze back to her.

"Surely anything you have to talk to me about can be said in front of my family," she responds with an accusatory glare.

"Not this." She opens her mouth to protest, but I continue, "It's about my last visit with our mother."

Her eyes widen in surprise, but she nods. "Can you two go out and get some more wood for the fire while I talk to Andres?"

"Sure," her mate, Michael, says. "Come on, River. Let's go see who can carry the most wood." The two of them race out the front door, each trying to beat the other.

"Okay Andres, what is this about?" Andrea asks once they are out of earshot.

"I need you to listen and not fight me on this," I warn her.

"Now you're scaring me," she responds, placing the dishes aside and taking the seat across from me.

"We all need to go into a slumber," I start.

"But River is only ten. We need to wait until she is an adult," she says.

"No. We need to go now. We cannot wait."

"Is this about the hunters? We've been careful." Like the rest of us, Andrea has been miserable under the new rule of secretiveness.

"It's not about the hunters," I say, then think again. "It isn't *really* about the hunters."

"Was this in Mother's last vision?" she asks.

"Yes."

She sighs but then shakes her head, resigning herself to the inconvenience and returning to her dishes. "We will find a spot and leave in the morning."

"That's not all," I say, dreading what comes next. I know it's going to be a fight. I would've known it was going to be a fight even without my mother telling me so many years ago. "River must slumber alone."

"No!" She slams the dishes down on the counter with a bang, turning toward me with a confused, murderous stare. "No, she absolutely does not."

"She must. Mother was very clear," I plead with her.

"Andres. She is only ten years old. She cannot slumber alone."

"Andrea," I sigh. "It's not what I want either, but that was the vision. Our mother was adamant that River must slumber alone, and that I must be the one to sing her to sleep."

"What?" she asks, her hand on her chest and her eyes filled with unshed tears. "I can't even put my own child in her first slumber?"

I walk over and wrap her in a hug. "I'm sorry. I wish it could be different. But no, you can't. You must—we must—trust in Mother's vision. She was right about everything else."

"Then this is the first time she's wrong, Andres," she says, stepping out of my embrace and shaking her head violently. "I can't—I won't—leave my daughter."

"Andrea," I plead. "We have no choice. If we don't follow her instructions, terrible things will come to pass."

"What, Andres? What will happen?" she begs me to tell her.

"I can't. You know this. Mother told me the vision was meant for me alone. I didn't ask what the repercussions of telling you would be, but I know she did not intend for me to share it." I am uncertain how to argue this with her when I am feeling only apologetic.

"No, Andres. I refuse. Vision, prophecy—whatever—or not, I will not be allowing my only child to slumber alone," she says without looking back at me. "We reject this prophecy."

"Andrea, be reasonable," I beg of her.

"Reasonable?" she exclaims and turns on me, her eyes alight with rage. "You want me to be reasonable? You're asking me to allow my only daughter to slumber alone. Alone!"

Her face is a mixture of sadness and rage. Both of which I understand but can do nothing about. Ever since River was born, I knew that this day was coming. I have had a decade to prepare, but my sister has not had that luxury. The pain and anger are still fresh and new to her.

"I know what I'm asking of you. Do you think I want to let River slumber alone? I love her just as much as you do. If there was anything I could do to change it, you know I would," I explain as I begin to pace across her wooden floor.

She slumps into a chair. "I know you do. It's just—this. It's impossible..." She sounds so defeated, as if I'm breaking her heart with my words alone.

I walk over and kneel in front of her. "I know it seems that way. I promise you that if there were any other way..." I take a deep breath to steady my emotions and take hold of her hands. "Trust me when I say she will be all right. Mother assured me of that. It's the rest of us I'm not sure of."

She blinks back her tears as she allows this thought to settle. The only thing I know for sure is that River will live long enough to meet her mate and become part of this prophecy. Whatever harm allowing her to slumber alone could cause, it will not keep her from waking safely when the time comes.

"Tomorrow?" she asks.

I nod. "Tomorrow."

I leave for the night to allow them to have time alone as a family. When I return in the morning, River is waiting.

"Uncle Andres, do I really have to slumber alone?" she asks, her big doe eyes glazed with the early morning light.

"I'm afraid so. But I promise I will stay with you until you fall asleep," I reassure her. "Give your parents a hug. We will leave soon."

With tears in her eyes, she turns to her parents. They wrap their arms around her, and I hear my sister's sobs as tears fall from my own eyes.

Through tears, Andrea crouches down and smiles into River's face. "My dear one," she says, clearly trying to assuage her daughter's fear. "I will miss you so much. But it will be just like a night to you. You will rest, and when you wake it will be as morning. We will be there to wake you."

When my sister rises to look at me, her eyes and tone are more stony and desperate.

"Somewhere safe," she pleads. "You'll stay with her until she's asleep."

"Of course, I will." I also walk over and wrap my arms around the three of them. I'm going to miss them as well. "You two also need to slumber. Find somewhere far away from here."

We stand there and embrace for a long while, but we can't stand like this forever.

"River, let's go," I say, stepping back far sooner than I would like. If I don't leave with River now, I'm afraid my resolve will break. I can't let that happen.

Being the courageous little girl that she is, she steps away from her parents and takes my hand. "How are we going to get there?" she asks.

"We're going to fly, of course," I tell her with a smile. She tries to contain it, but her body begins to vibrate with excitement.

We shift and fly together to the north. We have both been unable to fly for too long, and I make sure we take the time to enjoy this journey. We stay hidden above the clouds, so there's nothing to stop us from doing a few loops and barrel rolls. River is so much smaller than I am, and she likes to flaunt it with a line of back-to-back flips. I am happy to give her this opportunity to stretch her wings before her rest. I'm not sure what the future holds. I only pray that we see each other again. If I am to believe what my mother saw, we will. When my will begins to waiver, that is the thought I turn to. I will see her again.

We are nearing mountains when I feel a tingle in my gut. It takes me a moment to place the sensation, but I realize it is what my mother warned me to look out for. This must be the place we are looking for. This is where River must go for her slumber.

I lower myself, cast about below me for an opening, and land on the ground while River follows close behind. That's when I see it. It is a large cave surrounded by forest. The opening is somewhat obscured by trees, and this area is uninhabited by man or animal. It is the perfect spot for someone to go for their first slumber.

I lead River in that direction, sniffing the air for any evidence that we may be intruding upon someone else's but find nothing.

We make our way through winding caves deeper into the cave. We come to a large, open cavern but can go no farther as the entrance is too small for us to pass through. We shift back into our human forms instead.

"Will you stay with me until I fall asleep?" River asks, sounding concerned as she tries to get comfortable in the corner.

"Of course, I will," I promise as I sit beside her. I brush her golden blonde hair back in soothing motions as I sing the lullaby of our people. The song is the secret to calming our dragons and lulling them into their long slumbers.

"Will we see each other again?" she asks between yawns.

"I hope so, sugar," I tell her, placing a soft kiss on the top of her head.

I sit there for a while after she falls asleep, watching as her body automatically shifts from the sweet, pale girl into her massive, verdant dragon. If it weren't for the brighter blue of her scales, she could blend in with the slate-gray walls of the cavern. I send a silent prayer to the gods that I live to see her again.

When I can't take it anymore, I give River a kiss on the scales atop her head and begin my flight south. I don't know where I'm headed. I just know that I can't stay close to River, or I will not be able to control myself. If I am near enough to find and protect her, I know that I will. I need to find a place to slumber so deeply that there is no temptation.

Eventually, I find a spot deep in the rainforest. There, in a cliff-side cave hidden by a waterfall, I settle my weary wings, impatient already to wake again. Something about this cave feels right. I guess that my mother was right about that as well.

My last thoughts as I fall asleep are of my family. I send up another prayer to the gods that my family survives whatever comes next. If need be, I offer myself up as a sacrifice.

I let the gods know I'd accept that deal. I'd happily die in place of any of them.

Chapter Two

Drusilla–Sixteen Years Ago

"Psst. Dru," my brother whispers from the door of my room. I turn my eyes to him and take in his appearance. His always-perfect blonde hair is styled messily, and his big blue eyes that match mine sparkle with mischief.

"Yes?" I whisper back, not entirely sure why we're whispering.

He looks both ways down the hallway before scrambling into my room and closing the door quietly.

"We're all going to a human party in town. Do you want to come?" he offers, and my eyes go wide.

"Me?" I point at my chest, and he chuckles and nods.

"Really?" I squeal, and he puts his finger to his lips, glancing back at the door.

"Mom and Dad don't know," he reasons.

"Oh. Okay," I whisper back. "Can Breanne come? Please." He groans, and I know he's already regretting inviting me. I know he's not Bre's biggest fan, but she's my best friend. As if I'd actually go to my first human party without her.

He groans again but nods.

"Yay!" I whisper excitedly, clapping my hands with exaggerated silence.

"We're leaving in an hour," he says and stands up.

"Thank you, Drakey," I say, climbing off the bed and wrapping my arms around his neck.

"You're welcome. If you two are going to sneak out to parties, I'd rather you come with me."

I pull back from his embrace.

"How do you know about that?" I whisper. We were planning on sneaking out to a party at some point this summer. The human kids have big bonfire parties on the beach every weekend. We've watched from afar, wishing to be included. Every time we've asked for permission to go, the answer is the same. No.

Drake chuckles. "I'm only two years older than you, Drusilla. You act like I don't remember what it was like to be sixteen."

"Yeah, but you only like to associate with vampires," I challenge. He's never wanted to make friends with any other species—humans or supernatural.

"That's still true. I don't want to make friends with humans. But, eventually, I will want to have personal donors. Drinking blood from a bag is getting old." He licks his lips at the thought of drinking directly from the source.

"Bagged blood is good," I say adamantly.

He wrinkles his nose. "That's just because you don't know any different."

"And you do?" I challenge. When a guilty look passes over his face, I decide I don't want to know. "Let's agree to disagree on that," I add, dismissing him. I turn to my closet and begin cataloging my outfit options.

Once I hear the door close once more, I rush over to the phone and dial Breanne.

"Hello?" My best friend's voice, made tinny by the phone, is a familiar greeting by now. As of Bre's last birthday, we both have phone lines connected in our rooms. That, among so many other things, may be why people accuse us of being spoiled. The accusations are not entirely incorrect.

"Bre! You'll never guess where we're going tonight," I squeal despite still whispering.

"Where?" she asks impatiently.

"Drake's taking us to a human party," I whisper into the phone, cupping my hands around it.

"What?!" she exclaims, her voice so loud that I have to pull the receiver away from my ear.

I chuckle. "Just put on your best outfit and get your butt over here." I hang up the phone to the sound of her heaving clothes and hangers out of her over-full closet.

I turn back to my own closet, assessing and trying so many outfits that they all seem to blur together until I hate them all. Eventually, I settle on my dark-wash jeans and baby-blue halter top. I had planned on wearing my miniskirt, but Drake probably wouldn't let me leave the house wearing it anyway. Besides, I look pretty good in blue.

I sit at my vanity and put on my makeup. Sparkly blue eyeshadow and thick black mascara highlight my eyes, and a little bit of blush pinks each cheek. After swiping some of my pink gloss over my lips, I crimp my hair with my hands to add some volume to my straight, blonde hair.

The door bangs open and closed quickly, and I am wrapped in a hug from my friend before I can even turn around.

I look at her wide, blue eyes in the mirror. Her platinum blonde hair is tucked up into a high ponytail, and her smile is so big that I think her cheeks may split open.

"I can't believe Drake's letting us go," she whispers.

"I know," I squeal, standing and jumping up and down with her.

A soft knock on the door makes us both stop.

"Yes?" I call out.

Drake steps in and studies us. His eyes narrow when he sees Bre in her miniskirt and tube top. I knew he wouldn't have approved if I dressed like that. "You two ready?"

I pick up my clutch and nod. "We were born ready."

As the three of us head out of the complex, Drake peeks around each corner to ensure that we don't run into our parents. As amazing as our parents are, they're also the leaders of the coven. Having their children sneak out to human parties isn't part of the image they want to portray.

Once we make it outside, we meet up with a few of Drake's friends: Colin, Matt, and Albus. I internally snort. There's something about the name Albus that makes me laugh every time I hear it.

Drake leads us through the wooded area behind our compound toward the public beach, and we all use our vampiric speed to make the trip incredibly quick. He stops just shy of the sand, spinning to face Bre and me.

"You two," he says, but I'm too busy looking past him. Dozens of humans are running around on the sand, playing football, splashing in the waves, and sitting around a huge bonfire. My body is thrumming with excitement. "Earth to Dru." He snaps his fingers in my face, and I scowl at him.

"What?" I shove his hand from my face. "That's rude."

"Now that I have your attention. You will not feed. You will stay with the group. No wandering off." Once we both nod, he turns on his heel and leads us the rest of the way.

"This is amazing," Bre whispers, and I nod, my eyes darting around, unable to focus on one single thing.

"Oh, and here," Drake says, handing us each a small vial.

"Why?" I ask, wondering why he's giving us blood right now.

"Put a few drops in your glass of beer. It's the only way you'll be able to keep it down, and it'll help you fit in." I nod, tucking the vial in my bra to keep it safe. Drake rolls his eyes at me but doesn't say anything as he and his friends head straight toward the group playing football. I watch with wide eyes as some of the humans greet him as they would a friend. Like they've known each other for years.

"I didn't think your brother liked humans," Bre says. I just shrug, not wanting to explain the reasons why he's suddenly so interested in mingling, and pull her toward the kegs of beer. I only recognize them from the movies I've seen, but I am still not completely sure how they work. Bre and I stand there with cups in hand, already primed with a few drops of blood, as we try to strategize where to start.

"Here. Let me," a musical voice says. Its owner reaches his hand out, grabs a long tube from somewhere on the contraption, and presses the little button on the top. Instantly, liquid fills my cup. I turn to him, my mouth dropping open. Holy shit. He's incredibly handsome. No. He's hot. His brown hair is shaggy and long enough to brush his shoulders, and his arms are thick with muscles and covered in dark, unfamiliar tribal tattoos. Oh, gods. His face is perfect. It is like an angel came down from heaven and is standing in front of me.

He notices that I am checking him out and smirks. I shake my head and try to un-drop my jaw. "Thanks."

"No problem. I'm Price," he says, sticking out his hand for me to shake.

"Drusilla," I respond, placing my hand in his. Instantly, tingles travel up my arm. A solid elbow to my ribs has my mind clearing quickly, and I turn in that direction to see Bre with an impatient, raised eyebrow. "Oh, and this is my friend Bre."

She doesn't seem as enamored with him as I am. It is probably a good thing since I'm pretty sure I would be upset.

After their introductions, she turns to me. "I'm going to go dip my toes in the water."

"I'll come," I say, not wanting to leave her alone.

"No. No. You stay here with Price. I'll be fine," she says it with a wink, and I blush.

"We can go sit on the rocks over there so we can see her," Price suggests pointing to a more secluded location.

"Okay," I squeak out, suddenly nervous. I am not in danger of being hurt, but this experience is entirely unfamiliar to me. I've never felt this attracted to another person in my entire life. The thought that he may be my mate slips into my brain. Vampires can't sense their mate with certainty until they are over eighteen and at full power. Until then, though, the mating bond presents as an intense and sudden attraction. The attraction, at least, is already certain.

Price and I sit and talk for hours about everything and nothing at the same time. He probes a few times about my family and school, but I keep my answers vague and turn the conversation back to him. There's no easy way to explain my living situation to a human. I tell him that I go to a private, girls-only school in Europe. He looks as if he doesn't really believe me. If I was smarter, I probably would've thought of a more believable lie, but I've never been in a situation like this before and panicked.

I am jarred out of our calm by the alarm on my watch. It beeps, warning me that it's time to go. I blink back my confusion. It can't be time already. After glancing back at my watch and once at the lightening sky, I see that time has passed more quickly than I could have imagined.

Something deep inside me rebels. I don't want to leave him.

"I have to go," I tell him, catching sight of Bre already walking toward us on the beach.

"Stay and watch the sunrise with me," he begs, and I turn to the water wanting nothing more than to watch the sunrise over it. I bet it's beautiful, but I shake my head.

"We snuck out and need to be back before our parents wake up," I explain.

"Surely they won't be up until after the sun rises."

I chuckle. "Oh, they'll be up." Little does he know that my parents will probably be just getting home after checking that the compound is locked down for the day.

"Well, then. Meet me here again tonight. Same time?" He brings his hands up to cup my face, merging his lips with mine softly. I moan and wrap my arms around his neck.

This kiss ends far too soon, and I bring my hand up to touch my lips. It is my first kiss, and it is incredible. Of course, I will find a way to meet him if this is what waits for me.

"I'll meet you tonight," I whisper and back away from him before I do something stupid like give away my virginity as the sun rises and burns me to ash. I turn back to him quickly. "Can you bring a friend for my friend?" I ask, gesturing toward Bre.

"Absolutely." He smiles and nods.

I step up on my tiptoes and place one soft kiss on his lips. "Until tonight," I say, walking away.

"Can't wait," he calls after me as I catch up with Bre.

"You're glowing," she whispers, linking her arm with mine.

"I think I'm in love," I admit. "I'm meeting him again tonight. He's going to bring a friend." I wiggle my eyebrows at her.

"I don't know..." she starts, and I pull her to a stop.

"Please, Bre," I beg, using the sad eyes that I know always work on her. "Pretty please?"

She rolls her eyes. "Fine. But you owe me."

I clap my hands in excitement.

We meet up with Drake and his friends and make our way back home without the smile ever leaving my face. Not once.

My first human party! My first kiss! It is the first of many, I hope. If the way I'm feeling about Price is any indication, he could even be my mate.

I fall asleep the second my head hits my pillow and dream of a life with Price.

*   *   *

I wake up before the sun goes down. It's early, but I am too excited to stay in bed any longer. I hop straight into the shower and spend a few extra minutes shaving. Even though I'm only sixteen, I know that there's a good chance things will go at least a little bit further tonight. I still vividly remember the way my body reacted to being near Price, and I have hopes that Bre will like his friend enough to give us some time alone.

I get out of the shower, dry off, and put on my prettiest underwear set underneath my sundress. I would have picked my miniskirt, but I saw the look Drake gave Bre last night. I don't have to tell him everything, but I know I'll need his help if I want to sneak out again tonight.

"Drusilla." The voice from the doorway startles me.

Speak of the devil.

Drake steps into my room and stands behind me at the vanity. "What are you doing?"

I turn to look up at him instead of his reflection. "I'm going back to the beach to meet some friends."

He shakes his head. "Nope. Absolutely not."

"Come on. You can't introduce me to all that fun and then expect me not to go again," I complain.

"Then I'll come with you," he says, getting up and walking toward the door. I grab his arm before he reaches the door and pull him back.

"You can't."

"Why not?" he challenges, raising an eyebrow.

"Because I'm meeting a boy," I whisper, pleading with my eyes for him not to go crazy.

"No," he growls out.

"Drake," I say, putting my hands on my hips. "He's just a human. It's not like I'm going to get hurt."

He scrubs his hand down his face with a groan. "I'll just stay nearby in the trees."

"No. I'm bringing Breanne with me. We'll be fine." I grab his hands and give him my most reassuring smile.

He holds my stare for a moment before he relents. "Fine. But if you're not home by four, I'm coming to get you."

I jump up and kiss him on the cheek. "You're the best big brother anyone could ever have."

He rolls his eyes at me. "Don't make me regret this."

"I won't. I promise," I say, rushing back to my vanity to put the finishing touches on my face. Drake settles on my bed with a sigh, but it's only a few minutes before I am ready for him to help me sneak out. I know it's going against everything inside him to let me go on my own, but I'm so happy he is.

We meet up with Breanne, and Drake leads us through the compound despite being silent and surly. His skill makes me wonder just how often he's been sneaking out on his own. At the edge of the beach, he turns me around to face him.

"Four o'clock," he says, a finger pointing at me in warning. He looks shockingly like our father in that moment. "Not a second later."

"Yes sir." I give him a salute, and Breanne and I rush off in the direction of the beach.

"Are you ready for this?" Bre asks, and I nod, slowing down as we reach the edge of the trees.

"Oh man, you have no idea," I respond, hip-bumping her.

I see Price standing at the water's edge with a friend and walk toward him faster. He opens his arms wide, and I launch myself into them. I am suspended there only for a moment before he shocks me by letting go. Bre is only a few steps behind me when I fall to the sand in a heap.

When I look up into Price's face again, I am unsure if I am confused, offended, or just angry. However, he no longer looks like the angel I met the night before. His mouth is pulled into a snarl that makes him look mean and ugly.

"What is—" I begin, but then look around and notice that it is not just Price and his friend on the sandy shore. Somehow, we're surrounded. There are at least a dozen men on the beach with us now. They are clearly adults, but they are dressed in black and many hold weapons.

"Price?" I probe, dragging my eyes back to his transformed face. "What is going on?"

He snarls, bringing his face down close to mine. "What's going on is that you're going to get exactly what you deserve."

What the hell does that mean?

Before I can question it, a metal collar is clamped around my neck, and a gag is secured in my mouth. I try to use my fangs to break through the gag, but it doesn't seem to work. I throw my head back, but whoever is holding me doesn't seem to notice as I fight to wrench myself out of their grasp. I don't know what material the gag is made of, but my fangs can't cut through it.

I catch a glimpse of Breanne being loaded into the bed of a truck. I am not sure where the truck came from, but I see her kicking and fighting just like I am. I cry out for her, but the sound is muffled by the material in my mouth.

Her eyes meet mine anyway and widen. I know what the look means. She is looking to me for safety, begging me to do some-thing...to save her.

I flail my arms, fighting with everything I have. I am no match for these men though. Even though I am supernatural, I am horribly outnumbered and unprepared.

An unexpected prick in my neck is a particular insult, and it has my eyes widening in rage before they blur into darkness.

My arms drop, and my knees buckle. I crash into the sand again as my assailant finally releases me. I have lost control of my limbs, and he knows I cannot run away.

Just before everything goes black, my sluggish mind dredges up a few senseless concerns.

How long do I have until sunrise?

My brother is going to kill me.

Chapter Three

Andres—Present Day

I return to the spot where I had left River to sleep for the hundredth time. The first time I rushed here after waking from my own sleep, I had expected to find her right where I left her, waiting for me to wake her up. As each time before, however, there is no sign of her. Against all evidence, the hope in my heart keeps leading me back to this cave. After leaving yet another message carved into the walls with instructions to stay here and wait for me, I abandon the site to continue my search elsewhere. Each time I return to this place, I stay for twenty-four hours before moving on, and each time I leave a piece of my heart in this cave at my departure.

I've searched the entire continent and found no sign of her. My next step is to expand across the ocean. If she were scared or searching for her parents, she may have gotten lost. Although she is a young dragon, she could theoretically still make it across the ocean. I get a running start and shift into my gray dragon. He's getting just as anxious as I am about finding her. I urge him to climb higher in the sky, and we use the clouds as cover before we surge forward toward the ocean.

After three days of nearly constant flying, I find myself above what they now call Europe searching for any sign of River, Andrea, or Michael. At this point, I'd be happy to find any of them. Of course, my focus is on finding River, but surely that search would move faster with her mother or father here to help. With no sign of them, I give myself one more day before I head back to the pack. I hope I'll make it before the hunters show up.

I'm flying above the clouds, sending out probes through my bonds with them, when I feel the overwhelming rage coming from Drusilla. I send out one last distress call to my family through our silent mental link and speed back to the pack, back to her. Although she doesn't even know who I am, Drusilla is the woman of my dreams. If she were any other person, I wouldn't be able to feel her emotions from this distance. She isn't just any other person though. She's my mate.

It's not like her to be full of rage like she is at this moment. Even during my slumber, I've been able to feel her emotions since the day she was born. It was my signal that my mate was alive somewhere in the world. At first, her emotions were the normal ones I would expect from any young person: happiness, sadness, anger, and excitement. At some point, though, something changed. She was constantly fearful, sad, and despondent.

I tried to wake myself. I was desperate to find her and help her, but nothing I did worked. Then, when Sebastyn and Sarah woke me, something in my mate changed once more. I could sense her becoming stronger, more confident, and even happy.

This sudden shift to rage is unexpected. I know she is safely among the Westwood pack with Sebastyn and Sarah. I can only guess this change means the hunters have arrived. They had expected this eventuality, but I pray they are ready for it now.

I'm growing more concerned by the minute and urge myself to fly faster. When I'm halfway there, the grief hits me, and I falter mid-flight. The pain is so intense that I feel my heart constrict. Oh, no. Surely she could only feel this kind of grief if someone close to her was injured or, worse, dead.

If something happened to Drake or Rayne, I may be in trouble. The prophecy depends upon their mating. I send a silent thanks to the gods that my mate is at least still alive and pray that her brother and friend are safe as well.

Hours feel like years, and I am exhausted by the time I land among the Westwood pack. The alpha house is before me, and I spot Drake and Rayne. The strong bonds now connecting them are visible to me, and I release a sigh of relief. If they are safe, why is Drusilla feeling this way?

"Oh, good. You two have bonded," I say, surprising them as I walk through the trees.

"Bonded?" Rayne asks looking from me to Drake. I guess I have put my foot in my mouth. That is the saying, right? I still have much to catch up on.

"It is one of the side effects of me turning you," Drake tells Rayne. "It's a perk if I say so myself." He's in for it. If he doesn't recognize the look that she's giving him right now, he will soon. I don't know her at all, but even I know what that look means.

"Drake," she warns but turns back to me. "Did you know that we would be able to walk in the sun when we bonded?"

"I wasn't certain, but I had my suspicions," I reply. I didn't know what the outcome of their bonding would be, but they are a part of the prophecy. I am not surprised that their bond has resulted in something special. Although Rayne does not seem aware of it, there's a dormant magic buried deep in her that sets her apart regardless of her relationship with Drake.

"Great. Just great. More people with suspicions," Rayne mumbles, throwing her hands up in the air before stomping away.

"You need to keep this among your trusted allies. No one can find out. Not yet," I call out.

"Or what?" Rayne challenges, turning to face me.

"Well, I would imagine there will be quite a few vampires who would love to be able to walk around in the sun. Just imagine what they would do to get that power," I reply before shifting and flying away. I'm utterly exhausted, but I don't trust myself not to drop a few secrets if I'm around them too long.

As they enter the house, I can feel relief replacing Drusilla's grief. She obviously feared one or both had died. Now that I've seen them both alive and safe and felt my mate's relief, I can return to my search for River. I long to go inside and be with my mate, but finding my niece is my main priority right now.

For the first week, I don't go far. I keep an eye on Drusilla's emotions. Luckily, other than flickers of loneliness, she's in relatively good spirits. After an entire week of calm, I head back over to Europe to continue my search.

It's another long, luckless trip across the ocean. Another week wasted. If I could get near enough to any of them, I'd be able to pick up a hint of their emotions. Everywhere I go, however, it is like they've simply disappeared. Until I've searched every corner of this earth, I will not give up hope that I will find my family.

With hope in my heart but nothing to show for it, I make my way back to Canada. As I get closer to pack lands, I feel it. There is a trickle down my familial bond. *River.* She's alive, she's...I search her emotions. She's happy. She's even excited. From the skies above, I try to pinpoint her location.

It can't be. Can it?

She's inside the home of Alaric and Phoebe.

What?

I crash to the ground, barely slowing for my landing. There's a rumble in my chest as a small girl with golden hair jumps off the steps and launches herself at me. I shift quickly, returning to human form so that I can hold my niece.

"Uncle Andres!" she exclaims. I wrap my arms around her,

holding her to me tightly, afraid that this might be a dream. Goddess knows I've dreamt of this enough times.

"My sweet, sweet, sugar. You're here. You're safe. I've been searching for you," I whisper as I drop to my knees. There are so many emotions caught in my throat, and I know they are not only mine but hers as well. We both thought we'd never see each other again.

She steps back and puts her hands on her hips. She is the spitting image of her mother at that age.

"Where were you?" she demands.

I look at her in awe. My sweet sugar has always been so sweet, but the girl standing in front of me isn't quite the same as I left her. She's hardened somehow.

"I've been searching for you and your parents since I awakened just over a month ago. When did you wake? Why weren't you at the cave?"

At the slight growl in my voice, her eyes soften and flit to the ground briefly. "I tried to stay at the cave and wait for you. Truly, I did. But then I heard these sounds. Beeping and whooshing. I just had to see what they were. I'm sorry."

I open my arms up wide, and she rushes back into them. "It doesn't matter. All that matters is that we're together now. Two dragons will find your parents faster than one," I tell her.

Once again, she steps back. "I know where they are. Well, where Mama is. Da is probably with her. But we can't go there. Promise me you'll never go there," Fear is plastered on her face as she pleads with me.

"What are you talking about? Where's your mother, and why can't I go there?" I am so confused. She's obviously scared, and I seem to have missed something very important.

As Drake and Rayne step down the steps, I instinctively push River behind me and growl. They both raise their hands to show they aren't a threat, but it's not until River slaps me on the back that I stop.

"Don't growl at them. They're my friends. They rescued me."

I swivel from Drake and Rayne to look at my niece. "Rescued you? From where? From whom?"

"Andres. Is there a chance we can talk for a minute?" Rayne says before River can answer. I glance up to see the slim, newly made vampire wringing her hands in front of her.

As much as I don't want to let River out of my sight, I'm not sure I want her around for what my reaction is going to be to Rayne's news. The guilt rolling off her and the concern seeping out of Drake's pores are worrying me.

"Okay, sugar. We can talk after. Go inside with Phoebe and Alaric. I need to talk to Drake and Rayne for a minute."

She nods. "I wanted to play with Riley some more anyway," she gives me a kiss on the cheek and whispers, "I missed you," before skipping back into the house.

We all watch until the door closes before we turn back to one another.

"Andres, I'm so sorry," Rayne starts but is quickly cut off by Drake.

"I told you that you are not to blame."

She sighs, but the guilt doesn't fade.

"Just spit it out," I say through clenched teeth, rising to my feet.

"My father had her locked away," Rayne says, looking at the ground. Her father? The hunter?

"How long?" I ask, unable to formulate full sentences. They share a look with each other. "Rayne, how long?" I repeat my question with more force.

"She said two years," she replies.

"Two years?" I scream, the rumble from my chest strong enough to shake the ground.

Rayne nods sullenly, her eyes on the ground. Drake watches me warily under tense brows.

"Where is your father?" I ask, ready to go murder the man who dared keep my niece captive.

"He's dead. Drusilla killed him," Drake explains.

I don't know whether I feel more relieved or angry at the fact he's dead. I would move heaven and earth to be able to watch the life leave his eyes. Knowing that my mate was anywhere near that man doesn't give me any relief.

I do not know much about Rayne's father, but my mind is already spiraling. A hunter had my niece. She was trapped with him for two years. I can't help but consider the things she could've been subjected to.

"You have more to say. You need to just spit it out before I jump to conclusions." I try to sound calm, but it comes out with more force than necessary. It still does the trick.

"You already know the hunters attacked two weeks ago—just before we bonded. My father shot me, and Drake turned me. Drusilla went on a rampage and slaughtered all the hunters in her path," Rayne begins, and tears form in her eyes. At first, I think she's mourning the loss of her father, but then she speaks. "When I was younger, my father captured a young vampire girl. He kept her locked in a shed in our yard for six years before I was allowed inside. I helped her escape, but I was never allowed back in the shed after that. I fooled myself into thinking that he wasn't keeping anyone else in there." She wipes the tears from her face, and Drake places his arm around her.

"Last night, we returned to her father's house," Drake begins, his tone souring over the word father. "We know the hunters have a facility somewhere—a lab—where they keep and experiment on supernaturals. With that group of hunters already decimated, we decided it would be safe to search for information there."

"We didn't find anything in the house," Rayne cuts him off. I can tell he's trying to make this story easier for her, but I do not have the patience for it. "We broke into the shed to search there too. That's where we found River. I'm so sorry, Andres. I didn't know." She is both pleading and ashamed. "If I knew, I would have released her. You have to believe me..."

I understand the guilt now. She believes she should have rescued River too.

"Rayne, it wasn't your fault. Everyone can understand why you didn't look too close after what you and Drusilla went through," Drake tries to console his mate.

"Drusilla? What does she have to do with this?" I ask, my eyes snapping to the house and back to the couple in front of me.

Rayne looks up at me with her tear-soaked eyes. "Drusilla was the young vampire girl my father held captive. The girl I set free."

The growl that comes out of me at the thought of either Drusilla or River being subjected to the hunters is ferocious. I shift and take to the skies, leaving them on the ground below me. I can't control my emotions or put a cap on my empathy right now, so it's better if I go somewhere to cool down. Feeling my rage is bad enough, but having to feel the guilt from Rayne is too much.

I land back at River's cave, and I sit at the edge of a hot spring I found during one of my previous stays. I understand Rayne's guilt, but I also understand it wasn't her fault. Being away from all their emotions is clearing the fog of rage from me, and I can breathe. But I still have questions.

What is this facility? Where is Andrea? Why doesn't River want me to find her? I need the answers, but I can't bring myself to be around anyone just yet. I need to find my center. So, I pray to Gaia for guidance and strength. I need both if I am going to confront the events of the past two years of River's life.

Goddess, two years. She's just a child. Why would hunters take such a small, innocent thing? What use could they have had for her?

I sit and meditate for a while, using the techniques my mother taught me to control my empathic abilities. I haven't had to do this in a very long time.

There is a trickle of water dripping down from the cave ceiling, and I match my breath to its slow drips.

In—Drip—Out—Drip.

Soon, I find myself in a remarkably familiar space. Here is the haven I have built in my own mind. I have not visited in a long while, but it is a relief to feel only my own emotions in this space. I can open and close the door at will, allowing myself moments of peace from the bombardment of emotions from those around me. I keep it locked up tight, not allowing any emotions but my own to flow freely.

Once I've gained a semblance of control over my emotions and hopefully the effect that others have on me, I head back to pack land to talk with River.

"Uncle Andres, you're back," River says, rushing to me.

"Of course. I just needed to gain some control. I'll always come back for you," I whisper to her as I wrap my arms around her.

"I know, and I understand. Mama always said it must be really hard to have a gift like yours," she murmurs back.

I nod. "Speaking of your mama...I need to ask you about where you saw her," I explain as I push her back a bit. I try to search her face for any sign of what she's been through, but she still looks like the little girl I sang to sleep so long ago. Tears brim in her eyes, and she shakes her head no. "I'm sorry, sugar. But I need you to tell me."

She takes a deep breath. "I saw her at the facility."

"The facility? The one Rayne told me about?" I question, taking deep breaths in and out to remain in control of my anger. I place a block on my empathy, so I don't have to feel the terror rolling through her at the mention of that place. Even with the block, though, I can smell it on her.

She nods her head.

"Did you talk to her?" I ask.

She shakes her head. "No. But she talked to me in my mind. She told me to be strong. She told me not to shift for them and to never return. She told me that you would come for me." Her voice breaks as tears well up in her eyes and drop down her cheeks.

"I'm sorry, sugar. You don't have to say more right now." She wraps her arms around me tight before beginning to sob. I rub her back and console her until her sobs slow.

"Thank you, Uncle Andres," she sniffs. "You're going to get Mama, aren't you?"

"I am, but I promise you I won't go alone. If your parents are still there, I will bring them back to you," I try to reassure her.

"Okay," she says.

We embrace one more time, and I can feel Drusilla come closer.

My mother warned me that she would need time and patience. It may be difficult, but I am willing to give her both. Rayne's brief retelling of their history explains some of the emotions I felt from her so many years ago, and I would at least like to tell her what we are to each other. From what I have learned of the present day, there's very little chance she will realize our connection the way I have. It doesn't seem fair for me to know so much about her without her even knowing I'm her mate.

I spot her hiding within the trees.

Her blonde hair shines in the low light of the yard, making her look like the angel she is. Her petite frame is easily hidden behind a tree, though I can see it clearly in my mind. She is so small, especially compared to my huge body. I suddenly feel hulking and brutish by the comparison.

I worry about the pairing, but then I remember that the gods would not have paired us together if we weren't perfectly made for one another. Her blue eyes sparkle with curiosity and hesitation.

She realizes I am looking back at her, and her rose-colored lips pop open in surprise before she darts back behind the tree.

My perfect little mate.

If I was a weaker man, the thrill of the chase would've overtaken me already. But I'm not weak, and I know that I need to wait.

Especially after what Drake and Rayne told me.

Chapter Four

Drusilla

When Drake and Rayne didn't return this morning after the trip to her father's house, I knew where they would be. Whenever they get caught out in daylight, they go to the pack. After all, there is a limited number of people who know their secret, and the chances of the pack gossiping to other vampires are slim. We're friendly, but not that friendly.

The shifters probably just assume they're wearing some kind of super sunblock. I wish that existed. It would make everyone's life so much easier. Living out an immortal life only at night can get boring. As we grow older, light becomes less and less lethal, but no one can handle direct sunlight.

Just as the sun sets, I am out the door and racing to Alaric and Phoebe's house. As I run through the forest, I reflect. It wasn't long ago that I would have scoffed at anyone who told me I'd be out running in the forest alone. The scars from my time in captivity may have faded, but the emotional damage remains. It's hard to trust again after being betrayed by someone you care about. Sure, I had only met Price the night before he broke my heart, but I thought I had found something real. I even thought he could have been my mate. I can't believe how wrong I was.

Rayne's return to my life has changed me in ways I cannot explain. I feel hopeful for the first time in years, and I have a renewed interest in life. For the first time, I believe I have a future, and I am excited to meet it.

After all, the chances of Rayne and I ever reconnecting were slim. If the goddess saw fit to place us back in one another's lives, it must be for a reason. I, for one, will not be taking it for granted. The fact that she is now my sister—as a result of being mated to my brother—is another matter entirely. They say the gods work in mysterious ways, and my hunter-hating brother being mated to the last of the Chasen hunters is evidence of that.

I slow my pace and leisurely walk toward the house, taking in the scenery. It's such a beautiful night. There is a clear sky, and I can see millions of stars shining around a thumbnail moon. The night is perfect and calm, and a pang of loneliness sinks into my chest. It is a feeling I am still unfamiliar with. I had become accustomed to it before I found Rayne again, but since then I have become dependent upon being surrounded by my friends and family.

Now that the threat of hunters on our doorstep is gone, Drake and Rayne are blissfully gliding through their honeymoon phase. I do not begrudge them the happiness they've found with each other, but it means I have been alone more often than not lately.

As the house comes into view, I realize that the large, gray dragon shifter has returned. He's standing on the porch embracing a young girl, and I quickly hide behind one of the trees.

I don't know what it is about him that makes the butterflies in my stomach go haywire, but—gods above—he is the most handsome man I've ever seen. The feelings he incites in me are both foreign and exciting, and I haven't yet figured out what to do about them. He's bigger than any other man I've met. He must be well over six feet, which easily dwarfs my five-foot-nothing frame, and it's shocking he can even find clothes to wear considering the way his muscles strain against them. His long, dirty-blonde hair falls freely in his face, and I can't help but wonder how sexy he will look with it tied up away from his face. Gods, the things I would absolutely love to do to this man.

A pang flows through me. I've had feelings like this before—sure they weren't this strong—but they were there nonetheless, and I got burned for them. When your very first kiss ends in you being kidnapped and held captive for most of your life, it really ruins the idea of romance.

I close my eyes with my back up against the tree, contemplating my next move. I take a deep, thoughtful breath. Sure, I've been around him before. But I've never been alone or with only one or two people. What would I say?

"Drusilla?" I hear a rumble of a voice saying my name from right in front of me. When I open my eyes, I'm startled to find him standing so close I can feel the heat radiating off his body.

"Yes?" I squeak. What the fuck was that? I sound like a mouse.

"I've been hoping to talk to you alone," he begins. His voice is velvet smooth, and his words are slow and intentional. It is the cadence of someone who has lived for eons and knows they will have eons more.

"You have?" I ask, my heart hammering in both fear and excitement.

"Yes. I wanted to talk to you about us," he says.

Again, my voice squeaks out. "Us?"

"Yes. I would like to talk to you about the fact that you're..." Before he can finish, I rush off. I have a feeling I know what he's going to say, but I'm not ready for that. Do I fantasize about him finishing the sentence, scooping me up into his arms, and flying us away into the night? Of course, I do.

Am I ready for even an iota of that much attention and vulnerability? Absolutely not.

I turn around once I reach the door, but I can still see the confusion on his face where he stands by the tree. I vow to be ready soon. Soon I will be able to love another. If Andres was going to say what I think he was, it will be him.

"Who are you?" a small feminine voice says.

I turn and see a young girl with golden hair and big blue eyes looking at me with curiosity. This was the one I saw embracing Andres.

"I'm Drusilla, but my friends call me Dru," I answer and stick my hand out for her to shake.

She tilts her head to the left and right and walks in a circle around me, studying me ponderously. "Aunty Dru. I like it," she says as she takes my hand.

"Uh..." I begin to protest. I'm no one's aunty unless there is something that Drake and Rayne need to tell me.

"Uncle Andres! Why didn't you introduce me to my Aunty Dru?" she aims this question behind me where Andres is walking up the steps to join us. Luckily, he looks just as shocked as I do. His step falters, and his mouth opens as he tries to determine what to say.

His eyes move from the little girl to me and then back again. "River," he warns, "we need to have a little talk."

"Why?" she looks at him with the same curious look she gave me.

"Not everyone shares our kind of knowledge, River," he explains, stressing the *everyone* with a subtle nod in my direction. "Sometimes you need to keep things to yourself."

The girl—River—laughs as if her uncle is joking with her. "Of course, she knows! How could your mate not know?" At her confirmation of my suspicion, I place my hand over my heart and take a couple of steps back.

"River!" Andres scolds once more. "Just because you know this doesn't mean you should share it." His eyes flit to mine in concern. He looks like he would like nothing more than to come closer and wrap his arms around me. Goddess, I bet it would feel amazing. Goddess, it makes me want to run.

"So, I guess I shouldn't tell Riley that he's my mate?" she asks with the nonchalance only a child can master.

"What? No! You most definitely should not. You're twelve years old!" he shouts.

"But he is," she argues. "Why should I keep this from him? You and Mama always told me that it's wrong to keep secrets from your family. He'll be my family, right?"

Andres looks lost for a minute. Hell. I'm lost too. She's got a point, though, you shouldn't keep secrets from family. With a shake to clear my head, I turn to her. For some reason, there is something inside me that is already attached to her.

"River, I think what your uncle is trying to say is that some people like to figure these things out for themselves. Just because you know them to be true—which I do expect an explanation for, Andres—doesn't mean you should share them. Do you understand?" I ask, crouching down to her level.

She looks to be contemplating my words for a moment. "I think so. You're saying that you would have wanted to figure out that you are my uncle's mate because of your feelings, rather than someone telling you?" she clarifies.

"Yes. that's exactly right," I say to her. "So instead of telling Riley that he's your mate, you should keep it to yourself until he discovers those feelings for you himself."

"I still feel like I would be lying to him, but I'll keep it to myself," she responds, wrapping her arms around me briefly before bouncing on her toes. "I'm going to play with the other children."

She rushes off, leaving Andres and me standing on the porch. I suppose I can no longer simply ignore him.

"Andres," I begin, turning to him.

"Drusilla, you don't need to say anything. River should not have told you that," he says before I can continue.

"It's okay, Andres. I already suspected as much. I'm just not ready. I won't be the mate you deserve," I lower my head in disappointment. "I'm broken."

He walks toward me and takes my hands in his. He lifts a hand, placing it under my chin, raising it up so that I'm looking into his eyes. The touch is intimate but somehow familiar.

"First, you are not broken." He waits for a beat, and I search his eyes for any sign of mistruth but find none. He doesn't know me or anything about me. I begin to lower my head at that thought. When he knows me, I will give the truth to his unintentional lies. He raises my chin up once more. "Second, I've been waiting centuries for you. I will wait as long as you need. I will be here when you're ready." His eyes shine bright with love that has already settled in. He doesn't know anything about me, but it makes me go weak in the knees anyway.

"It's very nice to say," I admit, "but you don't know me. You can't be sure."

"In the years I have slumbered supernaturals lost the ability to recognize their mates. Well, all except the shifters. Vampires could once recognize their mates by the smell of their blood, and witches would know with a simple touch of skin. The dragons in my family have the ability to see bonds. I can see, for example, a familial bond between you and your brother. There is another between you and Rayne that is forged of pure, simple love."

I smile at the thought. I do love Rayne, but there's some comfort in hearing that love verified by an outside source.

"The strongest bonds are the easiest to visualize," Andres continues. "The bond between true mates is impossible to miss.

That is what I—what River—saw between us. I know you have gone through a lot in your short life, and I am willing to give you all the time you need to be ready. However, if you want to spend time together and get to know one another, I would enjoy that very much."

He doesn't sound nervous, but I can tell it is a speech that he has rehearsed and considered carefully.

"What if I'm never ready?" I hope that won't be the case, but I have to ask.

"Then I'll be part of your life in whatever capacity you will have me," he answers without a moment's thought.

Swoon.

Can he be any more perfect? He is everything I could ever have wanted in a mate. If only I had met him before Price and the damage he inflicted.

The heat in his gaze makes the butterflies in my stomach flap their wings erratically. Goddess, the way this man makes me feel would be proof that we are mates even if River hadn't already blurted it out.

Unable to control myself, I take a step closer to him. "I..."

"There you are!" Rayne says, coming out onto the porch and breaking whatever spell I was under. I quickly step away from Andres and drop my hands to my side.

"I..." I stumble looking back and forth between Andres and Rayne. "That is—we..."

"I was just asking Drusilla for her help with River. I thought she could talk to her since they were both held captive by your father," Andres says, and I look at him in shock. I had no idea that River was held captive. I turn to look at the little girl. She is in the yard playing with the boys, and anger overtakes me at the thought of that monster touching her. Somehow, I school my features and nod, pretending that is what we were talking about.

"That's a good idea," Rayne agrees. "Come on. We want to get the kids ready for bed before we start going over the blueprints for the laboratory."

I look at Andres in thanks, and I don't miss the slight look of disappointment on his face before he smiles at me. I didn't mean to make him feel like I would be ashamed for people to know that he is my mate, but I fear that is exactly what I have done.

I follow Rayne and enter the house.

"There you are. We were expecting you before now," Drake says, coming to greet me.

"The sun just set," I argue.

"Like half an hour ago."

"Drake, leave her alone. Andres was asking her to help River deal with...what they both went through," Rayne interrupts, a flicker of guilt flashing on her face. I know she's always blamed herself for not getting me out of there earlier. River is just a child, and I am sure she feels even worse about her capture. I make a mental note to check in with my bestie later. She's going to need to vent. For once, she's going to need me and not the other way around.

"Drusilla, if you are unable to relive that time in your life, no one will think any less of you," Drake says with compassion and protectiveness in his eyes.

"Drake, I think I can set aside my issues to help a girl. Who knows, it may even help me," I say and place my hand on his arm. "But thank you."

Phoebe and Alaric get their children prepared for bed and leave to tuck them in. Andres decides that he and River should stay here for a while because she seems comfortable, and the kids are a nice distraction for her. The alpha pair welcome him as a guest, so he joins them to tuck River in for the night.

While they are upstairs, I pull Rayne aside.

"I didn't want to pry when Andres was talking to me, but what did he mean when he said she was kept captive by your father?"

"We found River in the shed," she says sullenly, and my breath catches. Immediately, panic and terror constrict my organs.

"What? But your father died two weeks ago. Are you saying she was in there all that time?" I ask.

She nods but adds, "Longer."

"How much longer?" Anger overtakes the panic of my rising memories, and the words come out more forceful than I wanted.

"She said she was in there for two years," Rayne admits, guilt lining her words.

"Two years?"

She confirms my question with another nod.

"She didn't go into detail about her time there," Rayne is hesitant to continue. "I expect—my father—probably like you—"

Gods, no! My stomach roils as the anger and panic rise and meet in my chest. Please tell me that sweet little girl didn't go through anything like I did.

I step away from Rayne and collapse into a chair where, head in hands, I'm pulled into a memory of that horrible time.

"Get up," the monster in human form snarls at me, approaching the cage that has become my home. Although it has been years, there's nothing but a thin scrap of cloth on the floor that I use as my bed. It doubles as a cloth when I attempt to clean myself. It is already too dirty, though, to do anything to help my filthy body.
I try to stand and stumble. They provide me with meager blood packs every other day, but the diet has made me so weak that my legs are almost unable to hold me.
"I said get up!" he shouts as the whip cracks down on my back. "One of these days, you'll learn to comply the first time."
I fall to the ground with the force of the whip hitting me, but the fear of the second blow has me rising to my feet faster.
"I'm sorry," I whisper, and the whip cracks again. This time it is

*harder and faster and draws blood. I hold my stance, though. If I fall
again, I know it will only increase my suffering later.*

*"Where is your coven?" he asks. It's the same question every day.
And just like all the days before this one, I remain silent. I shake my
head and refuse to give up the location. Though I'm not even sure if
I would remember the way at this point. My time here has blurred
my memory, and I can hardly imagine a time when I lived outside
of this prison.*

*What I do remember with shocking clarity is a boy with bright
green eyes and dark brown hair with lips as soft as silk. He was my
first kiss, my first love. He is also the reason for my imprisonment.
How could I have been so stupid? I allowed not only myself but my
best friend to be captured.*

*Somewhere Bre is suffering. Somewhere my family is mourning me.
We are all suffering because I was foolish enough to believe a boy
had feelings for me. Of course, he didn't. Why would he? I'm
nothing special.*

*The next two lashes from the whip sting, and I flinch and sway with
the force.*

*"How many more monsters are there?" he demands. He really
should come up with some new questions or stop asking altogether.
Again, I remain silent.*

*I hope that Breanne has been able to stay silent as well. I believe she
must. If she had told them what they wanted to know, they wouldn't
still be torturing me.*

*Tears leak from my eyes until the cracks of the whip stop. "You will
answer one of these days," he tells me calmly before locking the cage
once more and leaving the room.*

As I sink to my knees, I pray to the goddess.

*"Please help me. I know I'm only one of your daughters. There are
probably others who need you more, but I'm begging you. I can't
survive this much longer. I need help," I whisper the words low*

enough that they cannot be picked up by any listening devices they have nearby.

My sobs are harder to quiet.

"Drusilla. Are you all right?" Andres is standing in front of me, his face and voice wrapped in concern.

The memory breaks, and I am brought back to reality. Unable to speak, I nod my head gratefully. Even after all this time, the flashbacks bring tears to my eyes. He looks at me curiously. I can tell that he wants to say more but doesn't. He offers me his hand and helps me to my feet.

"Thank you," I tell him quietly, wiping my eyes before we head into the kitchen to discuss the plans.

We need to free the people being held in the laboratory. I need to know for certain if Breanne is there. I'm already responsible for her being kidnapped years ago, and the guilt of not knowing where she is now is becoming overwhelming.

Chapter Five

Drusilla

"These are the blueprints we found for the facility near Orillia. It looks like it's massive. If I were to guess, it's likely underground," Drake explains, as he flattens a roll of paper over the table.

The lines and abbreviations are so jumbled that it takes my untrained eye time to even recognize them as the outlines of a building.

"This looks like it could be a block of cells," Alaric adds, pointing to a section on the blueprint.

"I thought so too," Drake nods.

"This room is huge. Am I reading that right?" Phoebe asks as she points out another section. "Is this some kind of studio or laboratory?"

"According to this, there's only one way in or out. Here," Rayne says, pointing to the edge. "It seems to have a stairway leading in. I'm just not sure if it's up or down."

I study the blueprints as they continue pointing out details. Instead, I count the number of boxes in the section Alaric believes to be cells. I get to fifty before I stop, and there is still another row.

Just how many supernaturals are they keeping there? Hopefully, not all those cells are being used.

A high-pitched scream cuts through the calm of our hushed meeting.

Suddenly, we are all alert, chairs screeching back from the table as we locate the direction the scream came from.

"Upstairs?" Phoebe asks.

"River," I whisper the words like a prayer, but they are lost in the rush of everyone fighting to get up the stairs. There is a kind of traffic jam caused by everyone's simultaneous movement, but I am small enough that I can crouch down and slip past the others.

I follow the sounds to a door and throw it open.

River is in bed, asleep but trashing.

"No! Please don't!" she cries out. "No, no, no."

I run to her side and, without thinking, scoop her up into my arms and try to soothe her.

"Shh. It's okay. You're safe," I rub my hands over her head and her back, trying to show her tenderness. I gently brush her golden hair away from her face and comfort her, anything to prove to her that she is no longer in that place. If her time there was anything like mine, she'll need it.

Her arms tighten around my neck, and she begins to sob.

"Shh, River. It's okay. I'm here. Your Uncle Andres is here. You're no longer in that place. You will never have to go there again. I promise you," I continue to whisper the words over and over as she sobs.

"He hurt me," she whispers, and I can no longer keep my own tears from falling.

"I know, baby girl. I know. He hurt me too," I whisper as sobs begin to wrack my own body. "He will never hurt either of us ever again. I ripped out his heart."

Maybe I shouldn't tell a child that. If she was subjected to the same torture I was, though, she's no longer truly a child and needs to know.

She sits back to look at me. "You did?"

"Yes. I'm sorry I didn't do it sooner. I should've done it when I escaped. He never would have had the chance to hurt you," I tell her, moving the now-damp blonde hair out of her face.

"It's okay. We're both safe now," she whispers and snuggles back into me, trying to comfort me in return. I look up to the doorway and realize the others have joined us now. They watch quietly, giving us a sliver of privacy in this moment.

I notice the tears brimming in Rayne's big, brown eyes as she watches us. I know she feels responsible for our pain. She should know that it is not her fault, but I know the guilt follows her.

I make eye contact with the rest of the group, saving Andres for last. Everyone watches us with some form of pity, and I dread what I will see on his face. As my eyes meet his, though, it's not pity I see. It's respect, tenderness, and rage, and it makes my heart swell. If I didn't already trust the gods to pair me with the perfect man, he would've just shown me with that single look.

"All right," Drake says, "no need for us to eavesdrop." He guides everyone except Andres back downstairs. Rayne looks back at me over her shoulder, and I give her a soft smile. I hope she understands what I'm trying to say.

It's not your fault, Rayne. Not even a little. In the end, you saved us both.

She returns the small smile before walking back downstairs with my brother's arms draped around her shoulders.

I shuffle awkwardly with River until we are both laying on the bed, wrapped in each other's arms. I feel the bed dip as Andres climbs in on the other side of River, sandwiching her between us.

"You two are the strongest people I've ever known," he says, pulling us both close.

My eyes shoot up to meet his in question. "Strong?"

"Yes. Strong. Not every person would be able to withstand even a fraction of what you both went through. I don't know the details, but I can imagine," he says.

I begin to pull away. Now is the time for me to leave and allow Andres and River to have this moment together. A small voice stops me before I can extricate myself from their arms.

"Please stay, Aunty Dru."

I search her pleading aquamarine eyes for a moment. Tears are still rolling freely down her pale cheeks, and it breaks my heart.

"All right. Just until you fall asleep," I compromise, relaxing back into the mattress.

"Will you be here when I wake up?" she questions, looking up at me with big, puppy dog eyes.

"I will if you want me to."

"Please," she pleads.

I sigh. "Okay. I'll be sleeping while the sun is up, but Phoebe and Alaric will be able to bring you to me if you need."

"Thank you," she whispers and snuggles back into my arms. Her thin arms are wrapped around me, and Andres has managed to pull us both into his enormous grip.

I close my eyes for a moment to savor this feeling. This is the first time in my life that I have ever felt truly needed or wanted. Sure, my parents and Drake wanted me. Then Rayne, when we reconnected. They had to. You hardly choose to want your family. These two, though, are two perfect strangers. They know little to nothing about me, and they want me.

I don't know when I'm going to feel this way again, so I soak it in. Goddess, does it feel good. It's like nothing I've ever experienced before. For the first time since I was taken captive, I think I've found the reason for it. I didn't believe the gods had a purpose for allowing me to be kept there for so long, and I cursed them for the things that happened to me. Now, I'm beginning to see it. They didn't want to, but they needed me to be ready for this moment. They knew I would need to be here when this little girl was rescued. I needed to know—truly know—what she had been through to help her past it.

As her breaths even out and she slips into sleep, I open my eyes to find Andres staring at me. The weight of his gaze throws me off momentarily, but I regain control as I slip from the bed and out of the room.

"Drusilla," Andres whispers from behind me. He has stopped in the doorway, carefully pulling it closed.

Without thought, I throw myself into his arms and push my lips on his. He is taken by surprise but recovers quickly, wrapping his thick arms around my waist. I can tell that he's holding back by the tremble in his body, but I'm grateful. His large hand roams up my back to grasp the back of my neck, deepening the kiss. The first touch of his tongue on mine has me moaning.

Goddess. It's been so long since I've felt the touch of a man. Even then, I have never felt this wanted. He is gentle, but I can feel the tension as he manages the space between us, trying to keep himself from taking it too far. A warning rumble from his chest proves just how much control it is taking for him to do so.

He pulls back breathlessly, places my feet back on the ground, and takes a step back. "I'm sorry."

"Don't be," I tell him, still breathing heavily.

"I just wanted to thank you for helping River. I never intended to pressure you into anything," he says, his blue eyes almost shining.

"Andres," I start and walk over to take his hands in my own. The gesture is unfamiliar to me, but I hope it seems natural to him. "You didn't pressure me into anything. I kissed you because I wanted to kiss you. If anyone should be sorry, it should be me."

He chuckles. "You never have to be sorry for kissing me, Drusilla. I am yours and only yours for the rest of my life," he brings my hand to his lips and places a soft kiss across my knuckles.

I place my other hand over my heart. "I have never felt as special as I do when I'm with you, Andres. It's not a feeling that I'm used to, and I will still need time to come to terms with it. But you make me feel things that I've never felt," I run my fingers over my lips softly. "And River. Well, she makes me feel needed. For the first time in my life, I think there may have actually been a reason for my imprisonment. If only so that I could be here at this exact moment to help her through this. That is, as long as the two of you are okay with that," I say.

"It's true that the gods have reasons for everything they do. Still, I wish that both you and River could have been spared this," he replies solemnly.

"Me too," I whisper.

We head back down the stairs, stepping quietly to avoid waking anyone.

"Is she okay?" Rayne asks.

I nod. "She will be."

She breathes out a sigh of relief.

"Is it okay if I stay here in the bunker tonight?" I ask Alaric and Phoebe. "I promised River that I would be here when she wakes up."

"Of course. If she asks for you, I'll bring her down," Phoebe responds with a look that tells me she's in full mom-mode. She wants to take River's pain away in any way that she can, and she will extend her hospitality to anyone to make that possible.

"Thank you," I reply. "What did you all figure out?"

"We think we have a general plan of what to do, but we're going to meet with the rest of the alphas tomorrow. Skarlyt, Axel, and Trixie will be here just after sunset so that you are all able to be present. We're going to need everyone if we want to pull this off," Alaric says.

As Alaric and Phoebe head up to bed, I slip out onto the back deck. I've always loved how the lake looks on a fall night, and I walk down to sit on the dock. Meditatively, I pull my sneakers off, then my socks. I push one sock inside of each shoe before dangling my feet off the edge of the dock. I close my eyes and lean back on my hands, soaking in the rays from the moon as I dip my toes into the cold water and contemplate everything that has happened.

A slight vibration goes through the wood, and I listen closer. There are footsteps coming near me. I expect both Rayne and Drake or possibly Andres, but I open my eyes to find Rayne walking alone.

"I asked them to stay inside so I could talk to you for a minute," she says, recognizing the look on my face. "Dru..." she begins, but I raise my hand to cut her off.

"It's not your fault, Rayne. None of it is your fault," I tell her.

She takes a few more steps forward, kicking off her shoes as she goes, and takes the spot beside me.

"You don't understand. That little girl was in that shed for two years. Two years. How many times did I walk by while she was imprisoned there? And you. You were there for six years before I found out. Am I such a monster that I didn't realize what was being done in my own back yard? You were in a cage, steps away from where I slept in peace, ate food, showered, and played games." She sounds disgusted, and there are tears streaming from her dark eyes.

If she were anyone else, I would think she was just feeling sorry for herself. She's not though. I know that she is genuinely haunted by these thoughts.

"Rayne, you look at me right now!" I say with force, grasping her face and turning it toward me. "You are not a monster. No one blames you. I don't blame you. River doesn't blame you. Would you blame Drake for Colleen releasing Price?"

At my mention of Colleen, her fangs drop. We have been

putting off dealing with her until we figure out what to do, and it's driving Rayne nuts.

"That's different," she hisses.

"Is it? The only difference is that instead of keeping Price prisoner without Drake knowing, she helped him escape without Drake knowing. Just like your dad kept me and River without you knowing," I try to explain. "It is not your fault. If you knew and did nothing, then you would have some blame, but you didn't. As soon as you found out about me, what did you do?"

"I helped you escape, but I should have done it long before that."

"How, Rayne? Tell me how you would have helped me escape when I was too weak to run on my own. You did the only thing you could have. You helped me get strong and gave me a fighting chance. If you would have released me before that, I wouldn't have made it two steps before they captured me," I tell her, placing my palms on each of her cheeks. "You saved me. You saved River. Sure, we both wish you didn't have to. But the fact is that when we needed you, you were there."

Tears flow down her cheeks like twin rivers, and I use my thumbs to wipe them away. "I'm going to need you to tell me that about a thousand more times before I believe it," she chuckles.

"I will tell you as many times as you need me to. It's the truth," I promise her.

"Okay," she straightens up, wipes the tears off her cheeks, and packs her doubts away for another time. "What was really going on between you and Andres when I came out onto the porch?"

I breathe out heavily, turning my face up to the moon. I knew this was coming. I just hoped that I would have a little more time before it did.

"He's my mate."

"What?" she exclaims. "How do you know? Drake had to taste my blood before he figured it out."

"Shifters know by looking into their mate's eyes, and apparently Dragons have other special abilities. I am not really sure. Even River knew as soon as she saw me." I sigh, trying to decide how to explain something I do not even understand. "Andres told me that vampires used to be able to recognize their mates by the smell of their blood, and witches by just touching. He said that knowledge has been lost. He—or I guess his family—can see the bonds between people. Which—I guess—would explain how River knew that we were mates."

"And you believe him? Or them?" she asks skeptically.

I nod. "I can't explain it, Rayne. It's like my soul knows it's true. The feelings that stir inside me when he's around are unlike anything I've ever felt before. And when we kissed..." I sigh. "It was like magic."

"Wow. That's amazing, Dru," she says, pulling me into a hug. "I'm so happy for you."

"I told him I'm not ready," I whisper into her neck.

"What?" she asks, pulling back.

"I'm not ready to love someone else when I don't love myself. It wouldn't be fair to him," I tell her.

"Dru..." she starts.

"Rayne, I know you think I'm this amazing person, but I don't. I'm not. I'll admit, since you came back into my life, I've found the strength to begin living again. But I've spent a long time just barely making it through. I've been coasting, finding random men from the coven to try and feel wanted, needed, anything other than the trauma. He may be my true mate, but I need to feel worthy of him," I admit.

"That makes sense," she pauses, digesting what I've told her. "But I want you to think about this. Hunters only take those who they deem a threat, and most of those are killed right away. They thought you were dangerous and valuable enough to capture and keep imprisoned for years. When they tried to break you, they couldn't. You still had the strength to befriend and forgive a lonely, little hunter girl, and you still had the strength to leave that place and make a life for yourself. You are stronger than you give yourself credit for. Any man should have to prove they are worthy of you. Not the other way around."

I repeat the same words she said to me earlier. "I'm going to need you to tell me that about a thousand more times before I believe it."

She chuckles and tells me the same thing I told her. "I will tell you as many times as you need me to. It's the truth."

I grab her into a hug and whisper, "Thank you."

"Anytime, babe. I love you, Dru," she whispers back.

"And I love you."

We sit there for a while and watch the stars dance on the water until the sky begins to lighten, and we head inside to bed. I head down to the bunker, and Drake and Rayne leave with enough time to make it to their home before dawn.

This time, when I pray to the goddess before I fall asleep, it is for River and not myself.

"Mother, please help her get past this. She has seen terrible things. Give her the strength to overcome her trauma. Let her be stronger than I was."

I am shocked to hear a whisper back, something that has never happened before.

"I hear you, my daughter. Do not fret. I have given the girl the tools she needs to be forged even stronger from this hardship."

A breath of relief escapes, and I start to ask more questions. If the Mother is in my mind, I need to ask her everything I can. What does she mean? What tools? Before I can form the question, her voice comes again, calm and measured into my drifting mind.

"I have given her you."

Chapter Six

Andres

Drusilla goes outside after Alaric and Phoebe head up to bed, and I watch her through the patio doors. Gods, she is beautiful. Not only on the outside but also in her heart.

When River screamed, fear took hold of me. I have spent so long trying to protect her, but the fear that she was in danger left me paralyzed. My mate was brave and strong enough to jump into action without pause.

Drusilla rushed right up to River, a girl she had only just met, swept her into her arms, and comforted her as if they were family. Watching them from the doorway only cemented what my mother had told me centuries ago. This woman is worth waiting for, and I intend to make her feel loved every second of every day for the rest of her life.

She thinks she is incapable of being the mate I deserve, but she's wrong. It is I who needs to prove—not only to her but also myself—that I am worthy of her love.

And that kiss. Gods above and below, that was the best moment of my life. I had to use every ounce of control not to take advantage and push for more. I can feel her emotions well enough to know she isn't ready for that, but her emotions after that soul-satisfying kiss proved to me that she is trying.

I watch as Rayne silently walks toward the end of the dock and sits next to Drusilla before I slip out the door and head toward the front of the house to search for Drake.

"Can I ask you something?" I ask. Old habit makes me expect him to be startled, but his supernatural hearing probably doesn't allow for any real surprises.

"Of course," he replies, turning his head to me briefly before looking back out at the trees.

"When Drusilla escaped, was there anything you did that helped her?" I am hoping he can give me some insights about how to help River through this.

He sighs and looks up at the sky. "I'll be honest. When Drusilla escaped, I wasn't in the proper mindset to help her. I was so full of rage and hate toward the people who took her that it was almost impossible to be there for her," he looks down at his hands and then at me.

"But I will say this. River will need patience and love. Drusilla shut down completely when she got home. She hid herself away from everyone, and we let her. I know now that we shouldn't have. We wanted to give her time to work through it, but all we did was make her feel like we didn't care. If I could go back in time, I would spend as much time with her as I could. I would show her she was—no, is—loved, wanted, and needed."

"It can be difficult to see what people need from you when they need it most," I offer him some advice of my own. "Do not be too hard on yourself."

He shakes his head, setting aside my words as if they mean nothing. "Since Rayne has been back in her life, she's been acting more and more like the old Dru. She's strong, independent, and caring. She thinks I don't know, but I've seen the look on her face when she thinks we aren't paying attention. She was away for so long. She doesn't know where she fits in this world anymore, and she desperately wants to feel like she belongs. Since Rayne and I mated, I'm afraid that I'm making things worse again."

As he speaks about his sister, I can see the pure love that he holds for her. He may not be the best at showing it. Based on my limited interactions with him, he seems closed off, possibly even cold-hearted. Right now, though, as his eyes light up while he talks about Drusilla, I see the truth. He just doesn't know how to express himself.

"Have you told Drusilla your fears?" I ask.

He looks at me like I've grown two heads. "Of course not. I don't want to make her feel like she has to pretend to be something or someone she's not just to make me feel better."

"Is that what she would do?" I ask. "Or is that simply what you would do?"

He nearly chokes on his next inhale and looks at me in confusion for a moment.

"Is that what I do?" he asks in disbelief.

"Drake. It's not my place, and I have no right to give any type of advice. Right now, my sister is being held captive by hunters in a facility where they are doing goddess knows what to her. But I am guilty of the same when it comes to her." I turn away, looking up at the bright stars in the sky. "As a big brother, you want to protect them from the world. From everything ugly and evil. When we fail —whether or not it is our fault—we accept the weight of the failure." I turn back to him with a look of understanding. "What you're doing is the same thing I would do—or likely will do when we rescue my sister. You want to fix everything so that she never has to feel any type of hurt again, but the damage is done. She was hurt. Instead of trying to take it all away, I think we should be making sure they always feel cherished. We can't fix them because they aren't broken."

His eyes widen as he takes in my words, and his mouth drops open.

"From the short interactions I've had with Drusilla, she seems to believe she's broken. However, she is one of the strongest women I've ever met. That is not your fault, but maybe if you treat her as if she is stronger and trust her with your fears, she will realize how much she is capable of."

"But..." He tries to interrupt, but I continue anyway.

"You don't want to burden her," I say. "That is about you. Not her. You said she desires to be wanted. How better to show her than by sharing your burden?"

Again, once I finish speaking, his emotions waver. This time he lands on a kind of frustrated embarrassment.

"So, are all dragons some kind of therapists? Or is that just you?" Before I can respond, he goes on. "I thought this was about River. Why are you trying to give me advice about Drusilla? What does it matter to you?"

There's the mask he loves to show people. The asshole he pretends to be.

I obviously hit a nerve.

"I suppose we did get off track, but isn't it the same thing at the end of the day? Drusilla was held captive and suffered much of the same abuse River did. What will help one will surely help the other."

She is my mate.

I want to scream it at the top of my lungs.

She is my mate, and you need to care for her until I can.

My anger simmers, though, as his complicated emotions settle on my own. I can understand his thoughts, and I know this must be a hard topic for him. Plus, I have the feeling that no matter what I do, she's going to need support from him before she can accept it from me.

"I suppose you're right. I'm sorry for being a dick. I wasn't always like this." He sighs and walks over to the stairs to sit down.

"You know, Drake, Drusilla wasn't the only one who experienced trauma," I tell him, and his eyes shoot to mine in question. "Just because you weren't taken doesn't mean you didn't suffer every day that she was gone."

"It doesn't even compare. What she went through is something I don't think I would have survived," he admits.

"Have you told her that?" I ask.

"No," he says sullenly.

"Maybe you should," I tell him, and he nods.

We sit in silence on the steps of the porch and stare out at the forest. Even in the dark, I can see that the leaves are already beginning to turn. Fall is upon us. The prospect of snow excites me, especially now that I've found River. She's never seen the snow— or maybe she has during her time in captivity—but I have a feeling she's going to love experiencing it while free.

"You should go lay with River so that someone is there when she wakes. The first night was the worst for Drusilla. She kept waking up, and she didn't know where she was. If you can be there when River wakes, it may help," he says.

I agree with his logic, so I tell him goodbye and head up the stairs to the bedroom.

River is just starting to thrash as I enter, so I quickly slip into the bed and pull her close.

"Shh, my sugar. Everything is okay. I'm here, and I'm not going anywhere," I whisper as she whimpers and snuggles into me. I try to block out her emotions, but they are so intense that they still trickle through. The fear she is experiencing in her dreams would be paralyzing to me. The fact that she has remained so strong has me in complete awe. She shouldn't have to be strong. She should be able to be a child—run, jump, fly, play—never knowing the evil of this world.

But that's not the case. If my conversation with Drake taught me anything, it's that I need to be open and honest rather than try to shield her. She needs to know that, although what happened to her is not okay, the fact that she came back to me shows just how strong she is.

I pray to Gaia as I close my eyes. "Goddess, please give them strength to weather this storm and protect Andrea. Tell her I am coming for her. Tell her to stay strong."

I don't hear a response, but a kind of golden warmth spreads throughout my limbs. It is a sign, and I know that she has heard me.

Stay strong, sister.

I will be there as soon as I am able.

* * *

Drake was right.

I am not sure how much time passes before I wake to River screaming, thrashing about in my arms.

"Shh, sugar. I'm here. It's me," I whisper.

"Uncle Andres?" she questions.

"Yes, sugar. It's me."

She spins around, eyes wild and flashing.

"Is it really you? Am I really free?" She wraps her arms around me tight. "I thought it was just a dream, and I was going to wake up there again." My heart breaks and emotions clog my throat, so I just squeeze her tighter to me and rub her bony back. I try to comfort her without thinking about the ribs I can feel through her thin skin.

My heart squeezes with anger and sadness at the way she was treated. I have no doubt that a week with Phoebe and Alaric will put the meat back on her bones.

We lay like that for a while before her sobs slow.

"You're going to get my mama, aren't you?" she asks.

"I am," I promise. "I don't want to pressure you, but I will need you to tell me everything you know about that place."

She gets a panicked look on her face, so I quickly continue. "Whatever you can tell me will give me a better chance of rescuing her."

Her emotions flicker with fear, but she overcomes it with determination and nods.

"There's my strong girl," I say. "Let's get up and get ready for our day."

After we spend some time familiarizing ourselves with the modern conveniences—running water, toothbrushes, toothpaste, even the shower—we dress in the clothes Alaric and Phoebe set out for us and head down to the kitchen.

"River!" a blonde little boy exclaims, running up to her.

"Riley!" she responds and looks at me with a huge smile before rushing and wrapping her arms around him. So, this is the boy who will be my River's mate. I know she agreed not to tell him that they're mates, but it doesn't seem like she needs to. He looks like he's just as enamored with her as she is with him and the golden bond thrumming between the two of them cements that. It's even stronger than the one running between Phoebe and Alaric, and they have already cemented their mating.

"They sure hit it off," Phoebe says, walking up beside me.

"About that..." I begin. Being his mother, she deserves to know. I will have to leave River here at least long enough to rescue my sister, and Phoebe will be tasked with watching over her then.

"What about it?" she asks.

"Can we talk on the porch for a minute?" I gesture to the door.

"Sure," she says skeptically, settling the baby down in her high-chair before following me out to the porch. "What is it? Do you have a problem with them being friends?"

"They're much more than that," I respond.

She looks at me with concern. "What do you mean?"

"They are mates," I tell her, and her mouth gapes open in shock. She looks back inside at them before turning to me.

"You don't know that. You can't know that," she argues. "They're only twelve. They won't know for another six years."

"My family is special. My father was a dragon, but my mother was the most powerful witch the world has ever seen. Because of this, we all have special abilities. Included among those, is the ability to recognize mates—not just our own. River recognized it first. Now that I have seen them together, I can see that their souls fit together perfectly," I explain.

She looks back inside again briefly, her eyes misting.

"Are you sure?"

"I'm as sure as I am that you and Alaric are the strongest true mates I've seen in a very long time. We will need to watch them, though. If I'm right, they are a part of the prophecy and cannot be allowed to bond until we are ready."

"The prophecy?" she asks, her voice rising to an incredulous shriek.

"*The lost daughter of air mates the first son born of magic and fire.* Your son is the firstborn son of a mage and a phoenix—magic and fire—is he not?"

"Shit," she says and begins pacing. "This is a lot to deal with before breakfast, you know?"

"I understand."

"*Alaric!*" she yells, and the man himself runs outside.

"What's wrong?" His hands and eyes roam her body, looking for the reason for her distress.

"Tell him," she says, her breathing rapid.

"Tell me what?" Alaric asks, full of concern as he turns to me for an explanation.

"Riley and River are mates," I tell him immediately. There's no beating around the bush while the phoenix next to us is nearly bursting into flames. Alaric's mouth opens and closes in shock.

"And the other thing," Phoebe adds, still frantically pacing beside us.

Alaric looks at me expectantly.

"The other thing?" I ask, feeling flustered for the first time in a very long time.

"My gods," she exhales in a frustrated burst. "The. Other. Thing."

"They are also the pair mentioned in the next line of the prophecy," I reveal.

Phoebe finally settles to watch as the news sinks in for her mate.

"No, that's not possible. They're only twelve. Wait. What is the next line?"

"The lost daughter of air mates the first son born of magic and fire. As I just confirmed with Phoebe, Riley is the firstborn son of a mage and a phoenix, and River was a lost daughter of the air. Unless you know of another lost dragon and a son born of a mage and a phoenix," I explain.

"Fuck," he says and goes to wrap his arms around Phoebe's middle. "So, what do we do?"

"Nothing. River has been told not to tell him yet. After seeing them just now, though, I don't think she has to. His soul is already calling to its mate. When they're older, we will have to explain that they can't complete their bond until we're ready for the next stage in the prophecy."

"Let's focus on Orillia, the laboratory, and freeing those supernaturals first. Then we can..." Alaric begins, but he's interrupted by a crash inside the house.

"*Boys!*" he yells, and the three of us head back into the house. There is evidence of a scuffle between the boys, but that's not what holds my attention. In the corner, River is crouched down with her head in her hands.

I rush over to her. "Shh," I whisper and scoop her up from the ground. "What happened?"

She doesn't say anything. She just shakes in my arms. I try everything I can to get her to speak to me, to look at me, with no success. Finally, when I'm about to lose my mind, she whispers, "Dru," and I run down the stairs with her in my arms.

We find Drusilla sleeping restlessly in the bunker, and I gently place River next to her. As soon as River hits the mattress, Dru's eyes open, and she wraps her arms around River. They both seem to calm with the comfort of the other.

"What happened?" Drusilla whispers, and I shrug my shoulders.

"I don't know," River whispers back, frustrated. "I don't know."

"The boys did something," I try to begin. "Did they scare you?"

"No," she says immediately. "It was too loud. He was angry." A sob catches in her throat. "I know he was angry, and I just couldn't breathe."

That's what it was? Alaric yelled, and it sent River into a panic. Surely she knows he wasn't yelling at her. He wasn't even truly angry with the boys.

"Oh, River," Drusilla says as she gently brushes the hair from my niece's concerned face "I understand. Loud noises, yelling, even just crying can startle me, but I promise it will get better." River quiets, but her breaths are still rushed and panicked.

"I know he wasn't yelling at me," River explains, still frustrated.

"Take a breath, little one," Drusilla commands calmly. "That is what happens. You know you are all right, but your body forgets. It remembers being afraid, and so it makes you feel afraid again."

"My body forgets," River repeats the words. It is clear she doesn't believe them, but she holds on to them regardless.

"You just have to remind your body that you are here and safe," she holds up three, slim, elegant fingers in front of herself. "You take a deep breath, and you try to list three things. Something you can see, something you can feel, and something you can smell."

"See. Feel. Smell." River is still uncertain, but she parrots the method back to her teacher.

"I can see the pattern on the beautiful quilt," Drusilla begins, gently guiding River's eyes to the bed and the quilt they are laying on. "The colors are bright and whoever made it must have spent a long time making it so beautiful."

"I can feel your hair on my shoulder," she continues, pulling the length of River's hair gently through her hands and gently braiding it into a loose plait. "It is soft and just a little bit wet."

She pauses for a moment, letting River settle in.

"And we can smell?" River eventually prompts her.

"I can smell..." she pauses, searching. "I can smell your Uncle Andres. He smells just like leather and caramel, and he's too nearby to miss him."

"Hey," I joke, seeing they are both recovering. "I have certainly smelled worse."

"Once you notice three things, you can remind your body that it is here and now—not then and there. You are here, with a beautiful quilt and your uncle. So, you cannot be in that cage too. You see?"

River smiles up at her, and I can tell this lesson has helped them both.

"The cage is not here, and the punishment that follows is never going to come," Drusilla promises solemnly.

What is the punishment that follows? What is she talking about? How were they punished?

River nods into her chest and the two of them settle.

"I'll be right back," I whisper.

If I were to try to say anything more, it would come out more forcefully than I would like.

"Is she okay?" Phoebe asks from the top of the stairs.

I nod but walk past her, straight outside to shift and fly.

I need to burn off some of this rage before I explain what happened. If I try now, I'm liable to rip Alaric's head off. It's not his fault. He was only being a father, but I am focused on River's feelings right now. I cannot see far past her fear and my own guilt at not being able to protect her.

Chapter Seven

Drusilla

Even asleep, I can feel the nightmare taking hold, but there is nothing I can do to stop it. I thought I had defeated them. I've been spending too much time alone, though, and they've started creeping back in.

This dream is no different. It begins gradually, twisting and distorting recent events until I'm back in that cage with that monster. This time, however, I am not alone. River is at my side. She is lethargic and covered in blood from the open wounds on her back. I lean down, ripping off a piece of my shirt and trying to clean the wounds with it. At each touch of the fabric, she flinches in pain.

That monster is just there, standing at the door of the cage. He brings the whip up to aim at her once more.

"I'll take her lashes!" I cry out.

His laughter rings out as he continues his movements. I throw my body over hers as the lash hits.

"Ahh," I scream out in pain with the first lash, and River begins to scramble, trying to push me off her.

I grit my teeth, hold my ground, and take lash after lash until...

I wake with a start, feeling the dip of the bed as someone joins me. I'm momentarily dazed from the nightmare, but I pull River into my arms as soon as I see her tear-streaked face. When she explains what happened, my heart breaks. I remember how bad it was in the beginning. My panic attacks could be triggered by any shouting or loud noise. Even doors slamming or pots and pans clanging together could send me into a spiral. I had hoped that she would be spared these attacks, but I guess not.

As soon as Andres leaves, River and I snuggle into the bed and fall fast asleep. This time, my dream is shockingly pleasant. Instead of my ritualistic nightmares, I dream of flying high in the sky on the back of a dragon. The sun is kissing my skin but not burning it. I don't know what the sun actually feels like, but I hope my dream is correct. It is a warmth that travels through my body, relaxing and awakening my muscles everywhere it goes.

With such an amazing dream, I allow myself to get lost in it.

* * *

I am ripped from this dream by River, terrified and shaking me awake.

"Aunty Dru, something is wrong," she whispers, her bright eyes large with terror.

"Why? What happened?" I sit up and look around. We're still in the bunker, and I can feel that the sun has set.

"There's a lot of yelling upstairs. What if—I think maybe the other hunters are here. What if they take us again?" Her voice is shaking with fear.

I wrap my arms around her. "Then they will die. I won't let anyone take you. I promise." As I say the last words, I pull back so she can look into my eyes and see the determination in them.

She nods, and the two of us get out of bed slowly. As we walk, she hides behind me, clinging to my shirt. We get closer to the shouting, and I begin to decipher the voices: Drake, Alaric, and Skarlyt. I turn to River.

"It's okay. It's just my brother and our friends," I tell her. I watch her try to be brave, but the tremble in her hands proves it's not quite working.

We crest the top of the stairs to find them still in a heated argument.

With my hand still on River's shoulder, I very calmly ask, "What the actual fuck is going on here?"

Everyone stops what they are doing and turns to look at me. I gesture with my head toward River, who is still visibly shaking, and they all deflate in shame.

"River, honey, are you hungry? Riley saved you a plate. It's in the microwave, and you can take it up to the game room if you want," Phoebe says sweetly, moving slowly toward the kitchen. River pokes her head out from behind me, and her stomach growls.

"It's okay. Go eat and play with the kids. I'll be right down here if you need me," I whisper, and she nods. She takes the plate from Phoebe and rushes up the stairs to join the boys.

"We're sorry..." Drake begins, but I cut him off.

"That girl has been tortured for years," I growl out. I do not raise my voice anymore, but I think the hiss of my accusations will get their attention just as well. "She has been taught to expect pain every time someone yells. Whatever the hell *this* was just terrified the ever-living fuck out of her. And for what? What is so important that you have to scream and yell about it?

"I'm sorry. It was my fault," Skarlyt admits, her eyes downcast.

"No. It was all of us. We apologize, Dru. It won't happen again," Alaric steps in. He does meet my eyes and nods his head as if he has just made a pact with me.

"I didn't know," Drake says, and I know he's not talking about River. He's talking about me.

How many times did he and Dad get into screaming matches

that sent me cowering to the corner? How many times was I paralyzed in fear as Drake would scream his rage at the sky? When I returned, I told him only a fraction of what I had been through, so it's no surprise that he didn't know. Now, though, he's having to see all of it, and I think he's realizing how hard the last years have been for me.

"I'm so sorry, Drusilla. What can I do?" he pleads with me, stepping closer.

I soften at the hurt and shame in his voice.

"Drake. There is nothing to be sorry for. You didn't know because I didn't want you to know. Just please, for the sake of that little girl, just calm the fuck down. At least for a while. I'm going to work with her on some triggers, and hopefully she'll be able to handle things like this better soon."

"I yelled at the boys this afternoon. Is that what happened earlier? She had a panic attack because of my yelling?" Alaric asks, completely horrified at himself.

"Yes," Andres growls from the doorway where he is just entering. If he's just now getting back, he was gone an awfully long time.

"I'm sorry," Alaric says once again, looking sick with guilt. Phoebe goes to his side to console him.

"She's upstairs eating in the game room," I tell Andres when I notice him looking around.

"Will you come with me to see her?" he asks, and I nod. Together, we walk up the stairs.

Just before we get to the top, we stop and listen. The kids are laughing, even River, and it is music to my ears. That's something I wouldn't have been able to do when I first escaped. Even now, I'm not sure I am capable of such easy joy. It means she's stronger than I am, and that is a good thing.

"Is she okay?" Andres questions, turning to me.

"She will be," I tell him.

"I have to ask her about her time in that facility," he says sullenly.

"I don't know if that's a good idea," I admit. "I don't think she's ready."

"I wish I didn't have to ask her at all. But we need all the information we can get, and she's the only one who has actually been there," he explains, and I nod.

"You can ask her, but it needs to be her decision," I say this firmly. If he plans on pushing her too soon, he can count on me pushing him right back. He readily agrees, however, proving again just how amazing he is.

"River?" he calls out, knocking on the door.

"Uncle Andres, you're back!" she says, rushing over and wrapping him in a hug.

"I am," he whispers to her. "We need to talk though."

"About the laboratory?" Smart girl. She already knew.

Andres nods.

"Will you stay?" she turns to me.

"Of course, I will," I tell her, and the three of us walk into the bedroom.

"It will be easiest if we sit on the floor," she says.

"What will be easiest?" I question.

"For me to show you," she responds simply. I look at Andres in question, but he is already sitting on the floor, legs crossed. I shrug and take a seat beside him.

"Hold hands," she commands.

"Wait. You need to explain what we are doing," I say to them.

"I'm going to show you my memories," she says, looking at me like I should know this already.

"And how are you going to do that?" I ask.

"I told you," Andres explains, "the dragons in my family are special. We have gifts. One of River's gifts is the ability to transfer her memories to others." I'm absolutely terrified of what I'm going to see and worried that it will cause my own trauma to come to the surface again, but then I look at River's determined face. The way her blue eyes shine with unshed tears and her thin lips are set in a firm line prove to me that she needs me to be strong regardless of what I see.

The three of us hold hands, and she shimmies her narrow shoulders and then hips as she tries to get comfortable.

"I haven't done this in a very long time," she admits.

Without warning, we are dragged into her memory.

Unlike my own dreams, which feel intensely real and present, this memory feels strange, like floating. Below me, I can see River despite the darkness.

I look around and realize that we're in a box or crate of some kind. The world around us jars and rocks, as if we are being driven on a rough, gravel road. There are a few openings in the crate—it is certainly a crate now—that let in thin rays of sunlight. I can see enough to know it is day without seeing anything else.

"We're on our way to the facility," River whispers. I find her and Andres across from me. We are all apparition-like, faded, ephemeral, and seemingly invisible to the other version of River who rests on the hard ground below us.

I take in her appearance, and it breaks my heart. Her hair is matted, and a metal collar is affixed to her throat. Her clothing is torn and dirty. It looks like she's already been in captivity for a while.

As the vehicle comes to a stop, I hear someone exit, slam the door, and walk toward us. Whomever it is starts to open the crate, and the River who is here with us now begins to shake in fear. I squeeze Andres' hand tighter. I have a feeling I know who is going to be on the other side, and I suddenly decide that I don't want to be here after all. I begin frantically looking around for a way to escape and, of course, find nothing. River, noticing my anxiety, comes and places her arm around me.

Dragon's Destiny

"He can't hurt us anymore," she whispers, and I allow her strength to wash over me.

Logically, I know that he's gone. I know that he cannot hurt us anymore because I hurt him enough to put an end to it forever. Still, the thought of seeing him, even in a memory, paralyzes me with fear. As he opens the crate and his face is illuminated, my hands begin to shake.

"It's okay," Andres whispers, coming up and placing his arm around my shoulders in support. I take some deep breaths to center myself and watch as one of the monsters who haunt my dreams roughly pulls River out of the crate by a leash affixed to her collar. My fear melts away and is replaced by pure, unadulterated rage. I wish I could bring him back to life just to kill him again. She is just a child, and he is a coward who thinks abusing her makes him stronger. As he pulls her forward, she whimpers, and I want to surge forward and rip out his throat again.

I can't though. He's already dead, and I am not even really here. This is just a memory, so all I can do is watch as he pulls River through a large field, heading toward a small building that could be an outhouse or a small hunting cabin.

I wish I could take the time to gaze up at the sun for the first time in my life or feel the warmth of its rays, but the fury burning through my veins stops me from feeling anything positive. The only thing that matters right now is being here for River.

As we enter the shack, I realize it's not a shack at all. It is just a mask for what's hidden underneath. At the back of the nearly empty room, he places his hand on a palm scanner. After a pause, there is a beep, and a solid metal door swings to reveal a set of stairs.

He leads, and we follow him down. Our travel is painfully slow. River—the then River—stumbles on weak legs, but he yanks on her collar occasionally to prod her to move faster. When Andres starts shaking, I know I'm not the only one bubbling with rage. For the sake of River, we keep it to ourselves. She already has to live

*through this a second time. There is no need to make it worse
for her.*

*She walks just behind the memory of herself, her eyes trained
forward.*

*After seventy-two stairs down, we come to a landing. There is
another door here with a keypad. I watch him closely, ready to
commit the code to memory. He enters 2-4-2-7-3-6, and the door
swings open. We step inside a sterile-looking facility and begin
walking down a long hallway lined with doors on either side.*

*Some of the doors are open, but River can only remember what she
actually saw. I peer into several rooms, but the memory only holds a
portion of their contents. Several have beakers and equipment I do
not recognize. Others look more like exam rooms you'd see in a
hospital. What the fuck do they do here? What did they do to River
here?*

*Suddenly, I question if agreeing to this was a big mistake. In my
nightmares, I often revisit and reimagine the horrible things that
were done to me. In hindsight, though, there is something far more
daunting about actually reliving it like this. My heart is beating
fast. Panic is building. What will I see here? How will it
haunt me?*

*I clasp River's hand, urging her to stay strong. It is ridiculous to
worry about my own fears when this little girl next to me has willingly dredged up her far more recent trauma. Right now, she is wide
awake and reliving it. Gods. I hope we're not making things worse.
Rayne's father leads us to the right, down another corridor with a
single door. He throws the door open roughly, and we enter to find
an office with another man working behind a desk.*

*"Ah, Ulysses." The other man looks up from the papers in front of
him. "You better be right about this one. The council is becoming
impatient with the issues you've caused. If you're not careful, they
will have you removed."*

"Have me removed?" His face turns red at an alarming rate, and the

sight of it makes me feel sick. "I am a Chasen, a descendant of Ullr. The council should be reporting to me—not the other way around."

"Yes. Yes. I am aware of your bloodline, Ulysses." The second man has mastered a longsuffering, condescending tone. "But it doesn't change the fact that your indiscretions are becoming somewhat of a habit. The witch..." the man begins.

"I already told you that I did not know," Ulysses challenges.

"Yes, I know what you said. Mistakes do happen. But you also bred with that witch and produced a daughter. If the Chasen genetics weren't so strong, she would be down here with the rest of these vermin," he says, his eyebrows pulled into a false look of concern.

He didn't just say what I think he did. Did he? Rayne's mom is a witch. But then why would a vampire kill her? I don't understand. Sure, there are vampires that have no qualms about killing other supernaturals, but not many. I feel like I'm missing an awful lot of information.

"You will not lay one finger on my daughter," Ulysses growls out, surprising me. I have only ever known him as a monstrous torturer, but it is clear he cares about Rayne. Although she is my dearest friend, it is not enough to make me feel any sympathy for him.

"Of course not. Your precious Rayne is protected. At least until the council tires of you and decides to make you disappear. After all, didn't she release that leech from right under your nose?" He sighs and shakes his head. "It doesn't look good for you, Ulysses."

My breath catches. They did know she helped me escape. Shit. I never thought to ask Rayne about her treatment after I left. Did they hurt her? Did they give her the punishments meant for me? Surely not if her father is protecting her from this man.

"Martin, you are walking dangerously close to a line that you really don't want to cross with me," Ulysses spits.

"Fine," Martin says, holding up his hands in a peaceful gesture. "I only wanted to warn you to be careful. If this girl ends up being a dud, the council is going to expect you to pay the price."

I can tell Ulysses is fuming, and I know from experience that it's best to get out of his way when he's angry. He doesn't care who becomes the target of his rage. I study the version of River who is currently bound to him and pray that he doesn't take it out on her. He pulls River's leash roughly, leading us back out of the office and down two more corridors to an area that looks like a cell block.

I glance into each of the cells, trying to sort out just how many supernaturals are trapped here. Some larger cells house bear shifters. Although they remain in their shifted form, it is obvious that they are malnourished and exhausted. Their furred skin hangs heavily from their bones. Other cells, as small as kennels, contain shifted felines and wolves with patchy, mangy fur.

The corridor ends in two gigantic cells that are cloaked in darkness. He tosses River in one and begins charging at her. I know what's coming next, so I throw my body in front of hers. I've taken his rage before and survived. I can do it again.

When he raises his hand for the first strike, someone calls out to him, and he turns to leave. Just before he closes the door, though, he glances back in.

"I'll be back for you soon," he snarls at River, who is now huddled in the corner and shaking in fear. He slams the door behind him, closing out the world around us except for the small, square window high on the metal door.

I can feel all three of our bodies vibrating with a mixture of rage and fear., The sensation is so strong that I think the building—or maybe the memory itself—is vibrating too. As the booms become louder and the quakes come closer, I realize there is something else making the world around us shake.

I watch as River runs to the single window in the cell door and peeks out. Andres and I do the same and catch a glimpse of the beast being held in the second gigantic cell. Not just a beast. A dragon. A tear slips from River's eye as she goes to speak, but the dragon shakes her head.

"No, my love," a voice rings out inside our minds. "You mustn't. They cannot know who we are to each other."

"But, Mama," River cries silently.

"Shh now, my love. It's okay. But I need you to do something for me," she says, her voice strong and calming in our minds. Through the small window, I can catch glimpses of her large form roiling in the shadows.

"Anything, Mama."

"I need you to be strong. Stronger than you have ever been before. You must get out of this place and never return. Find your Uncle Andres. He will protect and keep you safe. But never come back here. Do you hear me?"

"But what about you, Mama?" River asks.

"I have hope that one day we'll be together again. For now, knowing you're safe will do," she responds.

"But I don't know how to leave," River explains.

"Whatever you do, don't shift. If you don't shift, they will take you somewhere else. Somewhere your uncle can find you or you can escape. They will try to make you angry or sad," her mother explains. Even though they are not spoken aloud, I can hear the despair in her words. "They may try to hurt you, my sweet one. No matter what, you mustn't shift."

"Okay, Mama," River cries, tears flowing fast from her eyes.

"Oh, my sweet, sweet River. What I wouldn't give to hold you in my arms and take away your pain. Right now, you need to wipe your tears and meditate. Remember our training. Center yourself. Remember that I love you always and forever," her mother's voice is growing weaker, farther away, by the second. I do not know what they've done to her, but it seems like she's too weak to keep herself awake.

"I love you, Mama," River whispers aloud, wiping her tears and sitting in the middle of the floor to meditate.

With a start, I open my eyes to the bedroom. The change is immediate and jarring. I quickly pull River toward me, and Andres scoops us both up. All our eyes are already wet, but we sit and cry for a while anyway.

Gods. The things this young girl has gone through in her short life break my heart. I would give up anything to take a fraction of her pain away. Hopefully, Andres memorized the layout because I couldn't focus on anything other than Ulysses and River, and I will not be asking her to revisit that memory ever again.

When we calm down, I look at River, studying her shining blue eyes.

"Why don't you come sleep downstairs with me while your uncle meets with everyone?"

She nods, her eyes puffy and red from crying. I take her into the bathroom and wash her face. Although her eyes are still red and tired, she looks more like herself as we head downstairs.

"Hey, everyone. River and I are going to hang out downstairs while you have your meeting," I say, waving to them as we turn to walk down the stairs.

"Wait," Skarlyt calls out, and we turn to face her. "I'm sorry for earlier. I'm Skarlyt. You must be River." River nods in agreement. "Well, to apologize for all the yelling, I made you something. Will you come with me so I can show you?"

River looks up at me in question.

"It's okay. Skarlyt's a friend," I tell her. She relaxes and takes Skarlyt's outstretched hand. I follow them down the stairs and into Skarlyt's workroom. Only it isn't a workroom anymore. It's now a living room, equipped with a sectional, TV, and video games. There is even a small fridge and cupboard with snacks.

"What is this?" I question.

"Well, I was trying to think of how to apologize, and Rayne told me that River likes to be close to you. I changed everything around down here to be set up for you," she tells me. "No sun. No weird bunker vibes."

I look around in shock. "What about your workroom?"

"I hardly use it since Lennox and I extended the cottage. Besides, I can teleport now, so I can just pop home to do anything I need," she says, waving me off. "The bedroom is through there, but that's boring. *This* is the best part."

River rushes to the door Skarlyt indicated and throws it open, revealing a large bathroom with an ornate bathtub, tiled shower, double sinks, and even a makeup vanity. It's everything a girl her age could ever want. Heck, it's everything I want.

River seems to vibrate with excitement before turning and rushing to the bedroom. Inside, we find the largest bed I've ever seen, and a large, mounted TV with all the streaming services.

"Look, Aunty Dru! It's big enough for you, me, and Uncle Andres."

"Yes, I suppose it is," I say, thinking of the three of us in her small bed the night before.

"Oh, I didn't think about him! I'll add another bedroom for Andres off the living room," Skarlyt interjects, raising her hand to ready the spell.

"Why?" River asks.

Skarlyt turns to her.

"I'm sure your uncle and Dru won't want to sleep in the same bed, sweetie."

I see River open her mouth and move my hands in a stop motion, but she doesn't seem to notice.

"Why? Don't mates sleep in the same bed anymore?" she asks innocently, and I hang my head.

There it is. I didn't want to tell anyone, but the cat's out of the bag now.

"Mates?" Skarlyt asks in a shriek, turning to me with wide eyes.

I nod, and River seems to notice her mistake. She claps a small hand over her open mouth.

"Can I talk to you for a sec?" I ask Skarlyt, and she nods. I pull her aside into the hallway.

"Explain," she demands, and I take a deep breath.

"I told him that I'm not ready, and he's willing to wait. I don't want Drake to know. Yet—" I tell her.

"How can you even know?" she interrupts me.

"Well, apparently dragons can tell. They just know." I try to explain. "I think everyone could sense it immediately a long time ago. The way Andres explained it, it sounds like we have forgotten how to do it over the years."

"What?" she whispers, and I nod once again.

"Please, don't tell anyone. Not yet," I plead. "I need to come to terms with this before I let everyone else know."

"Why do you want to wait, Dru?"

"Skar, I just got my life back. I left my home for the first time in years less than a month ago. I need to learn to live in my own skin. I need to learn to love myself before I can love another person. Right now, I'm not strong enough to be the mate he deserves," I tell her.

"It seems to me that you already love another person," she challenges and gestures toward River. I suppose she's right. That little girl has taken up residence in my heart very quickly.

"You're right," I sigh. "But that's different and you know it."

"I'll keep this to myself. Of course, I will," Skarlyt agrees. "But I want you to think about it, Dru. Not every person finds their true mate. Even those who do may reject it." There's a pang of sadness and guilt through my chest at her words. Both she and Lennox were rejected before they found each other. She grips my hands tightly in hers. "When I found Lennox, I thought I needed to wait. Now I know that was just time together that we lost. We almost lost each other forever because I was forcing myself to wait."

In a pack as busy and accident-prone as this one, people move on quickly. However, I have obviously heard the tale of Skarlyt meeting Lennox, her second-chance true mate, only days after delivering the child of the true mate who had rejected her just months before.

"Skar," I begin, unsure how to accept her earnestness in this moment. "I appreciate it, but you know the situations are not the same."

"It's similar enough," she insists, lightly slapping my arm with her open palm. It is a playful gesture and more like herself. "You want to learn how to love yourself? Sure, you can teach yourself how to do it, but it's kind of stupid when the Mother sent you the best teacher right when you need it." She gestures meaningfully to the ceiling above us. "Don't let your past trauma keep you from accepting this gift. I've been there, and I will keep your secret. But I wish I had just run into Lennox's arms the first time I saw him."

With that, she gives me a hug and walks back upstairs. I am left reeling in the wake of her words.

Is that what I'm doing? Am I letting my past hinder my future?

Chapter Eight

Andres

Seeing Andrea in River's memory is harder than I thought it would be. I've never seen my sister so weak, and I am concerned that she seems to be stuck in her dragon form. We need to get to her soon. My dragon rumbles his agreement, and I can tell he is ready to leave already. He is ready to take off into the night, storm that facility, and burn it to the ground. I agree with him, but I know that's not possible.

We risk hurting Andrea if we do that, I try to reason with him. *We will need help. There are too many hunters. We could get captured and risk leaving River unprotected.*

He huffs in disagreement, but I know he understands and would never willingly hurt Andrea or leave River in danger.

I want her back just as much as you do, I promise him. He slinks to the back of my mind, curling his long, spiked tail around himself. It's a brief reprieve from the strong emotions he's been projecting onto me, and I'm grateful. I don't think I will be able to focus on anything if he continues bombarding me with visions of what he wants to do.

When I reach the bottom of the stairs, I give River and Drusilla's hands a squeeze as they head down to the basement with Skarlyt and head to the table to talk with the group.

"I apologize, Andres. I didn't realize how raising my voice would affect her," Alaric says as I step up.

"It's okay, Alaric. All of us will need time to learn. We don't know what happened to her, so anything could be a trigger," I tell him, mastering my own, earlier anger. "But she did provide me with some information about the facility that I think will be useful."

I gaze over the map and blueprints strewn across the table.

"Here," I point to a spot on the map. "There is a hut or shack of some kind in the middle of the field. The entrance is hidden by that shack. When you get inside, there is a panel. If it recognizes the handprint on the screen, it opens a door to lead you down a set of stairs."

"Biometric lock?" Drake clarifies. "That's going to be difficult to bypass."

"Easier just to knock down the door," I agree.

"What if we could get the hand of someone with clearance?" Rayne pipes up.

We all turn to look at her.

"What are you thinking?" Alaric asks.

"I'm thinking that I know plenty of the people who would have access—the so-called head of the families. It shouldn't be too hard for us to obtain a hand from one of them. We wouldn't necessarily have to kill them," she adds with a shrug.

Only Drake and I are unfazed. Everyone looks at her with wide eyes. I guess they didn't realize just how bloodthirsty Rayne could be. But we did.

She may seem all snark and attitude, but she thrives in bloodshed whether she wants to or not. Her soul is a bright pink, streaked with red and black. She's ruled by her heart but isn't afraid to make hard decisions. The red and black streaks were worrisome when I first met her because of what they signify. They are evidence that she has taken life and, given the amount of black, a significant number of lives at that. After getting to know her, I know that she has killed out of necessity. However, I would imagine she did get satisfaction from a few.

"I suppose that could work," I tell her. "Could that be a task for you and Drake?"

Drake and Rayne share a look and answer together. "Yes."

Perfect.

"That's settled. The next thing is the stairs. It's deep. Over sixty steps before you come to a landing. There's another door with a keypad. This door is just a code: 2-4-2-7-3-6."

"That's my last name," Rayne says, interrupting me.

Again, we all look at her.

"What?"

"On a keypad—like your phone—2 is a C, 4 is a H, 2 is A, 7 is an S," she trails off. "It's Chasen."

"Does that mean the codes are different for each family? Each person?" Phoebe asks.

"The Chasen line is important, but I'd wager that at least each family has their own code. Not all of them would be vain enough to use their last name," Rayne says thoughtfully. "We may need more than a hand from our prey, my love." She looks lovingly at her mate and gives him her hand as if they are starting a dance.

"Sounds like fun," Drake responds, giving her hand a kiss.

They really are perfect for each other.

"That's settled," I begin, getting back to the task at hand. I point out the area on the map. "Once you're inside, there are a series of doors lining this long hallway. Some have equipment and machines inside. Others look like exam rooms in a doctor's office. Those rooms will need to be cleared as we enter," I say, watching each of their reactions. Understanding and rage alight in their eyes. I can only imagine what horrors are performed in those rooms.

I open myself up to feel the emotions of the group. I find exactly what I had expected except for the fear coming from one of the bear shifters. The large man, Axel, has a mixture of varying emotions. I watch him closely as he opens and closes his fists a few times. I wonder what that is about. I'm going to have to watch him closely if he accompanies us.

"They keep shifters in those rooms?" Phoebe asks.

"No," I admit sadly. "They are like exam rooms—not holding cells. The doors are unlocked, and they would be too comfortable. They are similar to the cells under your shed, Alaric." I explain, trying to give them whatever details I can. He showed me his own holding area when I went to meet Drake's prisoner in an attempt to assess her soul. I can tell the comparison makes Alaric uncomfortable, but there was no hope or remorse in her soul. Thus, she remains down there even now.

"Straight ahead," I point out the place on the blueprints, but it's only a large, empty rectangle. "there's a large office. The door was closed—no window. I don't know his last name, but the office belongs to someone named Martin. He seems to run the place."

"That will be Martin Tanburg," Rayne verifies. "He's an asshole."

"Is he going to be a problem?" I ask.

"Not once I get a hold of him," she says with a smirk. "I know exactly how to deal with him."

I don't even want to know what she means by that.

"Moving on. I don't know what is down that corridor, but there are a lot of cells to the right. All filled with supernaturals. Bears, wolves, mountain lions, and more. And, in this one—" I pause to take a breath, my finger resting on the lines that mark the largest cell. "This one holds my sister, Andrea."

Everyone sucks in a breath, their eyes softening as they watch me with pity. Amid the rush of pity, I can sense something strange coming from Axel again. He glares at me with something akin to jealousy. I cannot comprehend this, but I decide to watch him closely; he could end up being a problem for us.

"So, she is there?" Rayne asks, pulling my attention away from the bear alpha.

I nod. "Yes. But I don't have a clear idea of *when* she was there. River's memory didn't give me a solid time frame. If the condition my sister was in worsened between then and now..." I allow my words to trail off. I don't voice out loud that I almost hope my sister is at peace. I would rather think that she had passed on from this world than been stuck in that place all this time.

Rayne comes around the table and places her hand on my shoulder.

"We have to have faith," she says, and I can feel the strength of her compassion. It lightens my heart and gives me hope. "We have faith that she is there and safe. We have faith that we will bring her home."

"Are they holding mountain lions there?" The female alpha, Trixie, asks.

"Yes." I point to the place where the smaller kennels were. "Wolves and all kinds of feline shifters were being held in these."

She narrows her eyes at the spot, and I'm grateful that she's a shifter. If she were a witch, I have no doubt that the blueprints would be incinerated.

"All right," Alaric begins, taking the reins back with ease. "We need information. We will scout the place out to try and get an idea of their comings and goings." He waits for Trixie, still staring daggers at the blueprint, to look up and meet his eyes. "That's where you and your pack come in. If we could have a team up there for a couple of days...Honestly, a week would be preferable. If it were my sibling, I wouldn't want to wait that long. So, if Andres is okay with giving us a few days to get things rolling..."

He looks at me expectantly.

"I will give us a week to get things in order. I'd rather go in with more information and a better chance at success than rush in and possibly lose our element of surprise," I tell him, and he nods.

My dragon perks up at my response and rumbles his disapproval, but I ignore him. This gives us a better chance of rescuing everyone in there. Not just our sister.

"Okay, a week. I can send Samara with you," he glances over at Samara and receives a nod. "You will leave in the morning. Check back hourly. If you don't check in, we will storm the gates to find you."

With that settled, Alaric's gaze turns to Drake and Rayne. "You two have your job already. The rest of us are going to be the muscle on the actual day of. Axel, I will ask at least twenty-five of your strongest to come with us. I'll bring the same."

"I want no part in this, Alaric," Axel says with a growl before leaving the house. We all glance at one another. It would've been easier with the bears, but we can't force them if they don't want to take part. Alaric looks angry, but he seems to set the emotion aside to deal with later. From what I have seen of the bear alpha, we may be better off without him.

"What about us?" Phoebe and Sophia ask in concert.

"You two will be needed outside," Alaric states, and I can tell he dreads the thought of bringing his mate near danger. "I'm not sure what happens if an underground facility catches fire, and I don't really want to learn. I think you'll both be more help out in the open. If any hunters try to escape, if they try to call in reinforcements, you two can handle them more safely than any of us could."

I admire this alpha's forethought, and I can see this wisdom in his plans.

"We will need you to stock up on tears between now and then. You and the coven will be waiting outside to receive the supernaturals we release. We don't know what shape they will be in, so we will need you two on deck," he looks at Sebastyn and Sarah, and they nod without hesitation. "I'm going to need you to make a barrier like you did in Halifax to keep everyone safe once they leave the facility, and then slowly start teleporting everyone," he says with a pensive look. "I'm not sure where to take them yet. We will have to figure that out."

"We can build a temporary shelter in the coven's clearing," Skarlyt adds, coming up the stairs. She couldn't have heard much of the plan thus far, but she's ready with suggestions. "We already have the temporary structures set up out there. If Sarah and I go out there over the next few days, we can set up something like a hospital triage for them to heal in."

Her eyes meet mine, and I can sense a strange emotion from her. Is it pity? Adoration? Either way, it's weird, and I'm not sure that I like it.

"Without the bears, the pack is going to need to send more members," Darren warns. He stands behind his mate, his chin perched playfully on her slim shoulder.

"We will arrange for a few extra coven members as well," Drake adds, trying to take some of the burden from the wolves.

"You know many of the witches will want to be underground fighting with you," Skarlyt agrees.

"It would be a lot easier if Axel were to come with us, but I understand why he doesn't want to," Alaric says sullenly.

"I don't," I rumble. "I saw a few bears in that place. Surely, he would want to save his own people."

"His father was killed by hunters, and his brother has been missing—presumed dead—for years," Sebastyn supplies.

"I don't understand. Wouldn't that make him want revenge even more?" I argue.

"Some would think," Skarlyt says, looking between Alaric, Darren, and her brother. "But..."

"But after his father died, he changed." Alaric finishes for her. "He's afraid. He'll do anything to protect his sleuth—even if it means hiding."

I don't pretend to understand that reasoning. Even if I didn't already know my sister was trapped there, I would be just as interested in breaking in. If his brother is missing, it's the best place to start looking. Then again, I don't have anyone other than River to worry about. Perhaps I would feel differently if I had a pack with hundreds of people relying on me. Either way, I can't imagine his bear is agreeing with his decision.

We spend time going over the plan in greater detail. The leaders name some of the people they hope to send from their packs. We discuss the best time to attack, keeping in mind that our vampires cannot risk being out too close to dawn, but our phoenixes will be hard to conceal in the dark. Eventually, I decide that I need some air.

All this planning is stirring up my protectiveness over my sister. How dare those monsters touch her? How dare they hold her? She is eons older than even their ancestors. Don't they know who they are messing with?

I am breathing heavily, feeling the need to shift and stretch my wings. Just as I open the door, though, I hear a scream and freeze.

Drusilla...

Chapter Nine

Drusilla

River and I decide to curl up together on the gigantic bed and watch a movie. We are both still weepy and weary from experiencing her memory, so we choose a comedy movie that neither of us is familiar with.

"Aunty Dru?" About halfway through the movie, River's soft voice interrupts my thoughts.

"Hmm?" I hum in response.

"Do you think my mama will still be there?"

I glance down, at where her head is laying in my lap, and stroke her long, golden hair.

"I have hope that she will be." I cannot promise her anything, so I do not. I will not be responsible for disappointing her or stealing her hope.

She nods in understanding.

"Can I tell you a secret?" she asks after a few quiet moments.

"Always."

"Sometimes, I hope that she's not there." She pauses, blinking back the tears that are quickly flooding her eyes. "If she moved on to the next world—if she was gone—"

She stops, searching for the words she needs to say, and I grip her hand encouragingly.

"The next world is nice, you know? It is nice there, and—and she wouldn't hurt anymore. I know they hurt her at that place. I know he did."

I pull her into my arms as both our tears start to fall.

"I know what you mean, little one. I understand. There were times when I thought death would be a relief as well. Your mama is strong," I say. Though I do not know her, I have met her brother and daughters, and I am sure she is worthy of them. "If she thinks she can get back to you, she'll do anything to make it."

"She is strong," River whispers in assent. "I miss her. I miss my Da too. I do not know where he is. They would have been taken together."

"We'll find him after we rescue your mama. We have to trust in the gods that everything will work out as it should. If they are no longer in this world—you are right—they are in a place of rest and peace. Hopefully, though, your father is out there somewhere looking for you just as you are looking for him."

She nods, laying back down on my lap.

I don't voice out loud what I'm thinking. Andres has been searching for his sister and her mate for weeks and found no sign of them. There are only two explanations. First, the hunters are using something to block the bonds of the supernaturals they've imprisoned. Second, they are no longer in this world for him to sense.

Long after River falls asleep, I stay where I am, holding her and gently caressing her hair when she cannot settle. She is so strong for someone so young. She experienced horrors during her time with the hunters, yet she is doing everything she can to help, reliving that awful time to help save her own mother.

Yes. I have seen horrors too. I was older, though, and better equipped to meet their abuse. This poor girl hasn't even gone through puberty yet. She's a child who has had to wake alone in an unfamiliar world only to be kidnapped and abused by strangers.

My eyelids become heavy, and I feel the nightmare gripping me even before they drift closed. I try to fight it, but it's impossible. Its hold is like a boa constrictor. The more I try to fight it, the tighter it becomes.

I will escape soon. I'm not sure how I know, but I do. I know Rayne will be coming to feed me today, and I look forward to seeing her. Each time she comes, I gain a little of my strength back.

She provides me with more than my allotted portion of blood as well as her surprisingly pleasant company. I don't know how she gets away with it, but I'm terrified she will get caught. It's as inevitable as the sun rising. I simply hope she figures out a way to escape— with or without me—before that happens.

I can survive their tortures, but I cannot watch her go through them as well. I never thought that I would call a hunter my friend, but Rayne is different. She hasn't been a hunter in truth since the first day she walked into the shed.

I stood in the back of my cell, watching as she and her father strode toward me. The horrified look on her face told me everything I needed to know about her. She was nothing like the man she called father.

As the door opens, a smile graces my lips to greet her.

"You're early..." I begin, but the face that greets me isn't Rayne.

"I take it that I'm not who you were expecting," he snarls as he watches my face fall. I scurry to the back corner of my cage, hoping and praying that he doesn't enter. Not today. He isn't supposed to be here today.

It's been a little over a year since Price took over the chore of administering my punishments. Rayne's father still makes regular appearances, but Price is much worse.

"It seems our little prodigy needs a reminder of who and what you

*are. I don't know how you convinced her to bring you extra blood,"
he chuckles and my heart drops to my stomach. "After this, she's
going to be more afraid of me than you. That's for sure."*

*My fear is overpowered by protectiveness. If they're punishing me
for Rayne's actions, I can take anything they want to dish out. As
long as she stays safe, I can meet this threat.*

*I watch his movements as his hand hovers over a wall mounted
with a variety of whips. There are so many: metal ones, leather ones,
and ones with spikes. I send up a silent prayer that he doesn't
choose the metal-spiked one.*

*That one is made specifically for separating flesh from bone. I know
this because Rayne's father used it on me before. Although I'm
much stronger now than I was, I don't know if I will survive that
with Price being the operator.*

*Just as I feared, his hand grips the handle of the spiked, metal whip.
As he lifts it off its place on the wall, he turns to me with an evil
grin. Although Rayne's father always hated me, there is something
even worse in Price's leer. He kissed me once on the beach before
dawn, and he looks at me like he wants us both to suffer for it.*

*"Let's show that perfect little princess what happens when she
doesn't follow the rules."*

"She didn't..." I start, but he just laughs and shakes his head.

*"I've noticed how much quicker you're healing after my visits, so
I've been following her. I know she takes an extra blood pack or two
at each drop-off," he shakes his head as if he's disappointed.*

*I want to deny it out of fear that she'll be punished as well, but the
look on his face tells me that denial will only make it worse.*

*My breathing becomes rapid as I anticipate his movements. The
cell door clangs open, and the whip scrapes along the floor as he
drags it behind him. I close my eyes and try to go to my happy place.
I have carved my own little slice of heaven out of my mind. That is
where I escape when they punish me. Today, though, my worry*

about Rayne keeps me present. I am afraid she will interrupt. I do not want her to see this. I do not want her to take my place.

As always, the first two strikes are the worst. I can feel each barb of the whip grasping my flesh and pulling it back from my body. I cry out in pain, unable to stop myself. I can feel the rivers of blood streaming down my back and pooling on the floor. At the fifth strike, I heave, losing all the blood in my stomach.

This weapon is usually limited to ten lashes. As Price passes the fifteenth, though, I know the old rules no longer apply.

I'm no longer standing or even kneeling. Instead, I'm laying flat on the floor in a pool of my own blood and vomit. I have a feeling I'm going to finally die in this cell. They are going to put me out of my misery. My only regret is not telling Rayne what a monster her father is—telling her to get far away from here—telling her thank you for trying to help me.

I have lost count of the lashes. I hear him pull back again, and I am sure that the next attack will be the last I ever suffer.

Then, I hear the door burst open. I raise my heavy head in concern, hoping and praying that it isn't Rayne. I'm not sure what she would do if she witnessed this, but I cannot stand to see her trying to stop Price.

It's not her, though, and I will never know how she would have reacted.

It's her monster of a father.

I let my head fall back to the floor. All remaining strength leaves me at once, and I close my eyes, embracing the feeling of death. Once, long ago, I feared leaving this world. Not anymore. Now, I embrace it like an old friend.

"That's enough, Price!" he yells. "We don't want her dead."

"Sir," my tormentor, Price, interrupts. "You said we needed to teach Rayne a lesson. This is a lesson." There is an animosity in the air between them that I do not remember existing before.

"I said I want to teach her a lesson. Not that I am ready to kill our guest."

"Sir," Price says in a taut assent. He leaves the cell without closing the door and hangs the whip back on the wall without cleaning it. I can hear the slow drips of my own blood as they fall to the floor. The older man snarls at me, coming closer so that I can hear his lowered voice.

"If you know what's good for you, you'll make sure my daughter is never inclined to give you anything. She'll be in here with you if she keeps it up, and I don't think either of us wants that."

With the little strength I have left, I sullenly nod my head. He is satisfied that I have understood his warning and walks out, leaving the door to my cell open.

He knows as well as I do that I have no strength left to escape. If that door had been left open even an hour earlier, I would have walked out without a moment's hesitation.

I try to sit up anyway. If nothing else, I want to clean myself up before Rayne comes in. She doesn't understand everything that happens here, and I think it should stay that way. I know if she walks in to see this, the effect will be the opposite of what they want. She will know—once and for all—that they are monsters. She will defy them even more, and she'll be in even more danger because of it. I know it is almost time for her to join me. As I raise my head to greet her, though, my nightmare shifts.

I am no longer the one laying on the ground. In the way of dreams, I am now standing in the doorway. I am no longer hurt, no longer dripping my own blood.

Now, River is laying in my place. Price, crazed and covered in blood, stands over her with the same whip that haunts me.

"No!" I scream at him. It is a kind of warning, but I am not sure who it is for. I am not sure if he hears me, but he pauses and smiles. His cursed lips pull upward into a smirk as he grabs her roughly by *the hair—long and blonde and stained red at the ends—and pulls her back.*

"I've enjoyed our time together, pet. Haven't you?" He drops her with the same force that he pulled her back, sending her sprawling back onto the bloodstained floor. "You're much stronger than the last monster I had to play with. Let's see if you can last as long as she did."

As he pulls the whip back, ready to strike, I scream again. I throw my body over hers, but the whip goes right through me, tearing River's flesh from her back.

She sobs softly, and I am forced to watch. I try to throw myself at Price, but I go right through him. I try to curse him, taunt him— anything to bring his attention back to me. He doesn't seem to notice my words.

I watch in horror as the scene unfolds before me.

I feel someone shaking me.

"Dru! Come back to me!" I know that voice...

As I open my eyes, they meet Rayne's brown eyes, large and full of concern. I'm still half in my memories though, and I cannot be comforted.

"No. Rayne, leave. Run. You can't be here. You can't see this. You have to go," I cry, tears streaming down my face as I back up on the bed until I hit the headboard.

She follows me, crawling on her hands and knees.

"Shh. It's okay. I'm here. No one is going to hurt you," she whispers like she's coaxing a feral animal out of its den. I flinch as she touches my leg. Her eyes fill with sadness, but she doesn't leave. "It's okay. I'm here. I'm not leaving you. You're in Alaric and Phoebe's house. I am here. So is Drake. Over there are River and Andres. You remember them, right?" she questions, and my eyes flick over to the doorway.

The first thing I notice is River, looking terrified in the arms of her uncle.

Shit.

What have I done?

I glance back at Rayne's wide, worried eyes to search for an explanation, and her gaze softens.

"There you are. It's okay, babe. I promise. It's all going to be okay," she whispers, wrapping her arms around me while I sob into her hair.

I thought I was done with this. I guess going into River's memory messed with my head more than I wanted to admit.

Chapter Ten

Andres

I race down the stairs to get to Drusilla, but I find a terrified River standing in the doorway with Drake while Rayne is on the bed with Drusilla, trying to talk to her. Drusilla doesn't seem like she's completely here. Her eyes have a glassy look like they are seeing something from her nightmare instead of her friend. I look down at River and note the tears lining her cheeks. I pull her trembling frame to my side.

She will be okay, little one, I say through our bond.

She looks up at me in question.

How do you know? I shouldn't have brought her into my memory, she responds.

I crouch down in front of her, gripping her shoulders.

"If anyone is at fault, it is me. I should never have asked either of you to relive those memories. I didn't know what the conse-quences would be, but I knew there would be some."

"We need to take her home to heal," she says with determina-tion like it is an obvious solution I have been putting off.

"Our home has been gone for centuries, sugar," I begin, suddenly unsure if she understands just how long we were asleep.

She is not deterred by the words. Her eyes sparkle with excitement.

"We can recreate it," she says simply. "Just like you and Mama used to do."

"River, your mother and I practiced for years before we mastered that skill," I say apologetically, finally understanding her. "I cannot build it alone. I'm sorry. We will have to find something else."

"I can help you. Mama taught me how to create worlds just for me and her." A pang of hurt slices through my chest at the thought of Andrea and how much she is missing out on with River.

I want to say no. River can't be strong enough, and I don't want to ask her to extend herself any further than she already has. As I look over at Drusilla and watch her cling to Rayne, though, I decide we must try. After all, in a pocket world, she would have infinite time to heal while being safe.

I stand and tap Drake on the shoulder, gesturing for him to follow us into the hallway.

"River and I would like to take Drusilla to our home to heal," I tell him, and his jaw almost hits the floor.

"To your home? I thought you were asleep for hundreds of years. Do you even have a home?" Drake questions. When he is caught off guard, he turns to being mean.

"You're right. Our home would have been demolished while we slept. However, River and I are able to recreate a pocket world where we could go. It would be exactly like our home was so long ago, and it would give Drusilla the time to heal without triggers," I explain.

"Okay," Drake exhales a deep breath. I do not fault him for that. The concept of interplanar travel can be difficult at first. "You can ask her. But I doubt she will want to go with strangers." The way he calls us strangers hurts a little, but I can restrain myself. I stop myself from letting him know that we are certainly not strangers. River, however, does not show the same restraint.

"Of course, she will go with us," she says, bouncing from heel to toe in excitement. "She's your mate and my aunty, so it'll be no problem!" Drake looks at her in surprise before his features darken upon turning to me.

"You're her what?" he growls out.

"I am her mate," I say proudly, not caring in the slightest how his fangs drop and glisten with murderous intent.

"Why haven't you claimed her? Are you ashamed? Is that why you didn't tell me?" He spits accusations at me without pause.

"It's none of your business, Drake," Rayne interrupts him as she joins us in the hallway. "If you must know, it wasn't his call not to tell you." I shouldn't be surprised that Drusilla told her, but I am. Drake's eyes soften at her tone. Smart man. I would hate to be on her bad side. "She's asking for River," Rayne says softly to me.

I look down at River and nod, watching as she skips toward the bedroom and my fragile mate.

"Is she okay?" Both Drake and I ask at the same time, causing him to shoot a glare at me. I don't react though, one day—hopefully soon—he will learn to accept me.

Rayne gives us both a little smile. "She is okay. Or she will be. Going into that memory made her relive her last day in captivity. Instead of me coming to save her, it morphed into her watching River go through the same thing. She doesn't know if it's real, and she needs time to sort through it. She just needs time to live peacefully—with River—to prove to herself that they are both safe. That little girl has wormed her way right to the center of Dru's heart," Rayne says, turning to peek into the room with a loving gaze.

"Andres and River want to take her to some..." Drake begins but is lost for what to call it.

"Pocket world," I supply. "It is a recreation of our home. It is separate from this world, so she would have time to live without danger or fear."

"I think that's a fantastic idea," Rayne agrees, turning to walk into the bedroom. Drake and I follow, and he mumbles about women driving him crazy. I internally chuckle at him and wonder if I'm ever going to get to that point with Drusilla. Will she drive me crazy and make me fall more in love with her at the same time? Though Drake grumbles, I have no doubt that's exactly what's happening.

As I walk into the room, I smile at the scene that greets me. Drusilla and River are on the bed embracing. It's beautiful, and it is a sight I hope to one day see with our own children. If, for some reason, my sister is unable to be rescued, I know that Drusilla will love River with a fierceness that rivals even her mother's. I must believe that is what my sister would want. If Andrea can be rescued—which I'm praying for—then River will have two women who love her fiercely enough to trample the world for her.

As if sensing me, Drusilla looks up and meets my eyes. There is an immediate heat behind her eyes that she blinks away as quickly as it appears. She offers me a soft smile before turning back to a very excited River.

"Aunty Dru! We're going to make a pocket world for us to go relax in for a few days," she exclaims.

"What do you mean?" Drusilla asks, looking between both River and me.

I walk up and take a seat on the bed next to them. "River thought it would be nice for us to take you to our home for a while. It'll give you both a chance to relax away from all the stress." I clasp her hand in mine, and she doesn't pull away. Her hand is warm and damp, perhaps sweaty from stress or the salt water of drying tears.

She looks down at our hands, and then back up at me with a soft smile. "It's a nice thought, but we are all sort of busy right now.

And—no offense—but your home was probably destroyed a long time ago."

"That's the best part!" River exclaims. "Uncle Andres and I are going to recreate it, just how it was. Aren't we, Uncle Andres?"

"Of course, we are. That is, if Drusilla wants to," I tell River, and she begins to bounce on the bed, looking between both of us.

"Of course, she does. Right, Aunty Dru?" River asks.

Drusilla chuckles and nods. "Of course. I would love to see your home."

"Yay!" River shouts, jumping up off the bed to pace around the room. "When do we leave?"

"Whenever Drusilla wishes," I state.

"What about Rayne and Drake?" Drusilla asks, her eyes finding theirs in the doorway.

"We have some stuff that we have to handle here," Rayne says.

"But..." Drusilla tries to interrupt.

"No buts, Dru. This will help you. Go. Spend some time with your mate and River." At Rayne's mention of her mate, Drusilla's eyes go wide with panic and flash quickly to Drake.

"It's okay. River let the cat out of the bag," Rayne says. Drusilla scolds River with a look, but when the child's eyes start to water, her look softens.

"I didn't mean to," River whispers.

"It's okay," Drusilla says, grabbing River into a hug. "We shouldn't have expected you to keep the secret."

"I'm sorry," River sobs.

Hearing the pain in River's voice, I lean over and join their embrace, easily wrapping my arms around them both. We stand there for a few minutes until River's tears slow.

"Okay. We still have a couple of hours of night left. Let's go out to the clearing to prepare while Drusilla talks with her family," I say, taking River's hand and bidding the others in the room good-bye. I think they need to spend a little time together before I whisk

Drusilla away for a few days. Especially Drake. I don't think it will be easy for him to let her be out of contact for any amount of time.

I'm not sure how to help Drusilla overcome her own terror, but I think being tucked safely away from reality will be a step in the right direction—even if only for a short time.

"Andres?" Drake follows me before we can reach the stairs, and I turn to face him. "You will take care of my sister, right?"

"Of course, I will. I will do everything in my power to help her and protect her, even if it costs me my own life," I tell him. He nods at me before turning back and heading into the house. I'm a little disappointed. I thought for sure Drake would put up more of a fight when he learned that I am his sister's mate, but fate works in mysterious ways. Perhaps he has learned that since finding his own true mate in a hunter.

"Okay, sugar. Let's go home," I say to River.

Together, we walk out to the front yard, but I stop just before the tree line.

"Ready to shift, little one?" I ask.

She looks at me with excitement before her features scrunch up.

"Uncle Andres," she says in a panic.

"What is it, sugar?" I ask, kneeling in front of her and studying her face.

"I can't feel her," she tells me, her eyes flying open, brimming with tears once more.

"What do you mean?" I ask. I have never heard of such a thing, and River has been able to shift since she was an infant. Something that drove her parents—and me—crazy as we sought to keep her out of trouble.

"I mean, I can sense that she's still there. It's like she's sleeping or maybe afraid," she starts, but her voice trembles. "What if I pushed her so far down when I was stopping myself from shifting that I lost her forever?"

I grasp her face in my hands, wiping the stray tears off her cheeks with my thumbs. "That's not possible. It could just be that she doesn't feel quite safe yet. How about you hop on my back, and I'll fly us there?"

"Okay," she nods, tears still flowing from her eyes.

"It will be okay, sugar. You'll see. We'll get her back. Don't you worry," I tell her. When her tears slow, I turn and shift in front of her. My gigantic dragon dwarfs her small body, and I curl my tail so that it's easier for her to climb up. We've done this thousands of times. It's always been just for fun—never out of necessity—but with practiced movements, she scurries up my body until she is seated in her spot at the base of my neck between spikes.

With a roar, I take to the skies. I fly left and right and up and down until I hear soft giggles coming from her. I knew that she wouldn't be able to hold out for long, but the two-minute flight to the clearing turns into a twenty-minute exercise for me. It's worth it. I need to lift her spirits even if only for a moment.

I land and shift back quickly, causing River to fall through the air for a moment before I catch her in my arms. She is shocked into another fit of giggles, and it is music to my ears. I'm sure we can coax her dragon back out with some peace and relaxation.

As if not a day has gone by since we were separated, we stand together with clasped hands and envision our home through our bond.

"Don't forget the flowers in the glen, Uncle Andres," she reminds me.

"How could I?" I ask.

Together, we envision our home the way it once was. The grass, the forest, our house, even the glen filled with wildflowers, and the small stream that cuts through it. I can almost smell the wood burning in the fireplace and feel the fresh air on my skin. With a little push, it all pulls together, and a small doorway opens right in front of us.

We must hold it open until Drusilla gets here, but River runs straight through. She is already laughing and rolling down the soft grass. I am surprised by the pang of nostalgia that hits me when I see our home again. I hadn't realized just how much I missed it all.

Luckily, we don't have to wait long. Within minutes, a stunned Drusilla is standing next to me, placing her small hand in mine.

"Are you ready to see my home, love?" I ask her.

She watches me for a moment, her thoughts indiscernible behind her beautiful, blue eyes, and nods.

Hand in hand, we walk through the doorway. As she takes in her new surroundings, the door closes behind us.

Chapter Eleven

Drusilla

T he doorway looks like a tear between worlds. On one side is the clearing here in Parry Sound, with large evergreens beginning to drop their needles and the wind whipping through everyone's hair. On the other side, there is another world, so vibrant and green that I can see clearly despite the night. I twirl in a circle with an enormous smile on my face, feeling freer than I have in a very long time. A gasp escapes me as I look up at the sky.

"Oh, my goddess. I've never seen so many stars," I whisper. It's the truth. I am used to looking up to see the sky with stars scattered through it. Here, though, there are more bright, twinkling points of light than there is black between them.

"This is what the world used to be like," Andres tells me, walking up behind me and snaking his arms around my waist while we look up together. "Before the smog and pollution of the modern-day conveniences like cars or plastics."

I allow myself to melt into him, momentarily forgetting my past and my hesitations. I allow the feeling of bliss at his closeness to surround me.

"It's so beautiful," I say.

"Yes, you are," he responds in my ear.

I bow my head shyly, the butterflies in my stomach going haywire.

"Aunty Dru! Come see!" River exclaims, grabbing my hand and pulling me closer to their home. It's a small, wooden cabin with a covered porch. It looks like something from *Little House on the Prairie*. Instead of opening the door, River scurries up a ladder on the side of the house. It brings her to the roof, where she impatiently beckons me to come with her.

Once I'm up on the roof, I look around and freeze. Immediately, I know exactly what she wanted to show me. Just above the trees, the full moon sits, closer and larger than I thought possible.

"Oh my," I whisper.

"This was mine and my mama's special spot," she begins as she lays down on the slant of the roof facing the moon. I walk over and lie down next to her. "She used to bring me up here on cloudless nights, and we would try to count the stars."

I look over at her and watch a small tear slip from her eye. I gently wipe it away. "Thank you for sharing this special spot with me."

"I'm scared," she admits, and I prop myself up on my elbow.

"Of what?" I ask, turning toward her. I do not mention the hunters, hoping that's not what is on her mind.

"I'm worried that my dragon is gone."

I suck in a breath. Well, that wasn't what I was expecting.

"What do you mean?"

She sighs. "I used to feel her. She was always with me. We weren't separate; we were one. She was me, and I was her. When Mama warned me not to shift, I would feel her coming to the surface, especially when they would... She struggles with the words, but I know what she is saying.

"When they would punish you?" I finish the statement for her, knowing what she is trying to say. I may not have had a dragon living inside me rushing up to protect me, but I had to push down my nature all the same. That's what they wanted. They wanted my fangs to drop and my eyes to turn blood red. They wanted me to hiss and thrash at them.

She turns to me, tears still brimming in her eyes, and nods. "She would want to break free to protect me, but I would push her down. It got to the point where, as soon as they would open the door, I would start to force her down into the corner of my mind. At some point, she stopped even trying to come through. Now it's like she's there, but she's not. I don't know when it happened, and I don't know how to reach her. I was just trying to do what my mama said and protect her at the same time. What if I pushed her so far that she's gone forever?"

I slide over closer to her, snaking my arms around her tiny frame. "Oh, River. If you went through anything like I did, your dragon will understand why you had to protect her. There was obviously a reason why your mama didn't want you to shift," I tell her and just hold her while she sobs. "Maybe she realized you were trying to protect her, and now she's trying to stay hidden to help you."

She leans back and looks at me with hope shining in her small eyes. "You think so?"

"Why not? You say that you were one. I think she would know why you did what you did and has been trying to protect you too. I bet that if you look really hard, you'll find her in there," I whisper, wiping the last of the tears off her beautiful face.

With a smile, she rolls back and begins pointing out the different stars she knows and telling me the stories her mom shared with her. We lay there for a while before she cannot hide a huge yawn.

"All right, little one. I think it's time to get you to bed," I say, standing up and helping her to her feet.

Andres is waiting at the bottom of the ladder for us as we descend. He scoops up a sleepy River and carries her into the house as I follow.

Stepping inside the small cabin, I instantly feel at home. It's simple: one main room with a stone fireplace equipped with a spit for cooking, a table and set of chairs, a small counter with a sink, and two doors along the back wall. Small windows are covered with cloth curtains and lined with potted plants.

I follow Andres as he carries River through one of the doors and places her on the bed inside. I walk around the side of the single bed, pulling up the simple, quilted covers as I go and give her a soft kiss on her head. She's already fast asleep with a look of peace settled on her face. This is how she is supposed to be. Not plagued by the horror she has had to deal with.

I stop at the door, leaning against the frame to just watch her. Goddess, how I wish I could take every single memory of that place—of those people—from her. I've lived with memories like that myself, so I know the damage they're doing. I have not forgotten the Mother's whispers. She claims I will be the one to help her, but I have no idea how I am supposed to do that. I don't even know how to help myself.

"Drusilla," Andres whispers, surprising me and causing me to turn away from River.

"Yes?"

"Will you come with me? I want to show you something." His large, strong hand is extended toward me, and his bright eyes are hopeful.

I nod as I place my hand in his, allowing him to lead me outside. We walk for a few minutes, hand in hand. As we walk, I take in the scenery. Everything is so...perfect. I do not know how to describe it, but everything is somehow exactly as it should be. The world around us is clear, clean, and quiet. Our home in Parry

Sound is incredible, but this is perfect. Even the clouds are fluffier and purer.

I'm still looking up at the sky as we come to a stop, and I force my eyes back to the ground.

We are standing atop a large cliff that overlooks a beautiful valley. There's a thin river running through the center of the valley. I can see for miles.

"This is my favorite place in the whole world," Andres says, releasing my hand and taking a seat on the ledge, letting his legs hang off the side. "I have always felt free when I sit here. It's like the breeze carries all the burdens and troubles on my shoulders away with it."

"I can see why this place would make you feel that way. It's beautiful," I admit, taking a seat next to him. I allow my legs to dangle off the steep edge. There's a slight panic as my legs hang free, but I swallow it down. I close my eyes and feel the wind as it whips past us. It lifts the stray strands of my hair and blows them around my face.

"Will you tell me your story, Drusilla?" Andres asks with hope in his voice.

I turn to look at him in shock. Panic begins to seize my chest. "I —I—don't know."

"You don't have to. I simply would like to get to know you," he tells me with understanding in his eyes.

I nod my head, looking away from his eyes and back out to the scene in front of us. I center myself with a few deep breaths as he gently positions me to sit between his legs.

"I don't know where to begin," I tell him.

"You can begin anywhere you want to," he says as he gently combs his large fingers through my hair, calming my racing heart.

"Well, I guess I should start at the beginning," I say with a small chuckle. "I had a happy childhood. My parents loved me with a passion, and Drake was always my protector and my best friend. Drake only cared about vampires, but I was more outgoing. I wanted to make friends with everyone—even humans.

"One night, Drake took me and my friend, Breanne, along to a human party. That was the night I met Price," I shudder at the mention of his name. "He was handsome, funny, and—most of all —seemed interested in me. I was a teenage girl, remember? Between my parents being the coven leaders and Drake being Drake, I was off limits. None of the boys in my coven cared about me, so I was elated when I met Price and he actually paid attention to me. I was drawn to him. I even thought he could have been my mate—"

Andres growls loudly at my admission, and I turn my head to give him a soft, apologetic look.

"Sorry," he says.

I put my hand on his. "It's okay. I'm sure that I would have had the same reaction if you said something similar about another woman."

His next breath is another rumble deep within his chest.

"Anyway, we now know that wasn't the case. At that moment, that's how I felt. So, when he asked me to sneak away the next night, I was overjoyed and quickly agreed."

I pause, closing my eyes and trying to gain the courage to tell the rest. With each soft touch of his fingers through my hair, my fear loses some of its hold on me.

"Drake didn't want me to go, but I convinced him. I know that's something he blames himself for to this day. He wouldn't have been able to stop me from sneaking out, and we would have both been taken if he'd come with me." I pause and take another deep breath. Although I know I am the victim here, I cannot help but feel like I am recounting my own sins when I replay all the awful choices I made that night. "I took my friend again. Breanne was just as excited as I was to be getting out of the coven and meeting new people. We giggled the entire way, imagining that the friend Price was bringing along may end up being her mate as well." My voice cracks over the description of our girlish fantasies.

"When we got there, there were at least a dozen men waiting. We tried to fight, but it was no match. They brought these gags and chains to secure us. I still remember looking into Breanne's eyes as they put her in the other truck. She thought I would save her. Her eyes—she was begging me to do something—anything. But I couldn't. I couldn't even save myself."

The tears are flowing freely now, and Andres snakes his arms around me.

"You don't have to continue," he says.

"I do. I won't be able to go through this again. If you are going to hear it, it has to be tonight," I tell him, turning to look into his eyes. He nods, and I take another deep breath. "I spent years in a cage, being tortured for information. The people they were looking for—the people they desperately wanted to find—were my parents. They chose the wrong girl to kidnap and question because I would have never given up my family."

A soft smile graces my lips at the next part. "One day, an angel appeared. A young girl—she was probably in her early teens at that point—would come in to deliver my blood packs. Instead of throwing them on the ground or laughing as I tore them apart, she would set the blood on a tray and push it gently into the cage before taking a seat. Every day, she would ask me my name and tell me things about her life. She was constantly talking, much like now," I chuckle a little at just how right I am. "Rayne was the first person to show me any sort of kindness during my captivity. She did everything she could to give me extra blood. Turns out, I was her first friend ever. She was so sad. Her life was so lonely."

I glance over at him, and he doesn't have pity in his eyes or even rage like I expected. Instead, there's something like adoration. I think his respect level for Rayne just went up.

"Her father was a monster, and, after a while, he figured out what Rayne was doing—giving me extra blood—that is. He put the man of my nightmares in charge of my punishments. Price, it turns out, is the worst kind of monster. He pretended to be my friend, to be interested in me, and then he became my tormenter," I hiccup a small sob, trying to even my breathing enough to continue.

"When they found out about the extra blood—that day, Price grabbed the barbed metal whip, and I knew what he meant. I thought he was going to kill me, but Rayne's father came in and put a stop to it. He made sure that I was still alive when his daughter came in for my feeding. It was his way of punishing her. Before he left, he told me that I needed to make her stop helping me or it would be her in my place while I watched. The fucker laughed as he left—not even bothering to lock the cage again. He knew I was too weak to do anything, but I was strong enough to make sure that Rayne didn't take my place.

"I couldn't let that happen. I was hell-bent on telling Rayne that she couldn't help me anymore, but then she came. She rushed in, lifting my broken body off the floor and cradling my head while she fed me her blood. It was just as I was about to tell her that she needed to stop helping me that she offered me my salvation. I wanted her to come with me, but we both knew that she couldn't. I know now that it would've only put me in more danger, but it was hard to leave her knowing exactly what kind of monster her father was. She assured me that her father would never hurt her, but—" I take another deep breath, entwining my fingers with his as I look out at the beautiful scene before me.

"After that, I returned home. Everyone was overjoyed. Well, everyone except Breanne's family. I came home, but their daughter never did. It's a guilt that I've always felt. Somehow I should've been able to save her."

"But she wasn't with you, there was nothing you could've done," he says, giving my hands a squeeze.

"I know that. I do. But it doesn't stop the guilt. What's worse, though, is that I allowed those monsters to rule my life even after I escaped. I didn't leave my coven. Not until I was told Drake was meeting with a hunter, and I felt compelled to go. For some reason, it was like I was being pulled there. So, I went and found Rayne. I admit I wasn't—and am still not—too happy with the position I found her in, but I could never be upset that I found her again."

I wrinkle my nose at the memory of finding my brother balls deep in my best friend and desperately try to shake those thoughts from my head.

"You know most of the rest except what happened the night of the battle..." I pause. Is he going to think less of me if I admit what I did? Even if he does, I have to get it all out. It will come out eventually, and it's better that he knows the monster they created now rather than years down the road. I glance at him, and he gives me an encouraging nod.

"When I saw Rayne's father that night, I was frozen. My fear paralyzed me. I don't even think he recognized me. He was smiling as he raised the gun and shot Phoebe. He kept it raised as Rayne placed herself between them. But then...Drake stepped in, placing himself in front of Rayne. He was protecting his mate, but she wanted to protect him too. I could have lost them both. I don't know if he meant to shoot Rayne, but he did. When I saw her laying on the ground dying, I felt a rage that I can't even describe. It was like I didn't even know what I was doing, I was cutting my way through the hunters, ripping out their hearts, slashing their throats until not a single one was left. They turned me into the monster that they wanted me to be. The monster they always said I was." I begin to sob.

Andres stiffens momentarily and I think that he's pulling away from me, but instead he clasps my chin, turning my head back and lifting it so that I look directly into his eyes.

"You are not a monster," he grinds out through his clenched teeth. "Just because you took your revenge on men that deserved much worse than the death you granted them does not mean you're a monster. You were getting vengeance for yourself but also for your family. For your sister who was lying on the ground; for your brother who was losing his mate. There is not a single being on this earth who would've done anything differently in your place."

I search his eyes for a long time, finding it hard to imagine the gentle giant behind me not being in complete control of his actions. "Even you?"

"Even me," he replies, his eyes softening.

I don't know what comes over me as he meets my eyes without a moment's hesitation, without flinching away. I don't care to know why or how, but I move like a blur. Suddenly, I'm straddling his lap and merging my lips with his in a demanding kiss.

Chapter Twelve

Drusilla

Andres breaks our kiss with a groan.

"Drusilla," he whispers against my lips.

I lean back and look into his heated eyes. "Yes?"

"As much as I want to take this further, you need to be sure this is what you want. I don't think you're there yet."

"You don't want me?" I whisper. My stomach plummets in a sudden, sick feeling. No one has ever truly wanted me. Why would I let myself forget that? I move to get off his lap, sudden shame making my heart race. Maybe the kiss at Phoebe and Alaric's was a fluke. Maybe the tenderness and attention he has been showing me tonight were out of pity. Maybe the whole mate bond thing is affecting me differently than him. Maybe...

"Drusilla," he snaps me out of my inner spiral, and I look into his bright blue eyes. "I want you more than you will ever know. I just want you to be sure. Once I allow myself to have you, I won't be able to stop my dragon from claiming you." As he says the words, his hands grip my hips. He smoothly rolls my hips toward him, allowing me to feel just how much he wants me. If the extremely large appendage I can feel swelling against me is anything to go by, it's a lot.

"Andres," I plead as I rock my hips back and forth.

"Drusilla," he moans out, closing his eyes. I speed my rocking back and forth, chasing the release that I know is right around the corner. His grip on my hips tightens, stalling me, and forcing me to stop. "Not yet, love."

I groan in frustration and roll off his lap in a petulant motion, determinedly turning my gaze to the valley below.

"Drusilla," he begins, reaching out and placing a hand on my shoulder. I pull away from his touch. I know I'm being irrational, but I'm way too frustrated right now. I am frustrated with him and myself. He basically told me that he doesn't want to go any further and then I forced myself upon him.

"What?" I snap. I don't intend it to sound as curt as it does, but I cannot help it. I am sexually frustrated and disappointed in my own lack of control.

His eyes darken a bit, but they soften as he blows out a breath before he speaks. "Is it so wrong of me to want to wait until you're ready? Is it wrong that I want the first time that you find your release with me to be intentional?"

I am still fuming, but I mull over his words. I understand what he's saying, but being sexually frustrated is not something I'm used to. Normally, I would just take care of myself. Something tells me that Andres wouldn't be satisfied with that either.

"I'm sorry—I don't—I just..." What do I say to a man I just met? Although he may be my mate, it feels impossibly vulnerable to admit what I want in this moment.

"I know what you need," he says huskily as he lifts me easily and places me between his legs again. My back is to his front once more, and his words tickle my neck as he speaks. My entire body shivers as his hands slide down to my thighs. "If this is what you need, who am I to deny you?"

His hands follow the curves of my thighs upward until he reaches the waistband of my pants. "Are you sure?" he asks, his lips grazing the top of my ear.

Unable to speak, I nod. I lean back into him, his muscled chest meeting my back. His hand slides beneath the fabric, and my breath hitches as he reaches my core. His fingers lightly explore my lower lips, and my eyes flutter closed as I focus on his deft movements.

His hand is deft and delicate; he studies my moans and movements as he explores. My breathing quickens as he gently begins to circle my swollen bud, and I groan as he stops to gather some wetness from my center before returning, easily bringing me back up to the cusp.

"Not yet, love. Just wait," he whispers. He slows enough to keep me on the edge. His calm and control just drive my frenzy further, and I begin to squirm against him. As much as I want to follow his directions, I want to cum more.

"Andres," I plead with him, trying to move my body so his skilled fingers are where I need them.

He lets off a small chuckle, and my eyes snap open.

I see the sky turning pink with the rising sun and, just as I'm about to say something, his fingers renew their efforts.

"Now," he says forcefully, "Cum for me now." That's exactly what I do. My entire body feels like it's falling over the cliff we're sitting on as the sun begins to rise. If today is the day I die, I'll die knowing that I just had the best orgasm of my life.

Andres gently removes his hand, bringing his fingers up to his mouth to suck them clean. I watch with rapt attention, my vision blurred with lust. He gives me a knowing smirk as he releases his last finger. He gently brings his other hand up and turns my head, forcing me to face the rising sun.

I begin to panic, but, as the light reaches my toes, all I feel is warmth. "Wha—what is happening?"

"In this pocket world, the sun will not affect you as it normally would," Andres whispers in my ear.

For the first time in my life, I watch as the pinks and reds of dawn turn to orange and yellow as the sun rises. The sunrises I've seen in movies and pictures don't do this justice.

We sit there in comfortable silence, watching the sun rise higher and higher. The warmth from its rays moves up my body until even my face is heated by them. I have never felt this at peace in my life. It makes me feel like the past can be just that—the past. It does not need to have any influence on my future.

"Drusilla," Andres interrupts my drowsing thoughts gently, "we should probably head back and get some sleep."

"Just a little while longer," I say, turning to look at his face. "Please."

He nods and squeezes my middle a little tighter.

I have a feeling my big bad mate is actually a big softy.

At least with me.

* * *

After a few hours of sleep—which is less than I need but more than I want—River wakes me up, excited to teach me how to meditate. I don't have the heart to tell her that I already know about meditation, so I allow her to bring me to a beautiful glen filled with wildflowers and lead me through the motions.

I breathe in through my nose and out through my mouth. I close my eyes and clear my mind. I've done this countless times, so I slip into my dreamscape easily. It's the one—wait, no—it's not the only place I feel safe anymore. Andres added this place to that list this morning. I guess I can say my dreamscape is one of the few places I feel safe.

After I escaped and returned home, one of the clan elders

taught me how to meditate. She was convinced that I would be able to overcome my fears if I were to face them in a dreamscape. I didn't have the courage to tell her that I was too terrified to even attempt it, so I just told her I was still working on it anytime she asked. I found the meditation helpful, but I didn't try to push further than that.

I spend a little time in my own safe space—now augmented with a more realistic sunrise than before—before I open my eyes to greet a smiling River.

"What are you smiling about?" I ask, a smile on my own face as well.

"I found her," she replies excitedly.

"Found her?"

"My dragon. She was there. It was just like you said it would be. You were right. She was hiding to protect me. I think...I think I can shift now."

She stands up and closes her eyes, and I watch in awe as magic swirls around her, transforming her into an aquamarine dragon, almost the same color as her eyes. She's stunning. Her scales are oval and almost translucent, shifting from sky to midnight blue with each movement like ocean waves.

"You're beautiful," I tell her, and she brings her large head down to bump my body.

I let out a giggle and give her snout a little rub.

"Go fly. Be free, little one," she doesn't need any more encouragement. Her large wings flap, and she sets off into a run before taking to the skies.

"I see she found her dragon," Andres says, startling me.

"She just needed to look for her," I respond, melting into his body as he wraps his arms around me from behind. I'm almost surprised by how easy it is with him. After this morning, I think things have changed for us. The combination of the orgasm and his acceptance of my story has made me feel safe with him beside me. It's like every fiber of my being wants to succumb to the mating bond. We stand there and watch River for a few minutes in silence. There is something calm and peaceful in simply being together like this.

"Drusilla, I would like to try something if you are okay with it," Andres begins.

"Like what?" I turn in his arms and question, hoping it's something like this morning. By the look on his face, I know it is not.

He blows out a nervous breath. "I would like to try a type of meditation to help you get your power back from the hunters. I want to try it on River, but I don't want to put her through anything unless I'm sure it will work."

I take a small step back. I know what he's saying. He wants me to do what elders suggested when I first returned. They wanted me to try and relive my time with the hunters while contorting it to allow me to take back some of the power I felt I'd lost to them.

I'd be lying if I said the prospect wasn't enticing, but even the mention of it sends me into a panic. Then I think of River...

I understand why he wants to test this on me before trying it with her. Ordinarily, I'd be pretty pissed about that. This is for River, though. If this works for me, it will work for her. If it works for her, it's worth it.

The goddess sent River to me for a reason—maybe this is it. I just need to find the courage to face it.

"Okay," I say, turning back to him. "What do you want me to do?"

"Are you sure? I don't want to pressure you into anything."

"I'm sure. If it works for me, it will work for her, and I would give anything to take away her pain," I tell him, looking up and spotting the tiny speck of her flying form high in the clouds. She deserves to feel powerful and free like that all the time.

He nods and takes a seat on the grass where River and I were just meditating. I walk over and join him. He holds his hands out to me, and I place mine in them.

"I want you to close your eyes and breathe—just like you would for meditation. This time, I'm going to guide you." He waits for me to nod. "I want you to remember you are safe. You are here with me. I'm going to hold your hands the entire time to remind you." I nod again and close my eyes.

"I want you to take a deep breath in through your nose, hold it for a count before letting it out slowly through your mouth." When I do as he asks, he continues, "Good. Now I want you to bring up your worst memory from your time in captivity," he says, and panic grips me until I focus on the feel of his hands in mine. I focus on the feeling of the calluses on his fingers brushing up against mine as I pull up the memory of my last day there. Price stands over me with Rayne's dad. I'm sprawled out on the ground. I am being lashed over and over.

I must make a face because Andres can tell that I am in the memory.

"Now I want you to take your power back," he says. I want to ask him what he means. He must know it's not that simple, but he continues. "Morph this memory. Create an outcome where you are the one in power. I don't know what the memory is, and I don't need to. You have every tool to take your power back. You can create a weapon out of thin air. You can make it rain or snow—anything you can imagine is possible. This is your place—your mind. You're no longer that girl they stole. You're a strong woman who brought her captives to their knees. You took their lives; you can take their power back."

I try to figure out some way to do as he asks, but with each lash, I feel myself shrinking down. Somehow, the memory becomes more and more real as I try to alter it.

Is it snowing? Yes. It can be snowing. The sensation of cold on my skin is lost in the memory of pain. White snow builds around my knees as drops of my warm blood hiss through it. How did the snow get inside? I pull away from that abortive attempt. I know there is a roof on that damned shed.

No. It can be raining instead. I hear it beat against the roof. A bad enough storm could send them away—force them to leave me alone. Instead, it traps them in the building with me. They have nowhere else to go but stay and torture me.

After my fifth attempt to conjure something—anything—to save myself, my memory morphs into my more recent nightmare. River takes my place on the ground, and that's when I get mad.

I attack Rayne's dad first, reaching into his chest and pulling out his heart. There's no subtlety—no finesse—to the attack, but the shocked look on his face is priceless. I do not stop to enjoy my work though. I'm not done yet. Price is still attacking River with a smug look on his face.

"You are done, Price," I growl at him.

"Oh, little Dru. Don't worry. It's your turn next," he spits at me, bringing the whip back for another strike. Unlike my nightmare the night before, I'm able to intercept his attack this time. As I stop his next blow with my hand, his shock is apparent in the look on his face.

"No. You will not hurt anyone ever again. I'm coming for you, Price. When I'm finished here, I'll be coming for you next," I growl as I plunge my hand into his chest and tear out his still-beating heart.

I laugh as he takes his last breath.

"This isn't over," he rasps out.

"It is for you. You will never have power over me again." I surprise myself with the words. They are not surprising to say. I have understood the concept for a long, long time. I am shocked, instead, to find that I actually mean them.

A weight I didn't realize I was carrying slowly melts away, and the nightmare morphs once again into my dreamscape.

Quickly, checking to see if it worked, I pull up another memory. Each one I examine has changed. There's something different in each one that allows me to take a step away from it—makes it less real, less harmful. Each time he brings the lash down, I laugh maniacally instead of crying out in pain. I have changed it so that the lash feels like a feather instead of a whip.

I eventually pull out of my dreamscape and open my eyes. A very concerned Andres stares straight at me over our clasped hands.

Rather than explaining, I launch myself at him, landing on top of him and kissing him deeply. Every stroke of his tongue or nip of his teeth feels *more* than before. Not better—just more. It is like I couldn't really feel the sensations before, not with the crushing weight of my traumas as well.

I'm sure that I will need more time to heal—this one time didn't somehow miraculously fix the years of abuse I went through —but there is a sudden weightlessness in knowing I don't have to be ruled by it.

Andres pulls away gently, studying my face with concern.

"Does this mean it worked?"

"I think so," I tell him with a smile on my face. "Only time will tell. It helped though. Every time I think of that time in my life, I either get angry and want to slaughter all of them or laugh at their attempts to rule me."

"Together we will make them all pay," he tells me before merging his lips back to mine. A different woman would be appalled by the idea of doling out justice, but not me.

It just turns me on even more.

Just as I'm starting to grind on him, ready to take it to the next level, a beautiful blue dragon shifts into a giggling little girl and jumps on top of us.

We both wrap our arms around her, bringing her into our hug.

"To be continued," Andres whispers in my ear, low enough that only I can hear.

I shoot him a heated look.

That's a promise I'm going to hold him to.

Chapter Thirteen

Andres

I groan and adjust myself so that my beautiful niece—who wins the bad timing award—doesn't realize just what she interrupted.

"Did you see me, Uncle Andres?" she exclaims.

"I sure did, sugar! You were fantastic. I knew she didn't leave you," I say with a huge smile.

"Your dragon is gorgeous," Drusilla tells her, and River giggles, wrapping her arms tighter around both of us.

"Can we fly together, Uncle Andres? Like we used to?" she asks, releasing us and sitting back. I look from River to Drusilla with a smirk, the idea already forming in my head.

"As long as your Aunty Dru will ride on my back," I say with a wink in her direction. Drusilla looks taken aback, and her mouth drops open in shock.

"I..." she begins.

"Please, Aunty Dru. Pretty please," River begs, her big, blue eyes shining and full of hope.

Drusilla sends me a glare.

"How about you and Uncle Andres go fly for a bit, and I'll join you later? I want to work on some meditation for a little longer."

My lips turn down into a frown, and I reach out with my empathy to gauge her feelings. She's not scared, which is good. There are so many different emotions in her that it's hard for me to read. Happiness, frustration, lust, shame, concern, and something else I can't quite put my finger on.

"Are you sure? We can always just wait until later," I say, clasping her warm, small hand in mine.

She looks at River's pouting face that she has now turned to me before meeting my eyes once more. "I'm sure. You two go fly. I'm a little hungry." She looks down at her lap as if she's ashamed of her diet, and I instantly understand. She doesn't want River to see her feed.

I nod and give her a kiss on her cheek before whispering in her ear. "There's a small fridge in the kitchen with some food in it for you," I tell her, and she perks up.

"Thank you."

"All right, sugar. You ready?" I ask River with a smile. She jumps up and claps her hands.

"Catch me if you can," she calls out, getting a running start and shifting into her dragon.

I chuckle and do the same, the shift overtaking me quickly. My dragon is more than willing to play this game with her, and he soars through the sky. I watch as she turns her big head to look behind her. She slows when she doesn't see me—that is until my large shadow covers her from above. She dives quickly, spinning and coming out the other side.

You'll have to do better than that, she chuckles through our bond.

Rather than respond, my dragon and I work as a team, tagging her quickly with one of our large wings and darting away just as fast.

Aw man, she pouts but doesn't let her disappointment of being tagged stop her as she flies after me.

We spend the evening playing tag until the sun has completely left the sky and the stars begin shining bright.

Time to head back, I say as she tags me for the last time. Her dragon lets off her tiny roar as we land in the field of wildflowers. I know she doesn't want to stop playing. Heck, I don't want to stop either. River is tired though, and I would very much like to continue what I started earlier with my mate.

"Aunty Dru?" River calls as we walk up to the house.

"Hey, little one. How was your flight?" Drusilla asks as River runs and jumps into her arms.

"It was great, but Uncle Andres said we had to come back."

Drusilla looks up at the sky, noting the stars, before giving me a heated look.

"You can always fly tomorrow. Come, let's get you ready for bed."

They hold hands and walk into the house, and I stand in the doorway watching. They act like they've known each other for years instead of the mere days it has been. I don't know what I would do without either of those beautiful beings in my life.

After a few short minutes, once I'm sure that River has put on her pajamas and gotten into bed, I walk into the room. The sight before me is something out of my dreams. The two of them are snuggled up tightly on the single bed, both snoring over an open book on River's lap. I think about moving one or the other, but as I gently tug Drusilla to me, River begins to whimper, causing Drusilla to pull her closer.

I place a soft kiss on both of their heads before walking out of the room and closing the door. I peek in the fridge and note that there are only a couple of packets of blood left within it—she must've been hungry today. I curse myself for not being tuned into my mate's needs better. At this rate, we will either need to leave after tomorrow or make another trip to the coven to get more. Either way, we're good for now.

I walk out in the middle of the glen and sit with my legs crossed before closing my eyes.

"Merciful goddess. Thank you for blessing me with a beautiful mate and giving me back my niece. I have no right to ask anything more of you, but I feel I have no choice. Please protect the rest of my family." I whisper the words, allowing them to be carried away on the wind, hoping that they meet the ears of any goddess that can grant my wish.

The wind whipping around me is the only response, and I can't help but think that maybe...just maybe someone heard me.

I make my way back to the house and settle myself in bed. I study the ceiling and think about all the ways the world has changed.

The first thing I did when I awoke was find a human town to absorb as much knowledge as I could. My mother had taught me a spell long ago that allowed me to absorb massive amounts of knowledge from any library. Instantly, every word held within the pages was inside my mind.

There was so much violence. So many unnecessary deaths. So much destruction. Each year brought technological advancements, but they also brought pollution. Coral reefs are dying. There's an entire island in the ocean made only out of garbage.

That was just the human world. The supernatural world was more difficult. I made my way to Egypt, where the oldest coven in the world keeps its library. What I saw there will haunt me for all my days.

I can't help but feel that the way things turned out is my fault. Humans may be killing our planet, but they are thriving. My supernatural brethren must hide, scavenge, and wither away, waiting to be picked off by the hunters. If I had ruled as my father did, if I had stood up and said no to hiding away, perhaps this world would've been different. But then everything my mother told me on her last day plays over in my head, and I know the truth. This is the way it was always supposed to be. Even if I wish it wasn't.

I don't remember falling asleep. When I wake, it's to two small bodies wrapped around me, and I smile. I hear them both giggling quietly as they hug me, and I smile.

"Good morning, you two," I whisper and then chuckle as they both jump back in surprise.

"We were going to let you sleep for a bit longer, but Aunty Dru doesn't really know how to cook," River says, and Drusilla looks sheepish.

"That's all right. Perhaps both you and Aunty Dru would like to learn?" I probe, hoping to get a smile out of them both.

"Absolutely," Drusilla says, and they share a beaming smile before rushing out the doorway and into the kitchen area, which really is just the wood-burning stove, counter, and sink.

I spend the rest of the morning trying to teach them to make pancakes. They have more flour on them than in the batter, but they haven't stopped laughing and smiling since we started, so I'm calling it a win.

"Okay, sugar. We're going to try meditation," I tell River as she finishes her fourth pancake.

"But I already know how to meditate," she says with a mouth full of food. Drusilla laughs, and I scowl.

"Pretty sure your mother taught you not to talk with your mouth full."

River gulps down her bite and smiles sadly. "She did. I'm sorry." A pang of guilt slices through me. I didn't mean to upset her. We were having such an amazing morning, and I know that what we must do next is going to be even worse.

"It's okay, sugar. Just put your plate on the counter and meet us outside," I say and take Drusilla's hand, leading her out of the house. As soon as we step outside, I clasp her around the waist and pull her up against my body. She giggles and reaches up, placing a heated kiss on my lips.

"I'm sorry I fell asleep last night," she whispers, reaching out her tongue to trace my lips. I moan out loud, pulling her closer and deepening the kiss. As our tongues meet each other with ferocious passion, we both moan.

I pull back breathlessly and lean my forehead up against hers. "It's okay; you were tired. Besides, I would rather us be alone when I claim you," I say, and she steps back to look at my face.

"Why?"

I pull her close once more, whispering in her ear. "So you don't have to be quiet and can scream my name as loud as you want."

Her breath catches and she squirms; her desire is so strong I have to push her back a little bit so that I can stop myself from claiming her right here and now.

She looks like she's about to say something when a bundle of excitement crashes through the door. I forgot how much energy this little one has. She's been like this since the day she was born. She never stands still. When we were still at the pack, the boys did a good job keeping her occupied.

"Ready?" I ask, and she nods. "We're going to try the same thing we did with Drusilla yesterday."

"What is that?" River asks, looking between Drusilla and myself.

Drusilla waits for me to nod before crouching down. "I took control back from the bad men. During my meditation, I pulled up some of my memories," Drusilla starts, and River cuts her off.

"Wasn't that scary?"

Drusilla nods. "It was. But you know what?"

"What?" River asks, her eyes wide.

"Your Uncle Andres taught me how to change the night-mares into something good. I had to go back to the bad memories, but I was able to change them. I was able to change them so that I didn't have to be the victim. Do you think you want to try it?"

River looks between us, and I keep an encouraging smile on my face.

"I think so."

"That's my brave girl," I tell her, leading her into the middle of the glen. After we sit down, I take her hands. "I can come with you the first time if you want."

She looks up at Drusilla, and I see them exchange a silent conversation. If I had to guess, neither of them truly wants me to see what they went through. If I'm being honest, I'm not sure I want to see it either. There is a part of me that wants to know everything that the two of them went through, but the other part of me is terrified of what I will see.

"Can I try by myself first?" she asks, and I nod.

I unclamp my empathy so I can keep track of her emotions and give her hands a squeeze. "All right, sugar. Close your eyes. Breath in—one two three—and out—one two three." I wait and watch as she does it, and I can recognize the moment she enters her dreamscape.

"I want you to remember that you're safe. Whatever you see, you are right here with me. Nothing can hurt you. This is your space. No one has control but you." She nods, but I feel a tremor of fear flow through her. "Now, can you bring up a memory from your time with the hunters?" I try to keep the growl out of my voice because I don't want to scare her further, but I can feel her tense up as she drops into a memory.

After a few moments, she squeezes my hands hard and starts sobbing. Tears slide from beneath her bunched lashes. Before I can say anything, Drusilla slides in behind River. She puts her long legs on either side of my niece's small body and wraps her arms around her middle.

"It's okay," Drusilla says, resting her cheek on the slope of River's shoulder. "I'm here. You're safe. They can't hurt you."

River's breathing immediately begins to even out. When Drusilla's eyes go wide for a second before falling closed again, I know that my mate has entered the dreamscape with her.

Drusilla growls, and River shakes. Drusilla's emotions flit from mad to furious in a blink. River's fear slowly begins to fade—making room for courage—and I smile, knowing it's my mate helping her feel that way. I wish that it could be me, but now I know why she didn't want me in there with her.

The minutes tick by. River's hands squeeze mine periodically, making me want to force my way into her mind with them. I am desperate to protect them, but I know it would only defeat the purpose of this exercise. River needs to know she can take back control on her own.

When they finally open their misting eyes, River turns directly to Drusilla and embraces her. The love I feel flowing between them is so strong that it's almost overwhelming. I sit and watch, just basking in the glow of their love for one another.

"Thank you," River says to Drusilla, sitting back to look into her eyes.

"You don't have to thank me. You were so brave. Next time you will be able to do it all by yourself. I'm sure of it," Drusilla responds, giving River a soft kiss on her head. "Now go fly off some of your adrenaline. We'll be here when you get back."

River doesn't wait to be told anything more. She simply stands up, stopping long enough to give me a quick hug before running and shifting into her dragon.

"Do I want to know?" I ask, both curious and scared of the answer.

Drusilla shakes her head, tears flowing freely out of her eyes now that River is gone. "I don't think so," she admits. I reach over and pull her into my lap as she begins to sob. Only moments ago, she seemed like nothing was wrong. Here, in my arms, though, she trusts me enough to let go. "It was so much worse watching her," she whispers, and I place my head on top of hers, rocking her back and forth.

I send a silent prayer up to the gods. I'm not picky, and I'll take help from whichever one is listening.

Please help them. They don't deserve to have gone through what they have.

Let me lessen their burden.

Chapter Fourteen

Drusilla

A ndres had promised that our kiss was "to be continued," but I hadn't expected it to take quite so long for us to pick up where we'd left off. After spending the day working with River on meditation techniques, we were both simply too physically and mentally exhausted to think of anything else. We find ourselves doing the same thing again: sitting in the middle of the glen surrounded by wildflowers and helping River take back control of her life.

I had hoped she wouldn't need me to join her in her dreamscape after that first time, but she continues to freeze up at the same spot in the memory and brings me in with her. I am happy to help her, but it is harder to watch her memories than relive my own.

As I had feared, River's worst memory does contain Price and his favorite whip. Now, more than ever, I can't wait to find him and rip his heart out of his chest. As hard as it is to watch her revisit this memory, the idea of letting her face the monsters alone is worse.

For what seems like the hundredth time today, I watch River

rub at her chest as though it's hurting. Even in the midst of her meditation, her face scrunches up in pain.

"River, are you okay? Does your chest hurt?" I ask as she comes back to the present.

She looks taken aback before hanging her head and nodding.

"It's Riley."

"Riley? What's wrong with Riley?" I ask, worried. Have we missed some kind of attack while we've been here enjoying this peace?

River's blue eyes snap up to mine. "I don't think anything is wrong...or I hope there's nothing. I just really miss him."

I let out a breath and reach out to her. She scurries into my lap, her little head resting on my shoulder as she weeps. I rub her back absentmindedly as Andres approaches, holding a plate of food for them to share and a blood packet for me.

That's one thing that changed quickly. At first, I was worried that feeding in front of River would scare her. She eventually pulled me aside and told me she didn't mind, so I've been feeding while they eat their meals. This is the last of my blood supply, so we will need to head back sooner rather than later.

His eyes land on the sobbing River in my arms and immediately widen with concern. It's one of the things I love most about Andres. He has a huge heart. He's so gentle and caring, but I know that is not always the case. He is also fiercely protective of the people he loves, and I am sure he is terrifying to anyone who crosses him.

I shake my head at him gently, trying not to disturb River.

"I think we need to go back. Even if it's just for a visit," I whisper when he gets close enough.

"What do you mean?" he asks.

"I think River and Riley's bond is stronger than we realized. She needs to see him," I say. We've spoken already about the bond that they share and our worries about them being so young. It is even more important if they're really part of the prophecy as we suspect. If that is the case, we need to try and delay their mating until we've gotten a grasp on what exactly we're facing. I think we should tell them everything soon so that they are prepared, but Andres doesn't agree. I highly doubt the others will agree either. River and Riley are both more mature than their years, and they've both already had to endure so much. I have no doubt that they could handle the truth, but that's a conversation for another day.

He looks between River and me silently before nodding. "We can go after we eat."

"Really, Uncle Andres?" River perks up, wiping the tears off her cheeks.

"Yes. If I knew the bond between you was this strong already, I never would have kept you from him for this long," he tells her as he passes her a sandwich and me my blood.

"Thank you," we both say at the same time and fall into a fit of giggles. River climbs off my lap to sit and eat her food. I don't know how it's possible, but my feelings for both River and Andres have only continued to grow. Each morning, I've woken up thinking that I was the happiest I'd ever been. When the next morning comes, it blows yesterday out of the water.

As if sensing where my mind is going, Andres looks at me with heat in his eyes. "Perhaps River would like to have a sleepover with Riley and his family?" I give him a devious smirk. I know exactly what he's up to, and I am completely on board.

"Could I?" she asks with her mouth full of food, earning a perfunctory scowl from her uncle. She swallows quickly, shooting him an apologetic look.

"We can ask Phoebe if it's all right. No promises though," I begin, but then I remember. What if she has a nightmare? What if I'm not there when she needs me? "Maybe we can spend the night in the basement again—in case you have another nightmare."

Andres hides his expression well, but I can tell he feels ashamed for not having thought of that already.

"But I haven't had a nightmare in two days," River says.

"That may be, little one. But we are all still new to this, so it is best to stick together. I think Drusilla's right. We can stay at the house with you for the night, and you can still stay and have a play-date with Riley during the day," Andres responds.

I scoot my butt closer to him and place a hand on his thigh.

"We will have our time. Don't worry," I whisper, and give him a soft kiss on his cheek. His face turns to mine, flames blazing in his eyes from the lust.

"Yes," he growls. "We will."

After that, we spend the rest of the daylight soaking in the sun. I try to make the most of it because I know the sun will become a death sentence for me again as soon as we leave this place.

I fear that I have ruined my sleep schedule. I've become accustomed to being awake during the day and sleeping at night—which should have been impossible for me to do. Since I have adapted to this schedule so quickly, it hopefully won't be that hard to set it right again.

Andres and River spend the day flying together in their dragon forms. It truly is a beautiful sight and something I never imagined seeing. Dragons—actual dragons—flying in the sky. Their huge frames block out the sun. I have yet to get on his back and fly with him, though I know he desperately wants me to.

My mate's rock-colored scales look dull gray in the dark, but they sparkle as if each scale is embedded with tiny diamonds when they are awash in sunlight. He doesn't shine as bright as River, whose iridescent, aqua-blue scales seem to reflect the sunlight, but both are gorgeous in their own way.

As the sun dips lower, they land and shift back to their human form. How they remain clothed is still a mystery to me. I am not a shifter, so I have never had to worry about transforming only to find myself in the nude. However, my lack of experience also means that their explanations are lost on me.

Andres told me that it was a form of magic and that all shifters —like witches—have their own. I obviously can't help but ask why all the shifters in the pack run around naked all the time, and he explains that they must have forgotten the magic they were meant to have. They've simply forgotten. The knowledge has been lost to time like so many things are.

At the moment, though, it seems like a loss. I would much rather be able to appreciate my mate's muscular form whenever he shifts. I can still only just imagine the bulking muscles sculpted into his beautifully tanned skin. I would enjoy nothing more than discovering each freckle or birthmark he's hiding as I roam his body.

"I think it's safe now. Ready to go?" Andres breaks me out of my mental drooling.

"Yes," I squeak out, and he raises his brow at me as I snap my eyes up to his from their perusal of his body.

"See something you like?" he asks with a chuckle.

I nod, heat flaring in my eyes before the moment is broken by an overly excited River.

"Can we go now?"

My eyes move slowly away from Andres as if every second they stray from him is some sort of crime. I think the true crime here is simply him looking like that. I can't wait to get this hulking man alone and naked in my bed. All the dirty things I've thought up over the last few days may actually come true as soon as we resolve our "hunter" issue.

"Yes, River. We're ready," I agree.

The three of us stand together, and River and Andres hold hands and close their eyes. I am there to watch this time as a small crack between this world and reality forms and grows until I can see the clearing we had left behind perfectly. Within that clearing is something that I didn't expect to see: our family and friends. Either they knew we were coming or were hoping. If it's the latter, it can only mean one thing...something went wrong.

Andres takes my hand as he assesses the group before us. I can tell by the crease in his brow that he is just as concerned by the gathering as I am.

Rayne notices us first, breaking into a sprint and running toward us the second we walk through. I didn't realize just how much I missed her and Drake until this moment as I break away from River and Andres and sprint to meet her. We wrap our arms around each other.

"I missed you," we both say simultaneously and then break out into laughter as Andres clasps arms with Alaric and then Drake.

"I don't understand. Did you know we were coming?" I ask, studying Rayne's face.

"No, but we were hoping that you would," she responds.

I take a step back. "Why? What happened?"

"So much. Like literally so much, but it's not for young ears. Let's get River settled with the boys before we talk," she says, linking her arm with mine. Drake starts to approach us, but Rayne clasps me to her protectively. "Mine," she says, shooting him a glare.

Okay. What is that all about? My brother is smart enough to slow his steps and walk a few paces behind us. I give him a soft smile, hoping to let him know that I missed him too. I'm not sure why Rayne is being so possessive of me right now, but I can admit that it feels nice to be wanted.

"What is that all about?" I ask quietly enough for only her to hear.

She sighs. "It's one of those things we need to talk about," she looks back at River and Andres, realizing that they're both still within hearing distance.

Obviously, that's something that she wants to talk about without little ears present, so I change the subject.

"I understand now why you didn't want to give up walking in the sunlight." She gives me a puzzled look, so I continue. "In the pocket world, I could walk in the sun. It's everything that I dreamed it would be and more. I know I won't ever be able to walk in the sun here like you and Drake, but hopefully Andres will bring me back there to visit occasionally."

"Really? That's so cool. How does that work?"

I chuckle. "I asked that too. All Andres told me is its magic. It's an artificial sun, so it doesn't have the same effect."

"That makes sense. Although it does seem like the answer to any question lately is just 'it is magic,'" she says with a small growl at the end.

We aren't even through the trees before River speeds past us, running straight for a sprinting Riley. As they collide in an embrace, my heart melts a little more. I look back to find Andres staring at me and give him a smile. He returns it, and my knees go weak. Gods, that man is sexy. He's sexy, and he's all mine. At least he will be once we can sneak back to our pocket world.

"Okay, the kids are gone. Spill," I say, turning to Rayne. She glances around, looking for something or someone.

"Seb, can you do that bubble thing?" she asks when she finds him amongst the crowd. He nods and waves his hands, muttering some words.

"What bubble thing?" I ask her, concerned. I don't want to be trapped in a bubble that is controlled by anyone.

"It's the coolest thing. Seb can make a soundproof bubble around us so that no one can hear anything we're saying."

"Are you sure?" I ask.

"Yup...watch this," she says with an evil smirk. "Drake has a small penis!" She yells it loud enough that the entire pack should have heard her. When I locate my brother still talking quietly with Alaric and Andres, I see no sign that he heard. Sebastyn, on the other hand, is trying and failing to suppress his laughter.

"Seems like Seb can hear you," I point out, and they exchange a look.

"No matter. He already knows most of what I am going to share with you anyway. He won't tell. Will you, Seb?" Her tone makes it clear he'd be unwise to do so. He nods once again.

"Spill," I command once she looks back at me.

"Well...we went to see Martin," I let off a small growl, knowing the role he played in River's memory. It seems like he runs that facility. "Don't worry. He won't be hurting anyone ever again." She places her hands on my upper arms and gives them a comforting squeeze.

"So, we went to see Martin to try to get the codes we need. Well, I may have gone a little crazy," she puts her thumb and index finger close together, trying to signal a small amount.

I snort. Her? Go crazy? No...never.

"I know. It's impossible to imagine, right?" she asks with a knowing smirk but continues. "In the end, he ended up killing himself rather than talking to me." She pouts a little at her words, and I imagine the look on his face while five-foot-nothing Rayne scared him so badly he'd rather kill himself.

"So...with him gone...we needed to come up with another plan," she begins, and I can hear the anxiety mounting in her voice again. My gut begins to churn. I'm not going to like what she says next. "Before you say anything, know that Drake and I talked about it already, and he agreed as long as you agree."

"Spit it out, Rayne," I grind out, understanding why there is tension between her and my brother right now. She's going to sacrifice herself again. As I think that thought, I begin to pace, unable to even look at her.

"I'm going to let Price take me into the facility and hopefully give Drake the code as I go through," she spits out the words so fast I'm not even sure I heard her correctly.

"You're what?" I scream, turning to face her. Her mention of Price has my skin crawling. Unlike before, when the mere mention of his name would throw me into a panic, I feel rage. There is only unadulterated rage and bloodlust. I want to ensure that no one else —supernatural or human—will ever fall subject to his evil nature. I don't believe for a second that someone who gets off on torturing supernaturals as much as he seems to only does it when he's told. No doubt he has his own little workshop where he plays with his own 'toys' or 'pets.'

"It's the only way, Dru. I promise I won't be in danger. Not even for a second," she pleads. I can see her mind is made up, but she doesn't know what goes on in there. She doesn't know the other side of the hunters and what they do to supernaturals. She has only seen bits and pieces of their evil, and that is mild compared to what they actually do.

"What if we can't get you out? What if you can't get the codes? What if they kill you before we can get in there?" I rattle off my questions. Instead of her pausing and thinking them over, I see her resolve harden.

"I can do this, Dru. I know Drake only said yes because he knows that you will say no, and he doesn't want to be the bad guy," she says with a nasty look over at Drake. She takes a deep breath. "Listen. If there were any other way, you know that I would go for it. There isn't. This is the quickest and easiest way to get in there without bringing down the building. It's deep underground. I'm sure that they have measures in place to protect it. If we barge in, they're liable to blow the entire place to smithereens. What would happen to all the supernaturals trapped inside? The vampires would be unable to die—just trapped beneath a mountain of rubble forever. The shifters would break and heal and break again."

With each description, I wince. It would be a fate worse than death to be trapped like that. Unable to die. Unable to move. Tears shine in my eyes at the thought. The tears begin to fall at the thought of Rayne getting hurt while doing this.

"Can you promise me that you'll come back? I've finally learned to take my power back from your father and Price. I can't lose you. I just can't," I plead with her, clasping her hands in mine. I am finally learning how to be strong, but I know for a fact that losing her would break me.

"You won't. I promise," she says, looking straight into my eyes. I can see that she believes it. Although there's no guarantee she can keep that promise, it's enough to know that she will do everything in her power to come back to me.

"Okay," I whisper. I'm probably going to end up regretting this, but Rayne is right. This is the easiest way, and I will do anything in my power to reunite River with her mother. Maybe Breanne is there too.

Rayne wraps her arms around me briefly before stepping back and shooting Drake a triumphant grin. I watch as his face falls, sadness coating his features.

As he turns to me, that sadness turns into something else. It is a mixture of disappointment and rage. He is upset with me for not choosing his side. He shouldn't have made it my decision if he didn't want her to go. I don't think anyone could have stopped her, but it would have been comical to see him try.

Chapter Fifteen

Andres

The emotions rolling off Drusilla have me confused. Happiness, rage, and sadness. Each emotion has me wanting to rush to her side and comfort her. If Rayne is telling her what Alaric and Drake just told me, it's something that she needs to process on her own. After all, if this goes wrong...I don't even want to think about the possibility.

"What do you think?" Drake asks me. I see the hope shining in his eyes that I will disagree with the plan. Honestly, if it were Drusilla who wanted to do what Rayne is suggesting, it wouldn't be a question. There is no way I would let her go into danger like that. Hell, even the thought of it has a rumble in my chest warring to escape.

"I know this isn't what you want to hear, but It's a solid plan. Your mate is brave and smart. This is probably the best chance we've got to get in and rescue those in captivity with the least number of casualties." My eyes soften as I look at him.

He doesn't answer, and he doesn't need to. The emotions he's expressing right now tell me everything I need to know. If anything happens to Rayne, he will follow.

I sneak a peek back at Drusilla. If that were to happen, I'm not sure she would survive it.

"I will do anything I can to make sure she is unharmed. I can help Sebastyn create a temporary mind link for you," I tell him. They had been uncertain about how Rayne would get the codes out once she got inside. I don't know anything about modern science or technology. But I do know magic.

"You can do that? We've been trying to come up with solutions while we waited to see if you'd return," Alaric states.

"I can't, but Sebastyn will be able to. It's not unlike how you create your temporary pack bonds," I explain. They both stand there in shock, but I don't have time to waste. I want to get this night over with so I can take my mate back to the pocket world and make her mine. "Speaking of Sebastyn—I must go find him."

I walk away, leaving the two men standing there in shock. It's sad to see all the things they have lost over the years. So much of the knowledge and magic they had are now foreign and unknown. In order to survive this prophecy, they will need everything back again. I will be the one to help them—just like my mother predicted.

"Sebastyn, can I talk to you?" I ask. His eyes widen when he sees the serious look on my face, but he nods and follows me away from the nearby witches. "Are you planning on accompanying us to the facility?"

"Of course, I am," he says with steel in his tone.

"Then, you need to control your empathy," I tell him. Once again, his eyes widen.

"How...How do you know? We've only told a few people."

"I know because I am an empath too. Tell me, can you feel any of my emotions?" I ask.

His face scrunches up for a second or two.

"No. I can't. Not even a trickle. How is that possible?"

"It's a gift from the goddess that we are unable to read each other. We would never know if the emotions we sense are our own, the other empath's, or a lingering emotion from someone they were with recently." He nods in understanding. "If you are planning on going into the facility, you need to be able to control your gift. Otherwise, you will be bombarded with the emotions of the prisoners. Based on River's memory, I can surmise that they won't be good. I will need to practice as well, so we can do it together."

"I didn't think of that."

"It's because your mother's potion is still dulling your senses. You mustn't take it again. Whatever you've taken already will be worn off by the time we go."

"Why? Why can't I just take another potion?"

"It's unnatural to suppress your gift. Right now, your magic is battling with the spell for dominance. The spell is limited, but your magic is not. Once it breaks, your empathic abilities will rise to the surface. It will only become more and more difficult to contain your ability. You will need stronger spells and potions each time you try to suppress your magic." I watch his face as realization kicks in. As good as the intentions were, that potion is more hindrance than help.

"What do I have to do?" he asks. I look back through the crowd, searching for Drusilla before I answer. My gaze lingers on her for mere moments before her eyes meet mine. She may not realize it, but that's part of the developing mate bond. Once it's cemented, our emotions will be linked and heightened along with our awareness of each other. We will be able to feel one another even if I have my empathy locked down.

I gesture to Sebastyn, then over to the clearing. She nods, understanding my meaning without words. Goddess, this woman is amazing. Our bond isn't cemented yet, but our minds are linked in a way I've never heard of. It's as if we don't require each other's bite to finalize it, but that's impossible. Isn't it?

Turning back to Sebastyn, I say, "We need to practice meditation." He keeps pace with me as we walk back through the woods to the clearing.

"If you told me where we were going, I could've teleported us here," he says.

"Why? Do you have on uncomfortable shoes?" I ask as I take a seat on the ground, and he follows suit. Just like with Drusilla, it seems meditation comes easily for Sebastyn.

"First thing we need to do is remove the effects of the potion your mother gave you."

His eyes fly open in panic.

"It's the only way we're going to truly be able to learn," I supply.

He nods. "I'm not sure I'm ready for this..."

"In the beginning, it may seem like a curse. Once you learn to control it, I promise you will see it as the gift it really is."

"How do I remove it?"

"All you need to do is close your eyes and focus on your empathic abilities. The more you pull them to the surface, the faster they will burn through your potion. The fact that you could realize that you couldn't feel my emotions means that it's already nearly used up."

He nods, closes his eyes, and scrunches up his brows in concentration. I watch as the muddy-brown color coating his bright yellow soul clears as he burns the spell away.

"I think I did it," he says, opening his eyes and letting out a deep sigh of relief. I nod, guiding him back into meditation. From there, I teach him to make a vault in his mind to lock his empathic abilities in for short periods of time. I explain how he can focus on a singular person within a crowd and allow all others to fall into the background.

We practice locking up his empathy and releasing it a dozen times until the process is familiar to him. There is nothing more we can do until we are surrounded by people. Good thing there is a large group just outside of Alaric and Phoebe's house.

"Time to test it out," I tell him with a grin.

"Every second that passes since we burned away the potion—I can tell that the empathy is already stronger. I don't think I can go through the agony again," he tells me with a sullen look.

"When your new powers were initially released, we were in the middle of a battle. No one here is hurt or crying. The worst you will feel is rage or sadness. Most of the emotions that come through will be happy. Besides, if you're still planning on going to Orillia..." I wait for his nod before continuing, "then we need to get it under control. The best way to do that is to practice in a controlled environment."

"Okay," he says, releasing a shaky breath.

"I know that you experienced the worst parts of the gift already. Let me show you how amazing it can be," I tell him, clasping his shoulder and turning to walk back to the group.

I walk slowly, constantly probing for emotions. As the first few emotions begin to trickle into my mind, I halt.

"Stop here for now. We'll start slow."

"We're so far away, we can't even see anyone."

"That's the idea. You should only be able to feel a small number of emotions from this distance, so it won't overwhelm you. Close your eyes." As he follows my command, I look around us and continue. "Send out your empathy. Envision it like a fishing net. Try to spread it further and wider until you feel emotions that do not belong to you," I wait and watch as his brows scrunch up in concentration.

"There...I feel...a bunch of different emotions faintly, but I can't pinpoint one specific person or emotion," he says with his eyes still closed.

"Try focusing on Sarah. Ignore all emotions and thoughts. Use your bond to find her."

He nods and scrunches his brows up once more. Seconds tick by before he gets a soft smile on his face. "I feel her. She's happy and nervous about something..." he begins. I use my own gift to focus on Sarah to confirm what he's feeling. "There's something else. It's not an emotion exactly...more like...I can't think of the right word. Awareness?"

I can sense the same, but I know exactly what it is he is sensing, and that is Sarah's secret to share when she is ready.

"Good. Let's try Darren. You share a strong bond with him as well. Let's see if you can find his emotions within the crowd."

This time it doesn't take him as long.

"He's feeling love and lust. My guess is that he is looking at Sophia," he says with a chuckle. After confirming this, we move to the next person.

"Since you brought up Sophia, let's try her next. This one may be more challenging since your bond with her isn't as strong."

"Got her. She's feeling content. It's just like with Sarah. She has that awareness too. I can't get a good read on it. Almost as if it's another being but without emotions," he says.

So close to the answer, but, again, it is not our secret to know.

I shift gears and we filter through the rest of our friends. Each time it seems to be faster and clearer. Finally, after what must be close to an hour, I tap him on the shoulder.

"Now we're going to go closer. I need you to practice opening and closing off your gift so that you don't get bombarded. We will stop once we can see the crowd and practice some more."

"How long did it take you to master it?" he asks as we walk.

"Years. Unlike you, I had my gift from birth. When my sister was born, it was a tough time for me because I would constantly pick up on her emotions. It was harder on my mom though. Could you imagine a two-year-old and an infant having meltdowns at the same time?" I ask him with a chuckle. "Back then, I couldn't separate the emotions. When she was hungry, I was hungry. When she was sad, I was sad. As I got older, I was able to lock her emotions away. Thank the gods I sorted that out before my teenage years. I wanted no part of feeling her hormones," I shudder at the thought.

I accidentally left my empathy open a crack the first time she brought Michael home, and it was horrible. It was almost as bad as feeling those lust-filled emotions coming from my parents. At least they tried to tamp it down when I was in the room. Looking back now, it's a nice feeling to know that your parents loved and desired each other even after hundreds of years together.

As the emotions of the group begin to get stronger, I lock down my empathic abilities and look over at Sebastyn. His face begins to flash with various emotions, and I know he is struggling to lock his own down.

"Focus on me for a moment and lock it up," I tell him, pulling him to a stop.

He looks at me, his eyes brimming with tears that aren't his own. I know someone in the crowd is crying and those emotions are overwhelming him.

"Breathe and lock it down, Sebastyn."

It takes him a few minutes, but, eventually, he does. Relief spreads over his features.

"That was not pleasant," he says with a small chuckle.

"No. I suppose it wouldn't be, but you did well. With more practice, you will get faster and more efficient. I promise," I tell him.

"Now what?" he asks.

With a small grin on my face, I say, "Now, you open it a crack. Focus on Sarah and only Sarah. Follow your bond. Let me know when you've found her."

He nods after a moment, and I know he's found her.

"Now send her an emotion. Anything you want her to feel." His eyes snap up to mine in question. "You will be able to do the same with others when you gain more control over your gift. You will be able to send calm emotions amid a heated argument and happiness when someone is overwhelmed with grief. For now, just focus on Sarah."

I see the devious look in his eyes and open my own gift up to focus on Sarah, curious as to what he will send her. Finding her within the crowd, I let out a small laugh when I see her knees buckle and a look of ecstasy flash across her face. She looks around, and I know she's searching for Sebastyn. Once she finds him, she gets a determined look on her face and comes stomping over.

"Sebastyn Moon!" she shouts. She has a furious look on her face, but her emotions say differently. She's intrigued and aroused.

"Yes, sweetheart?" Sebastyn coos as her knees buckle again mid-stride.

"You and I have some business to take care of," she says firmly before adding, "Now."

I chuckle once more, leaning over to whisper into Sebastyn's ear. "Try opening the bond so that you can each feel each other's emotions during times of pleasure."

I watch his eyes go wide with mischief, and he nods quickly before sweeping his mate away for some alone time. With enough practice, I have no doubt his own abilities will surpass mine. Before that can happen, he needs control.

Without thinking, I search for my own mate, desperate to catch a glimpse of her beautiful face. We find each other at the same time and heat flares behind both of our eyes. I don't need to be an empath to know what she's thinking. I can't wait for this night to be over so I can spend some much-needed alone time with my mate to cement the bond.

Chapter Sixteen

Drusilla

After agreeing to Rayne's plan and dealing with an extremely pissed-off Drake, I'm exhausted. Physically and emotionally. As much as I love those two, they can be a lot to deal with. Add in the fact that I've become accustomed to sleeping at night and enjoying the sun during the day with Andres and River, and I'm desperately wanting to fall asleep.

Here, in the midst of my family and friends and under the light of a thumbnail moon, there is a peace settling over me that I didn't know I was missing. All those years I spent trapped inside my own head—inside the past—seem like a distant memory and a colossal waste of my life. What I wouldn't give to go back and teach myself how to regain my power earlier. Could I have learned this when the elders first suggested it?

If I changed the past, would I still have all of this? I glance around, noting each person. I realize that I wouldn't be able to truly appreciate this gift that I have here if I hadn't suffered through my past.

I wouldn't have Rayne—my best friend and sister. I wouldn't have the same bond with my overprotective brother. Sure, it would have saved all three of us a whole lot of pain, but changing the past can affect the future. If I changed my past, who knows if I would have ended up right here—where I am supposed to be.

I watch River pause in her running around with the boys to yawn. She covers her face with an arm to try and conceal it, but I know she's just as exhausted as I am. After flying all afternoon with Andres, she is likely even more tired.

I am just about to go to her when a concerned Riley stops and rushes to her side. Their bond is so strong you can almost see the threads connecting them. Their souls call out to one another without being truly aware they are doing so.

If they are the next couple in the prophecy, we will need to be ready by the time they hit eighteen. Even with explaining why they need to wait, the strength of the demands on their body and souls to claim one another will be extremely difficult for them to ignore. I know my own body and soul are demanding that I bond with Andres. I have not even tasted his blood, but it has been agony to wait this long.

Our waiting is nearly over now. Once River is tucked into bed and we get a few hours of sleep, we will slip away just before dawn to our pocket world to be alone.

Speaking of which, I should probably talk to Phoebe about that before I just assume she will watch River for us. I search her out in the crowd and casually walk over to where she and the girls are talking with a disheveled Sarah who has just rejoined them.

"Dru!" they all exclaim with smiles on their faces.

"Hey, guys," I smile back. I look at the group and my eyes widen. "Felicia, I think you've gotten even bigger in the last few days. How is that possible?"

She shrugs her shoulders and chuckles. "Apparently, I'm having twins."

My eyes go wide with shock. "Twins? I didn't think that—does that happen?"

"They don't—or didn't. It's a perk of having a phoenix as your luna apparently. Multiple births, increased health, and longer life expectancy too. At least that's what Gran reported from the elders in the Alberta pack this morning," Phoebe adds with a proud smile. Felicia isn't smiling.

"I'll take the longer life, sure. Twins? What am I supposed to do with two? I watch you, Charleigh, and Skarlyt struggle with one baby."

"Hey, don't worry. It takes a village to raise a child. If you look around, we have one awesome village," I tell her, wrapping her up in a hug.

"Besides, you won't be the only one with another baby," Skarlyt adds with a smirk.

"You're pregnant?" Sophia asks, and Skarlyt nods.

"I am too!" Sophia, Samara, Charleigh, Sarah, and Phoebe all speak at the same time. A second of shocked silence later, there is a chorus of "What?"

I laugh at their antics, but a slice of pain flows through me at the thought of all my friends having children while I am left behind. As the pain gets stronger, a new feeling surfaces, and I know it's not my own. A feeling of rightness washes over me, and I search out the source. I find Andres leaning up against a tree watching me. I send him a soft smile before turning back to the excited women.

"Phoebe?" I tap her on the shoulder. I don't want to disturb their discussion. After all, this is a very exciting time for all of them. Literally, all of them. At least eight new babies in one pack. I wonder if increased fertility is another perk of having a phoenix as the luna.

"What's up?" she asks, pulling me a step away from the group.

"I was wondering if you would watch River for us tomorrow so Andres and I could spend some time alone?" I say, feeling the blush creep up my neck.

"Are you going to cement your bond?" she asks with a giant smile on her face. I can't bring myself to say the words, so I nod. She begins jumping up and down in excitement. "Of course, I will! We all will. You take as much time as you need. In fact, why don't you go now?"

She spews out words faster than humanly possible. It's a miracle that I caught any of what she said at all.

"Thank you. We want to wait until dawn so that we are here in case River has a nightmare," I tell her. She pauses in thought momentarily.

"Why don't we just let her and Riley sleep in the same room? Their bond is so strong; I am sure he would be able to soothe her." I look around, unsure of what to say. I know she will be safe here, but I am still afraid of not being there when she needs me.

"I think that is a wonderful idea, Phoebe. Thank you," Andres says from behind me, and a blush creeps back up my neck. The butterflies in my stomach are flapping at full force. "Let's go say good night to River," he takes my hand, and we walk toward her together.

"We give her a choice," I say, pulling him to a stop. "If she wants us to stay until morning, we stay until morning." He agrees with a slight nod of his head.

River is glowing, sitting between Riley's legs while he plays with her hair. It is just about the sweetest thing I've ever seen. The way he gently combs his fingers through each strand and her relaxed posture...it's beautiful.

After explaining Phoebe's offer and letting her know that it's her choice, she suddenly seems more awake. She stands and starts jumping up and down in excitement. There's a chorus of "yes, yes, yes" and "thank you" as she, Riley, and Ryker run upstairs to prepare their fort.

"That's our cue, love," Andres whispers into my ear. His

breath tickles my neck, sending heat down my body and pooling in my core.

I turn to him, more than ready. Together, we begin to walk toward the clearing and our little pocket of heaven. We only make it a few feet inside the woods before I pounce on him.

I merge my mouth with his, wrap my arms around his neck, and cinch my legs around his waist. It takes him a couple of breaths to catch up, but his hands settle under my ass pulling my body up against his. He rotates us so that my back is up against a tree.

I hold on to his shoulders tighter, giving myself the traction to grind against his impressive manhood and moan into his mouth. He takes that opportunity to sneak his tongue inside, massaging my own. I move my body faster, chasing my orgasm.

"Drusilla. If you don't stop that, we won't make it to our haven," he says as he pulls his mouth back.

"That's okay with me," I say, pushing my mouth back toward his and resuming my grinding.

"I don't want to claim you up against a tree," he growls out. He stills my movements but kisses me with a heated passion. I hate to admit that he's right, but he is. As much as I don't want to wait, I know it will be worth it if we can have the privacy we desire for this.

I push him back, breathing heavily.

"What are we waiting for, then?"

He doesn't put me down. He simply turns away from the tree and sprints to the clearing. He's fast, but he's not fast enough. The sexual tension between us only builds the longer it takes us to get there.

He places me down gently with a quick kiss on the lips as we arrive in the clearing. It only takes him a moment to reopen the doorway to the pocket world. I admire him as his arms move through the controlled motions. The muscles in his back tense and release deliciously through his shirt. Next thing I know, I'm being picked up fireman style and thrown over his shoulder as he sprints through the door. I watch as it shrinks closed behind us. Magic really is a wondrous thing.

I thought he might bring us to the cottage so that we could explore each other in bed. Instead, he slows his pace and walks toward the cliff we visited on our first night and places me down.

There is nothing left to say before I latch onto him again, moaning into his mouth with each touch of his fingers. His hands roam over my legs and ass, leaving tingles in their wake and sending sparks directly to my clit.

Without losing contact, he sits down with me still attached to him and gently tugs the hem of my shirt. I force myself to remove my mouth from his for a moment to remove my shirt and tug at the hem of his to do the same.

I had planned on continuing our kiss, but the sight of his rippling muscles has me gasping. Never in my life have I seen a man this well-defined. His muscles really do have muscles. I move my hands from his shoulders, over his pecs, and down to his abs, my fingers tracing each one as I go.

"You're so beautiful," he whispers as he moves his mouth to my neck and begins sucking and licking a pathway down to my breasts. He pulls my bra down to give him free access and sucks a nipple into his mouth, twirling his tongue around the peaked nub.

Reluctantly, I remove my hands from his body and reach around the back, unclasping my bra and slipping it over my arms so that it falls on our laps. A rumble builds in his chest, vibrating his entire body and mine through extension.

"Oh, goddess!" I cry out, the pleasure from that vibration jump-starting my release. I grind on him, slowly moving my hips in a circle while he moves from one nipple to the next, lavishing it with the same amount of attention as the first.

My movements pick up speed, and soon I'm on the cusp of my

orgasm. He grabs my hips to halt me. I quietly groan in frustration before he picks me up and lays me on the ground.

"I need to taste you," he says with a gravelly voice. I didn't think it was possible, but I almost had an orgasm from that statement alone. Never in my life have I desired someone so much and had them desire me with that same passion.

He places small kisses down my chest to my stomach, while sliding my leggings and panties down over my ass. His mouth follows, kissing everywhere except where I need him to be.

He works his way down: over my hip, to my thigh, down my calf, and back up the other. When he reaches the intersection of my thigh and core, he pauses and places a soft kiss once more.

"This is where you will wear my mark," he says, the rumble in his chest returns with the last word. He continues to place kisses on my skin in every spot except my core, and I begin to writhe and squirm with need.

"Andres," I warn breathlessly.

Without hesitation, he secures his mouth to my clit, pulsing his tongue in time with my moans. The ecstasy I feel is indescribable. Out of nowhere, I get a glimpse of his emotions as well. I sense his desire to please me, and his satisfaction with each moan he coaxes out of me.

Just when I think I'm about to die with the sheer amount of pleasure I'm experiencing, my orgasm overtakes my body. My legs begin to shake with the force of my release. His mouth slowly moves my clit, his tongue slips between my folds and thrusts inside. It seems to thicken and grow with each thrust until I feel it pressing against my G spot, massaging it with shocking dexterity until I am tumbling over the edge once again.

Before I come down from my high, his teeth pierce my leg, and the orgasm comes back with a vengeance as I am marked as his mate. My own fangs drop in anticipation of doing the same.

"Goddess!" I cry out.

He laps at his mark, pressing a soft kiss over it before snaking his body upwards. I don't know when he removed his pants. Maybe he magically removed them. I don't care. All I care about at this moment is the fact that his impressive cock is now pushing up against my core, requesting entrance.

"Please, Andres," I plead and push myself downward, sheathing his cock between my folds. "Gods above," I say as I allow myself a moment to revel in the feeling of fullness.

He slowly begins to thrust in and out. Each time, I feel both of our pleasures strumming within our bond. He adjusts the angle slightly by lifting my ass off the ground so that his cock hits the delicious spot inside me, heightening the intensity for both of us.

I run my tongue over my fangs, my mouth salivating with the need to mark this man in all his sweaty glory.

"Do it, love. I can't last much longer. You feel so good," he growls, and the vibrations from his cock on the inside quickly have me tumbling over with my release as I sink my fangs into his neck.

The taste of his blood on my tongue is the best thing I've ever tasted. Any other blood will pale in comparison. As we cling to each other with our releases, wings spring from his back, beating to lift us up off the ground.

A feeling of weightlessness settles over me as Andres secures my frame to his as we soar higher, still connected. Reluctantly, I remove my fangs from his neck and lap up the trail of blood dripping down his chest. I look up into his eyes.

"I didn't know you could partially shift," I say, watching the stars as we fly by.

"Neither did I," he whispers in awe as well.

I kiss him again, pushing all my love for him through our now-established bond as he does the same, and I feel his cock harden once more.

Time for round two of a thousand.

As long as I live, I will never tire of this man.

Chapter Seventeen

Andres

Waking up in the middle of the glen wrapped around my mate—my fully bonded mate—is incredible. A feeling of completeness I've never experienced settles within me, and I allow myself to revel in it as I watch her. I run my fingers through her hair. I am reluctant to remove the evidence of our lovemaking in her tangled blonde hair but am unable to resist. These have been the best twelve hours of my existence. It's as if I was simply drifting through the last thousand years. I slept for half of that time, but my mind was plagued with memories of the past and fears of possible futures even during my slumber. Now, with Drusilla at my side, my life has meaning once more.

As I watch the rays of sunlight move across her beautiful skin, I can't help but wish I could give this to her permanently. She deserves the ability to walk in the sunshine for the rest of her life. She's soaked in as much as she could over the last few days, and I've seen how much it means to her. She loves the sun and the feeling of it on her skin.

I pause for a moment as an idea sparks. What if I could give it to her? What if, like Drake and Rayne, our mating allows her to walk in the sun? Why would the goddess pair us together only to have us live in separate worlds? How can she live in darkness while I live in light? If our children inherit my genetics, they will want to live in the light as well. I have to believe that the goddess has a plan, but all that matters is that we are together.

"My love," I coo as I brush the hair out of her face.

She groans her displeasure at being woken up, and I chuckle.

"We need to head back soon," I tell her.

"Ten more minutes," she growls and rolls over. She's so adorable.

"Love, River will be waiting for us." At my mention of River, her eyes go wide.

"Yes. We should go," she moves to get up, but I pull her back down.

"Not so fast. It's not yet dusk. We have a few minutes left to enjoy each other," I tell her, and she giggles.

"I wonder if I'll get to walk in the sun like Drake and Rayne after they mated," she whispers.

I do not disclose that I had the same hope myself. I know it is unlikely, and I don't want to get her hopes up.

"We can test it out when it's safe to do so."

"Really? You think it's possible?" I can feel her excitement and hope thrumming through our bond.

"It is possible. Drake and Rayne were part of the prophecy, and we aren't. I don't want us to get too excited. I've also never heard of a dragon being able to partially shift, and that was certainly something that was made possible by our mating."

"It's enough that we can come here to walk in the daylight. I won't lie and say that I don't want the sun, but my life is already more than I dreamed it could be because we are together," she says and merges her mouth with mine in a slow and passionate kiss.

"Me too, love. Me too," I whisper as we break apart.

"Andres?" she whispers after a second.

"Hmm?" I hum in response.

"Do you think any children we have will be hybrids like you?"

I ponder that question for a moment before I answer. "It's a very good question, but I don't know if I have an answer for it. Because I, myself, hold two different types of magic inside me, it's more likely that our children will hold only one of the three."

"I suppose," she says, turning back to watch the setting sun.

"No matter what type of magic our future children hold, they will be loved." I don't know why I feel the need to say that, but I do.

"Yes, they will," she agrees.

"How are you feeling, love?"

She lets out a soft sigh as she smiles. "I didn't think I would ever feel this at peace."

I nod. "I know exactly what you mean. Mated couples always talk about how different they feel when they cement the bond, and I chalked it up to them just being in love. Now I know what they mean..."

"It's like everything is just as it's meant to be. Like my entire life was just preparing me for this. The calm after the storm," she whispers, closing her eyes and soaking in the last of the sunlight.

"If anyone deserves a calm after the storm, it's you."

She turns to look at me, tears shimmering in her gray-blue eyes. "I love you, Andres."

I pull her close to me, wrapping my arms around her tightly.

"And I love you, Drusilla. More than you will ever know."

"Really?" she teases. "Why don't you show me just how much."

I take that as my cue, flipping her over so her back meets the ground and peeling off her clothes as I do. If she were human, there's no way she would be ready for more already, but she is not human. As I dip my finger into her wetness, I can tell just how ready she is.

"Andres..." she moans loudly as I lower my mouth to her clit and push two fingers into her core, quickly bringing her to the edge of ecstasy. She clenches around my fingers, sucking them deeper inside her. It makes me groan, wanting nothing more than for another part of my body to be in their place.

When her legs finally stop shaking, I remove my mouth and fingers from her core, bringing them to my mouth and sucking them clean. The taste of her is so delicious, like the nectar from honeysuckle.

I begin to move my body up hers, but she uses her speed and strength to slip from underneath me and push me down onto my back.

"Dru..." I begin but am cut off by the feel of her mouth wrapping around me. Her tongue moves quickly around my head. As she increases her suction, I am brought quickly to the edge.

"I'm going to..." I begin, trying to pull myself out of her mouth. Rather than stop, she uses her speed to bob her head up and down my shaft at a rate that can't be natural.

I cum with a roar, watching her as she swallows each drop of my release. When she finally releases my member with a *pop*, she licks the tip and then her lips like she enjoyed that as much as I did.

I pull her up my body so that she's laying across me and take her mouth with mine, savoring the taste of our combined releases.

"You didn't have to do that, love," I tell her as we break apart.

"I know. I wanted to," she says with a smile, bringing her mouth back to mine as if she enjoys the taste of us as much as I do.

After what feels like far too little time, we separate and pull our clothes back on. We sit at the edge of the cliff, with her back to my front and both of our legs dangling off the edge. We sit and watch as the sun sinks until its last rays are just peaking over the horizon. Then we stand, and I open the doorway back to the clearing.

Just like the pocket world, the last rays of sunlight are just visible when Drusilla sprints through the doorway. I rush to stop her, but I'm not fast enough. The rays hit her, and I watch as she turns toward them without flinching. She closes her eyes and soaks them in before turning to me. The smile on her face is as large as the Grand Canyon, and it's the best thing I've ever seen.

I quicken my pace toward her, but River beats me to it as she launches herself into Drusilla's waiting arms.

"Aunty Dru! You're walking in the sun!"

Drusilla laughs as she twirls River around in a circle and—just like that—my life becomes even more complete. Watching the two most important women in my life so happy makes warmth spread throughout my entire body.

"Uncle Andres! Do you see? Aunty Dru is walking in the sun!" River exclaims as I get closer.

"I do, my sugar. How amazing is that?" I ask, wrapping my arms around both of them.

The sun dips below the horizon as Drake and Rayne enter the clearing.

"Rayne! Drake! You missed it!" River runs toward them and jumps into Rayne's waiting arms.

"Missed what, honey?" Rayne asks.

"Aunty Dru can walk in the sun too!" she exclaims loudly.

"She can do what?" Drake asks, looking between the little girl in his mate's arms and Drusilla.

Drusilla nods at him, and he grins before rushing over and wrapping her in a hug. I didn't think it was possible for her smile to get any bigger, but it does. I don't need to search her emotions to know that she's happier now than she has ever been.

"There is so much we will be able to do now!" Rayne shouts as she joins Drake and Drusilla's hug. "Just think of all the things I can show you. We can go shopping—we can have spa days! Oh, the possibilities are endless." I feel a slight panic coming from Drusilla, but her happiness and excitement are more dominant.

"I have a feeling we're never going to see our mates," Drake groans to me. I just nod with a smile on my face. If Drusilla is happy and comes home to me each night, that's all that matters to me.

As one, we walk back to join the pack. I am already homesick for our pocket world, but I know that the pack needs us here to get ready for our attack on the laboratory.

I slow Drusilla down, pulling her aside for a moment.

"I think we need to stay here for a while if it is all right with you, love. We need to be here to make sure everything is ready."

"I know," she says. "I think that's the right thing to do."

She clasps my hand with hers, and we fall toward the back of the pack. I send out my empathy to gauge her emotions. As I expected, there is a small pang of sadness. Other than that, I can only feel her resolve to do the right thing.

"It is," I agree, bringing our clasped hands up to my mouth and placing a light kiss on the smooth skin of her hand.

Chapter Eighteen

Drusilla

Running through that doorway was probably the stupidest thing I've ever done in my life. What if the sun had burned me? Would it have been serious enough to kill me? For some reason, my body seemed to know that I was safe. With each step, my feelings of doubt disappeared.

Spinning and laughing in the last rays of sun—real sun—with River was the absolute best feeling. Knowing that it's one more thing I will be able to share with her and my family is the best gift the gods could've given me.

"Thank you," I whisper to whatever god or goddess granted me this gift. As usual, I don't get a response. I do not need one though. If they heard me, that's all that matters.

We walk back to Alaric and Phoebe's house to meet with the rest of our group. There are only a few days left, and we need to catch up on the plan. Besides, I need to spend as much time with Rayne as I can. She promises she's going to come back to us, but we both know that's a promise she can't really make. Anything could go wrong.

Once we arrive, we are quickly put to work. Andres, Sebastyn,

Drake, and Rayne go somewhere quiet to work on the communication spells they'll need to transmit the code. I end up helping Phoebe, Sophia, and Skarlyt set up the triage area for the injured.

We enlist the help of the rest of the witches to construct an enormous structure in the middle of the clearing with beds lining each wall. It will take us the last days we have to get the rest set up. When they go to Orillia, Opal and I will be staying here to receive patients. Sophia and Phoebe will be waiting outside the hunter's facility with Sarah to use their tears on anyone whose condition is too dangerous to be teleported.

"You look happy." I'm startled out of packing away supplies as neatly as possible by Skarlyt's voice.

"I am happy," I respond, turning to her with a smile.

"I'm so glad." Her eyes shift away from mine like she is embarrassed. "We haven't had much time alone, so I haven't had a chance to tell you that I'm sorry."

"Sorry? About what?"

She looks down at her feet before her eyes meet mine again. "Sorry that I didn't come and see you after you came home. And sorry that I left you to face it all alone."

"Skarlyt, you have nothing to be sorry about. Trust me. I wasn't very good company in those days and probably would've turned you away anyway," I tell her honestly.

"Still. What kind of friend doesn't at least try after everything you went through? I just didn't know what to say or do." Tears brim in her eyes, and I can tell she genuinely feels guilty about not coming to see me.

I wrap her in a hug and squeeze her tight. "Oh, Skarlyt. I know you, and I know that you were with me in here." I tap on her heart while still squeezing her.

"I was. I thought of you every single day. I was just so worried that I would say the wrong thing. The more time that passed, the worse I felt. I couldn't bring myself to visit, and it just got harder the longer it went. I thought for sure you would hate me..."

She steps back to look at me, but she has to brush tears away from her eyes before they focus on me.

"When I saw you at Alaric's and you weren't mad at me, I felt even worse. You should've had a friend to lean on. You needed a friend to confide in, beat up, anything—and it should've been me."

"Stop that. I'm telling you honestly that nothing you could've done would have made a difference. I probably wouldn't have even agreed to see you. I was so lost inside myself, inside my past. There were days when I wouldn't even let Drake and my parents see me. If you still feel that you have something to be sorry for, then you're forgiven," I say, wiping away the tears that are still falling down her cheeks. "But I promise you there's nothing left to forgive.

"I love you, Dru. You're a better person than most," she admits with a small smile.

"And I love you too, Skarlyt. Now, come help me make a list of all the supplies we need." I grab her arm and drag her over to the supply table.

After about an hour of making lists and taking inventories, I discover that the witches need a lot more than just bandages and antiseptic. Just the herbs on Skarlyt's list covers two full pages. We split the lists to make our work quicker, and Skarlyt thankfully takes the longer one. I am left with a meager half page, and she waltzes away with a list that is—well—long as fuck.

As I head toward the door, I decide to invite some additional help.

"Hey, Opal. Want to run to the store with me?"

She turns in confusion but smiles when she realizes it's me asking.

"Sure, Dru. I'd love to."

With that, we head to the twenty-four-hour drug store to load up on anything and everything we might need. We fill a small cart with bandages, butterfly stitches, antiseptic, painkillers, and anything else that we could think of. We spend more time than we had planned, but we have quite a bit of fun while doing it. I had forgotten just how nice it was to spend time with—well—with anyone.

"Dru?" Opal begins once we are done packing our supplies into the SUV.

"Yeah?"

"You should know—I'm sorry too." I turn to her in confusion. "I heard the conversation between you and Skarlyt earlier. You and I weren't as close as you and her, but I still should've tried to visit. It felt like one of those things, you know? Are we close enough friends for me to visit after something traumatic happens? How much trauma is too much trauma?"

I pat her leg.

"It's okay, Opal. Like I told Skarlyt. I wouldn't have wanted to see anyone. I heard...I heard you were going through a hard time when I got back anyway."

I turn to look at her, and she begins wringing her hands in her lap.

"Yeah..."

"Hey," I say, getting her attention. "You don't have to tell me anything you don't want to." I didn't mean to bring up a sensitive subject. Even when I couldn't be bothered to contact them, I kept up with stories about my old friends over the years. I heard about how Opal left. When she returned, she had changed—and not for the better. The woman sitting in the seat next to me now sounds nothing like the one I heard about then.

"My mate rejected me," she blurts out, and I suck in a breath. My hands tighten on the steering wheel.

I take a couple of deep breaths to calm myself before I speak.

"You don't have to tell me if you don't want to. When did this happen?"

She sighs. "It was just after my eighteenth birthday. I ran into him in the woods on the way home from Supernatural. He was everything I didn't know I wanted. As soon as the bond began to form, he rejected me and took off."

"That's horrible," I whisper.

"Yeah, but the things I did after that were worse. I acted like a complete psychopath. If the Moons weren't as amazing as they are, there's no way they would have forgiven me. Hell, I wouldn't have forgiven me."

"You know, Opal, over the past few days I've learned some things. First, fate works in mysterious ways. Sometimes terrible things happen for a reason." She snorts in disbelief at my statement. "No, seriously. I used to curse the gods for allowing me to be taken and tortured by those monsters, but now I know it was for a reason."

"Why would the gods have allowed that?" she asks, tears forming in her eyes.

I pull over to the side of the road, putting the car in park before turning to look at her. "Because of River. If I hadn't gone through what I did, no one here would've known how to help her. If I didn't go through what I did, Rayne never would've questioned the hunters. She never would have left them—never would have met Drake."

Opal stares at me in wonder, and I can see the gears in her head whirling.

"I would happily go through all of that again if it meant that things would end up here. I'm happy. I have my family. I have the love of an amazing man." I pause as she flinches away from that statement. It is a subtle shift, but I maybe shouldn't have brought that up. "My point is that sometimes bad things happen to pave the way for good ones in the future."

She nods. "Okay. What is the second thing?"

"What?" I ask, confused.

"You said you learned a few things recently, and you only told me the first."

"I guess I did. The second thing that I've learned is that no matter what life throws at you, it's your life. You are the one with control. If someone has taken that power from you, you can take it back."

She nods her head, but I don't think she's quite ready to take her control back yet. That's fine. I wrap my arms around her and pull her in for a hug.

She gasps like I've burned her and pulls back from my touch.

"What?" I ask, concerned.

"Nothing," she says quickly, but I can tell by her expression that it is definitely not nothing.

"You can tell me."

She sighs. "Sometimes I get these flashes when I touch someone or something. It can be visions of the future or the past. I never know what it is, and I can't control it."

"What did you see?"

"I saw part of the day Rayne set you free," she whispers, tears misting her eyes.

"I'm sorry you had to see that," I say, grabbing her hand and giving it a squeeze.

"I'm not. I think I was meant to see it so that I could truly believe what you were telling me." She wipes more tears away but quickly adds, "Only my family knows about these visions—I haven't told anyone else."

"Your secret is safe with me," I promise, putting the SUV back in gear.

"Thank you," she says as we pull back onto the road.

It's well past midnight by the time we return and put away the supplies. As we work, a feeling of foreboding sets in with the knowledge of my friends and family heading into that place with all those monsters. I don't mean the supernaturals—I mean the hunters.

I feel desperate to stop this from happening, but I know why it is so important. Even if we didn't already know that River's mother was locked in there, even if I didn't have hope that Breanne is there, someone needs to shut that place down.

From River's memories, we know many supernaturals are being held there. As I play through the various scenarios in my mind, I am not sure which is worse.

If they are all still captive there, we can save them. It would mean, though, that they have had to endure so much pain while waiting for us.

"Are you ready to head back, love?" Andres snaps me out of my thoughts.

I nod my head and try to suppress the yawn building in my chest. I fail miserably, and Andres scoops me up to carry me back to Alaric and Phoebe's.

When we reach the house, we stealthily creep up the stairs to check in on River. When we open the door to her room, she's nowhere to be found. A slight panic overtakes me before I abruptly turn and move to the room across the hall. As quietly as possible, I inch the door open to find toys strewn everywhere. It's like a bomb went off in there. Still, the kids are nowhere to be found. The panic is gripping me harder now. Not only did I somehow forget to say good night to River—I have somehow lost her too.

This time there is no stealth. I rush over to the game room and throw open the door. My terror recedes as I find the most adorable sight I've ever seen. Riley, Ryker, and River have created a blanket fort supported by the gaming table and chairs and are sleeping peacefully beneath it.

My hand moves to my pockets, checking for my phone. I need a picture of this. This is one of those memories that you must document. My phone isn't in my pocket. In fact, now that I think about it, I haven't seen my phone in days.

I turn toward Andres to ask if he even has a phone, but another voice comes from behind me.

"Phoebe already took pictures. They're adorable, aren't they?"

I turn toward Alaric in surprise. I didn't even hear him come up behind us. I nod and turn back to the sight before me. The three of them are in a row, their arms wrapped around each other.

I slowly make my way over to their fort, grabbing the end of a blanket and pulling it up over them. River sighs with a small smile on her face, and my heart melts. The bond that River and the boys share already is too strong to be broken, and I can't help but think that we—and hopefully River's mother—will need to get used to life among the Westwood pack sooner rather than later.

Silently, I turn back to the doorway. I take my mate's hand in mine before turning to Alaric.

"Is it okay if we sleep downstairs?"

"Of course," he replies, and I give him a nod of thanks before pulling Andres down the stairs with me.

Chapter Nineteen

Drusilla

When we make our way down the stairs into the kitchen, I find Rayne waiting impatiently.

"Took you long enough."

"What?" I ask looking at Andres and then back at her.

"Sorry, big guy. I'm stealing your mate for the night," she says, linking her arm with mine and leading me down the stairs. I glance back at Andres, but he gives me a big smile and nods. I blow him a kiss over my shoulder before turning back to Rayne.

"What's going on?"

"What's 'going on' is the fact that we need to celebrate your mating," she says, leading me into the bunker. We weave through the kitchen and living room, and I freeze at the doorway to the bunkhouse. I am accustomed to finding rows of bunk beds inside, but they have been replaced with a large dance floor, a DJ booth, and rows of tables with snacks. All the women in my life are waiting for me just inside—including my mom.

"Wha—" I start but am immediately cut off by the entire group of women.

"Surprise!" They all yell the word in various volumes and tones before rushing to embrace me.

"We all thought it would be nice to celebrate your mating and have a real girl's night before..." Rayne begins, but my mom cuts her off.

"You know, it would've been nice to hear of my daughter's mating from my actual daughter," she says, a hand cocked on her hip. "Don't worry, though, Colin was kind enough to let me know."

She's trying to pretend that she's upset, and maybe she really is. The smirk on her lips says differently.

"I just haven't had the chance," I explain. "It's been a busy week."

She drops her hand, rushing over to me and wrapping me up in a big hug.

"I remember very well how consuming it can be when you meet your mate," she says with a wink as she steps back.

"Ew. No. I don't want to hear that from my mom," I say, shaking off the icky feeling that comes over me.

She just chuckles and heads over to the tables. I see a row of shots lined up on the bar and take a step toward them.

"These are all for us," Rayne explains as she motions to the array. "They have a single drop of blood in them. Somehow everyone else is pregnant, so they're all party poopers." She sends a wink in the direction of Phoebe, Sophia, Skarlyt, and the others who are happily munching on snacks.

"More for us," I say, grabbing one of the shots.

"That's the best thing I've heard all night," Opal agrees, joining us for a cheer before we all down a shot.

"All right, bitches. Let's get this party started," Rayne yells, walking over to the DJ booth and tapping on the attached laptop to start the music. Rayne knows every word to the songs on her playlist, but Opal surprises me by joining her performance. They begin our own personal concert of *Shoop* by Salt 'n' Pepper.

Even those who are not quickly getting drunk are more than happy to take to the dance floor and let loose. There's something comforting about being so loud and silly all together.

After far too many shots, Rayne pauses the music, interrupting with her slurring words.

"All right. All right. It's time for speeches."

"Speeches?" I whisper to Phoebe and Charleigh. They are standing next to me, and both raise their shoulders in an identical, sympathetic shrug.

"Just go with it," Charleigh says with a wink.

"I just wanna say that you bitches are the best friends a girl could have," Rayne stumbles through the words. A round of cheers goes up, and she holds up her hand. "No, really. I never thought that I would have such an amazing group of women to call my family."

I can see that she's starting to get emotional, so I make my way up to her. Good friends let their friends know when they need to sit out a round.

"There she is," Rayne exclaims when her clouded eyes find mine. "You know, if it weren't for this woman right here, I definitely wouldn't know any of you. This woman—she took a lost, little girl and gave her purpose—showed her right from wrong."

"Rayne," I say softly, hoping to coax her down.

"Not only are you my best friend, Dru. You're my sister. You're the salt to my pepper—the leaves to my tree. The laces to my shoes. The lightsaber to my jedi…"

"I think we get the point," I interrupt her, causing a round of laughter to ring out.

"What I'm trying to say is that I wouldn't be who I am without you."

I wrap her in a hug. "That's the nicest thing you've ever said to me."

"I love you, Dru," she whispers before raising her glass. "To Drusilla. May she and Andres live happily ever after."

Cheers travel around the room, and I discreetly wipe away a stray tear. No one seems to notice except my mom who sends me a smile.

"And Opal. Opal, tonight I found my second soul sister," Rayne shouts, looking around the crowd. Her lips tip up in a giant smile upon finding her. Opal looks flattered but shy and raises her hands in an indecisive motion. "If you sing like that, then you are my sister too. You and I are going to take on the world." Rayne cheers before running over to Opal and wrapping her up in a hug.

I take that as my cue and turn on the music. Rather than being upset, both Rayne and Opal begin screaming out the lyrics to the song.

"That was quite the speech," my mom says with a chuckle.

"It was," I say, watching my best friend with a smile.

As I glance around the room, I can't help but agree whole-heartedly with Rayne.

We do have the best friends in the world.

* * *

After the party of the century—as Rayne started calling it—the next two days fly by. When we aren't planning and getting everything ready, Andres and I are sneaking away to have some time alone together.

I am laying in bed, wrapped in the scent of my mate as I watch him sleep. I am entranced by the small crinkling of the skin between his brows and the way his long, blonde hair is tussled from sleep. This may be the first time I've woken up before him.

I often wake to the feel of his soft kisses or his fingers playing with my hair. Usually, I grumble about getting more sleep. Today, my anxiety is at a record high. Today is the day I watch as the people I love head off into danger without me.

I know that I wouldn't be much use in an actual fight, and my skills can be put to better use here. Andres and I already agreed that we could not both leave River. If he doesn't come back—the thought makes me sick—I will be responsible for protecting River. Although it is my worst fear, we both know it's a possibility. That is why Andres and I discussed it at length. If he does not return, I will take custody of River. He asked if I would take care of her as if she was my own. Of course, my answer was yes.

With the knowledge that this could be our last morning together, I run my fingers over his face. I sweep the stray strands of hair off his forehead before moving down his cheeks and tracing his chiseled jaw. I'll never know how I got so lucky to have this god of a man as my mate, but he's mine. I'm going to give him a reason to come back to me today.

I follow the path my fingers just traveled with my mouth, placing soft kisses down his face and jaw. I continue, traveling lower to his neck and chest. I make it as far as his abs before he wakes up.

"Morning, love," he says huskily.

Instead of answering, I slip his boxers down and lick his cock from base to tip before sliding my mouth over it. I slowly move my mouth up and down, increasing and decreasing my suction in time with his moans. I swirl my tongue around the tip and savor the taste of him before moving down and increasing my suction once more. After a few more bobs of my head, he explodes into my mouth.

I swallow down each and every drop.

"Come here, love," he says, and I shimmy out of my shorts before climbing up and straddling his waist. He merges his mouth with mine as I lower myself down onto his still-hard cock. He reaches between us to rub his thumb over my clit, and I release his mouth with a gasp. I move up and down slowly, savoring the feeling of fullness that only he can provide.

I rock my hips back and forth, quickening my pace, and chasing my orgasm. As I tumble over the edge, he flips us over and begins thrusting in and out of me with vigor. He doesn't let up, prolonging my orgasm. After what feels like hours, but is likely only minutes, he follows me over the edge.

His large, muscled arms reach across me, grabbing a towel from the floor. He uses it to clean me up as he slips out of me.

"Goddess, I love you," he says.

"I love you too, Andres. I love you more than it should be physically possible to love another person," I whisper back.

He kisses me then, slow and passionate. Each swipe of his tongue and brush of his lips is evidence that he feels the same. How did I get so lucky?

"I have to get ready to go," he whispers as he pulls back. I nod with tears brimming in my eyes, remembering why he is leaving me, and where he is going. "Don't worry, my love. I will come back to you," he whispers as he swipes a stray tear from my cheek.

"But—" I start, but he places his hand on my mouth to silence me.

"We have a plan—a good one—and the strongest supernaturals alive coming with us. I will be coming back to you, I promise," he vows.

Not trusting my voice, I nod and pull his head down to mine for a kiss. Just like with Rayne, I know this is a promise that he can't really make. I know with all my heart that they are both going to do everything they can to come back to me. I need to trust in just how strong they are.

Breaking apart from our kiss, he leans his forehead into mine. We stay like that for a few minutes—just being close to one another. I send a silent prayer up to the goddess that she keeps my family safe and brings them back to me today. I don't know if she can hear my prayers among the others that must be going up from all around the pack, but I have hope that she will do whatever she can.

We get ready quickly and begin making our way to the clearing. We are joined by others on our way, but everyone is quiet. It's not until I see Rayne standing just outside the triage building that I break apart from the group, speeding my way to her and pulling her into a hug.

A small sob escapes me at the thought that this could be the last time I see her, and she rubs my back.

"I'm not going to leave you," she says, emotion thick in her own voice.

"You don't know that. You can't know that." I cannot stop myself from voicing the fears that are rattling around in my head.

She pushes me back to look into my eyes.

"I will walk through the gates of hell to get back to you if I have to."

I nod my head, trusting that she means exactly what she says. She gives me one last squeeze before she is replaced by Drake pulling me into a hug.

"Please bring her back to me," I whisper.

"There is no way in hell she is leaving either one of us," he says, stepping back and looking into my eyes. I see the determination there. If he has to sacrifice himself to save her, I know he will.

"I don't want to lose you either," I tell him. He doesn't say anything—just pulls me into another embrace.

He lets go and turns to walk away as Andres steps up, wrapping his arms around my waist.

"I'll bring them back to you, my love," he whispers, putting his finger under my chin and raising it up so that our lips meet.

"I need you to come back to me too," I whisper. He nods, reluctance shining in his eyes, but he walks away to join the rest.

I feel an arm slip around my shoulder and look to see my mom, emotion shining in her own eyes.

"They'll come back to us," she whispers, and I nod. I glance one last time at my family and see that my father has joined Drake.

"Please bring them back to me," I whisper, hoping and praying with everything inside me that we can all celebrate my mating with a proper ceremony when they get back.

"Come on. Let's get busy," my mom says, stepping back with a clap of her hands.

She's right. The busier we are, the less we'll worry.

Chapter Twenty

Andres

L eaving Drusilla and River behind while I head off to storm the laboratory is the most difficult thing I've ever done. I would never want either of them to accompany me there, but I can still feel the emotions seeping out of their pores. They are anxious and worried. I would give anything to take those feelings from them, but the only way to do that is to keep my promise and return to them.

I cannot get distracted by thinking of them now. Drake, Alaric, Sebastyn, and I are hidden at the edge of the wooded area that surrounds the underground lab.

We are farther away than I would like, but we need Price to get all the way inside with Rayne and come back out before we can snatch him and make our way in. Other small groups are positioned in the surrounding trees—hopefully far enough apart to avoid detection. They will take their cue from us. When we make our move, they will join us.

I lock down my gift and tell Sebastyn to do the same. The emotions coming from Drake are those of a crazed man. I do not blame him. His mate currently has her hands cuffed behind her back, a bruise on her cheek, and an escort to the underground laboratory. It doesn't help that the man roughly handling her is the same one who spent years torturing his sister.

"Alaric," I whisper, and he snaps his head to me. I gesture to Drake, who is currently pacing. Alaric nods, understanding immediately what I am saying. We may need to restrain him.

Alaric steps in front of Drake and places his hands on the smaller man's shoulders.

"Drake, you need to calm down. She is okay. This is part of the plan. If you aren't thinking clearly, you won't be able to hear the code." Sebastyn and I both place our hands on him and try to send him waves of calm. It works as well as can be expected—which isn't much. There isn't much that would calm me if I were in that situation, but he begins to slow his breathing and the glossy look in his eyes recedes.

Once he nods, we all take a step back. He collects his cool just in time because Rayne begins firing off the numbers of Price's code. He must be entering it in front of her just inside. Drake repeats the numbers aloud, and Alaric plugs them into his phone to ensure we don't forget it—as if any of us would. It's better to be safe than sorry.

"Anything?" Alaric asks Drake after a moment.

"Nothing," he shakes his head. "She's shut down the bond. I can't feel or hear anything that's happening," he says with a grim look on his face. The rest of us look at one another too. We all know there's only one reason Rayne would do that, and it isn't anything good.

"We know there's something about the facility that can block bonds," I offer. "She may have just gone too deep inside."

The sky is darkening by the time Price returns to the surface and heads toward his car. I look to Alaric who nods to Drake. Out of all of us, he is the one with the biggest reason to want that man dead. Personally, I would rather see him suffer for a few years for his actions. Luckily, Drake must have the same thoughts. He speeds toward the unsuspecting hunter and simply knocks him out before throwing him roughly over his shoulder and carrying him back to the shack.

"Anyone willing to stay up here and guard him while we go in?" he asks. "I think both Drusilla and Rayne are going to want to take part in the fun."

Alaric assigns four shifters to stay and guard him on the main level once we use his hand to gain access to the door. Once we enter the code on the next landing, there is no turning back.

The hallway appears empty, but Drake, Alaric, Sebastyn, and I approach the closed doors, throw them open, gather any staff inside, and secure them in a single room before moving on to the next. If they put up a fight, they die. The ones who seem weak or scared are handed off to other shifters to contain.

They do not seem to have expected us, but there are fewer hunters here than we had anticipated. Although we are neatly emptying the rooms behind us, there is no way to keep our presence a secret. I hear an alarm whining in the distance, but it is only seconds before it is suddenly blaring in my ears as well. Lights flash a red warning across the now-empty hallway.

By the time we've finished with the first and second hallways, there are more than twenty hunters laying dead on the floor, but there are still no signs of any supernaturals.

We are quickly approaching the place we expect the prisoners are being held. On the blueprints, the cages appeared like cells in a prison. I open my bond with my sister wide. I can tell that she has shut down her side of the bond because it takes more force than I expected to open myself to her. When I do feel her, she's incredibly weak. She is so weak that I'm not sure she would've lasted even another day.

Not caring about the plan anymore, I surpass our allies and rush to her. What I see breaks my heart.

My sister is in her dragon form, covered in scars that should be impossible. Her healing should've kicked in long before scars could form. She is not alone. Rayne is laying, bleeding and unconscious, on the ground next to Andrea. My sister's massive tail wraps protectively around the vampire's small body. I spot the electric panel next to the cage's door and rip it from the wall. There are sparks and a solemn hum in the air as the electricity winds down. I grab the door itself next and use my strength to pull it off its hinges.

A growl emanates from Andrea as she wraps her tail tighter around Rayne.

"Andrea," I whisper, unable to keep the emotion out of my voice. She doesn't seem to recognize me at first. "Sister," I add, hoping that she will snap out of it and remember me.

It takes her a few moments, but I see when recognition sets in. Her body slumps, all her strength from only moments ago is gone. As her pulse begins to slow, I walk over to her and rub my hands over her enormous head. I send as much strength as I can spare down our bond.

"River?" Weakly, she uses our bond to ask me about her daughter.

"Safe," I say out loud. I see the relief on her face, and her body begins to shut down. "No, Andrea. Not yet," I spit out quickly. Her eyes flutter open. She's trying to stay awake, but she's too weak.

"You need to shift," I tell her. Her eyes slip open. It looks like she's trying, but it's not working.

"*Shift!*" I scream, using my influence as the king of dragons. The role was passed down to me by my father. Even if I never intended to sit on the throne, the power is always sitting there, waiting to be used. I push every ounce of strength and power in my body into the command. I know this is going to leave me weak, but it's worth it. I cannot have come so far just to lose her. River is waiting for her. I just need to get outside to Phoebe, and she will be fine.

Her shift is agonizingly slow and painful to watch. After a few short minutes, my battered and bruised sister is laying naked on the ground next to a now-conscious Rayne.

Rayne looks disoriented but is quick to think on her feet. She glances between the two of us, shucks off her overshirt, and drapes it over my sister's body.

"Thank you," I say weakly. I've used every last drop of my own strength to force her to shift. "I need someone to take her to Phoebe. I can't carry her."

I look Rayne in the eyes. I can tell she's weak too. Now that she is wearing only a dark tank top, I can see the slices on her back and shoulders.

I do not have time to ask her about this before Drake barges into the room. His eyes are red with bloodlust, and he is breathing heavily. I watch the moment he sets his sight on Rayne. In one swift movement, his arms are around her and his mouth is crashing onto hers. She hisses in pain as his hands brush against her back. His eyes somehow seem to be even redder when he hears his mate hiss in pain.

She grabs his face in her hands.

"I'm okay. I'm okay," she repeats over and over to him in a calm voice. He forces himself to take a few deep breaths before he is calm enough to turn her around to look at her back. Like me, he sees right away that the skin is already knitting itself back together. That is probably the only reason he is able to stay calm.

He finally notices me and my sister on the floor, and his face falls.

"Andres," he says, rushing over to me. "What can I do?"

"Take Andrea to Phoebe. She needs her tears, or she won't make it," I tell him as I attempt to stand. I slip back down and decide to simply stay down until I have enough strength back to make it upstairs.

"What about you?" Rayne asks.

"I just need a few minutes to regain my strength. I'll follow shortly," I tell her.

She nods as Drake scoops up Andrea and rushes out of the room.

Rayne stops just outside the door, turning back to me.

"We'll be right back for you," she says before she rushes off after her mate.

I don't doubt that they will be back. In my thousand years, I have never experienced a bond like this outside my family unit. The bond that I share with not only Drake and Rayne, but Alaric, Phoebe, Darren, Sebastyn, and the rest of the pack and coven is unique. As I allow my body to slip into sleep, I find some peace in this thought. Perhaps this is my role in my mother's prophecy. This bond I share with them could be our salvation.

As I try to conserve my energy, my eyes fall closed. I lose control and feel my head being tilted back. Someone grips my jaw to open it wide.

"Please don't let him drown," someone whispers. It sounds like Rayne. The liquid flowing down my throat is smooth and fruity.

"What?" she scoffs at the person holding my head. If I were a betting man, I'd wager it is Drake. "We're pouring liquid down an unconscious man's throat. What if he breathes instead of swallows?"

I want to smile but can't find the energy.

Drake chuckles. "I'm pretty sure his reflexes will keep him from drowning."

"What if they don't? Then what, smart ass? If I kill your sister's mate, she'll kill us."

"No one is killing anyone," I whisper hoarsely, my energy quickly refilling.

"Oh, thank the goddess," Rayne exhales, standing up and reaching her hands out to me.

"What did you give me?" I ask, wondering as my body seems to repair itself remarkably fast. When my magic is depleted, I need to slumber for a few days—sometimes longer—before I can recover. I feel good as new.

"Skarlyt said it was a potion to replenish strength or some shit," she responds with a shrug.

"I feel better now than I have in years. Let's get everyone else free. Then we go home to Drusilla," I say with a laugh as I walk out the door. "By the way, I don't think she'd ever kill you."

I wait at the junction of the hallway for the two of them, knowing that it is my turn to keep them safe as well.

"Where are you going?" Drake asks Rayne as she turns down another hallway and walks past the numerous cells filled with supes that we are supposed to be rescuing.

"I don't know," she responds, never looking at him or me. She keeps her gaze forward. "I just know that I need to go this way."

"That's not ominous at all," Drake sighs, looking at me. I shrug, and the two of us follow her anyway. We crisscross down countless hallways until we are standing in front of a singular door. There are no supes or hunters this deep in the laboratory, and we are now far removed from the noise of the fighting above.

And that's when I feel it. The slight pulse of the magic behind this door is so familiar that it makes me stumble. I haven't felt this magic in—

I close my eyes and try to focus. It can't be. As I open my eyes, I see Rayne dreamily reach for the handle. Drake places his hand on top of hers.

"Wait. Let me go first."

She moves her hand, and we both watch with bated breath as Drake opens the door. Chained to a cement wall, with nothing but a small cot and filthy toilet beside her, is an adult woman.

It is not who I expected, but her magic is the same. She's an oracle and, more than likely, descended from my mother's bloodline. I instantly feel the connection between us grow and watch as a silver thread sparks between us. It can only mean one thing. She is family and is meant to be protected.

"Mom?" Rayne whispers, adding an additional shock to finding someone from my mother's bloodline in this cell.

I watch as the woman's eyes fill with tears. She takes Rayne in, neither of them blinking. My vision is blurred by the tears brimming in my own eyes.

"Please stop. Please," she begs through her sobs. "I can't take any more of your tricks. Please, just leave me here to die."

"What do you mean? It's me, Mom. It's Rayne."

"Please, Martin. I'll do whatever you want me to. Just please stop torturing me with visions of her. Please."

Rayne runs her hand soothingly over her mother's hair and rests her palm on her sallow cheek. She crouches down to meet her eyes.

"Mom, it's me," she promises. "Martin is dead."

Her eyes fly open, and recognition shines in them.

"Rayne? Baby? Is it really you?" She tries to reach her daughter's face, but the chains securing her arms to the wall won't allow it. Rayne moves her face to rest in her hand.

"Yes, Mom. It's really me. Have you been in here all this time? Did Dad know?"

For a moment, I feel as if I'm intruding on a private moment, but I can't find it in myself to care. This woman is my family too. Even if we are generations removed from one another, Rayne and her mother are my family. I had thought the silver thread connecting me to my mate's dearest friend was only because of Drusilla's connection to her, but now I know that it is not.

She's preparing to answer when Drake walks up and rips her restraints from the wall so that the two of them can truly embrace.

"Let's get her to Skarlyt," he explains. "She can remove the shackles, and you can continue your conversation."

The older woman looks up at Drake curiously.

"Is this your mate?" she whispers.

"He is. Mom, this is Drake. He's a..." Rayne begins.

"He's a vampire," Rayne's mother supplies. "I had a vision when you were a baby that your mate would be a vampire." With unexpected grace, she gives Drake her hand and allows him to help her stand.

"A vision?" Rayne asks, dumbfounded. "Are you a witch?"

"I am, and so are you. We have a lot to talk about. Right now, your mate's right. We need to leave this place."

I take that as my cue and scoop her up in my arms.

Both Drake and Rayne nod their thanks, and the four of us walk up the stairs. I hope that Skarlyt has more of that potion ready because I can feel this woman fading fast.

"Your mother wanted me to tell you how proud she is of you," the woman whispers, and my steps falter as I look down at her.

"How?" I ask the question even though I already know. She is an oracle, and she has unlimited access to her ancestors who guide her.

"She came to me in a dream a few days ago. I thought she was wrong—thought she was selling me false hope. She said that her son would help lead others to my rescue," she chuckles and clutches her side.

She must have at least a few broken ribs, and it is clear she has been malnourished.

"Thank you..." I whisper, not knowing what to say back.

"Valerie," she supplies, and I nod.

"Thank you, Valerie."

We retrace the steps of our trek through the underground facility. From the blueprints, we know already there is only one way out. Thankfully, Skarlyt's potion has given me the strength to climb the many stairs with Valerie in my arms.

While we traveled deeper into the laboratory, the others must have been quickly clearing out the upper levels. We pass by the dead and wounded inside rooms in various states of disrepair. There are still shifters searching through those rooms for any additional information, but the sounds of fighting have ceased.

As we crest the top of the stairs and exit the building, Valerie stiffens in my arms. She closes her eyes, relishing the feel of the breeze on her skin. I set her down on her feet, and she opens her arms wide, tilting her head up to the moon. After a few moments, we head toward Skarlyt and Phoebe where they are standing deep in conversation. They watch us in confusion, but they must recognize the resemblance between Rayne and her mother because they quickly spring into action and rush toward us.

The first thing Skarlyt does is wave her hands, and the shackles from Valerie's wrists and ankles release. I watch as she rubs each of her thin wrists before looking up at Skarlyt with a smile.

"Mom, these are my friends. This is Skarlyt and Phoebe," Rayne says. Phoebe and Valerie both stick out their hands to shake before Skarlyt sweeps in to hug the older woman tightly to her chest.

Skarlyt jumps back abruptly as if she's been burned.

"You're an oracle?" she whispers in disbelief.

"I am," Valerie confirms. "Or I suppose I *was*. I haven't received any visions since being imprisoned, so I'm unsure if the next oracle has been born or if the gods were protecting me by not showing me the things to come."

"Wow," Skarlyt thinks aloud. "I haven't heard of any new oracles being born. The last oracle we know about disappeared—like—twenty years ago."

Valerie gives Skarlyt a look I now recognize from Rayne. It's a patient sort of *ta-da* face.

"Holy shit! It's you? You're the last oracle. Oh, my Mother! Wait until my mom hears about this...Actually, let's go right now. I can take you to her," Rayne places her hand on Skarlyt's arm to halt her ranting.

"Actually, Skar, I wanted to talk to my mom for a few minutes before the wolves—or witches—descend on her."

"Of course," she says, trying and failing to keep the disappointment out of her voice. "Here, take this first." She pulls out a vial and hands it to Valerie. She takes it and smells it quickly before downing the contents. Her smile is wide as she hands the empty vial back to Skarlyt, and I see the changes in her appearance immediately. The raw skin on her wrists returns to a normal hue. Her hair even becomes shinier and looks healthier.

"Where in the world did you get phoenix tears?" Valerie asks in amazement.

"That would be me," Phoebe says, stepping up with a humble wave.

"Oh, my," Valerie says, clasping Phoebe's hand and closing her eyes. I know what she's doing. She's reading her. I remember seeing my mother doing the same many times. It's both painful and heartwarming to see.

"I promise I'll bring her back," Rayne says with a wink. She links arms with her mother and takes her toward the woods.

"I'll stay here and help," Drake says, snagging Rayne by the arm and placing a brief kiss on her lips. "Please be safe."

"Aren't I always?" she asks with a smile.

Phoebe, Skarlyt, and Drake all scoff their disagreement at the same time, and I chuckle. She's definitely not fooling anyone in our group.

"Well, I promise I will this time," she says, using her fingers to trace a cross over her heart.

"I'm going to go with them," I whisper to Drake.

"I don't..." he begins, looking from Rayne and her mother back to me.

"It will be fine," I tell him and turn to walk away, keeping to the shadows. I know that Valerie will know that I'm following, but Rayne might not. Either way, I'm far too curious about her to not follow. Especially since I feel so connected to her. If she was just a distant relative, I wouldn't feel this strongly. It's almost as if she carries my mother's magic inside her, and I can't help but want to be close.

"I'm so happy to see that you have more of my personality than your father's," Valerie whispers to Rayne.

I watch Rayne struggle to find words for the first time since I met her, and I cock my head to the side in curiosity.

"My sweet girl," Valerie stops walking and takes Rayne's face in her hands. "I already know he's gone. I felt his death. He was my true mate."

"What do you mean?"

"When your true mate dies, you feel it—even if they are millions of miles away," she says, and a tear slips from her eye.

Rayne brings her hand up and wipes it away. "I'm sorry."

"Now, you listen to me. What happened in the past doesn't matter. All that matters is that we are together now," she says, placing her hand under Rayne's chin and raising her face so that their eyes meet.

"You don't understand. Mom, I'm the reason he's dead," Rayne sobs, and now I understand why she struggled with the words. Knowing that you're the cause of the death of someone's true mate would be hard. Knowing that it was your own father would be impossible.

"What do you mean?" Valerie asks.

"I mean that my friend...Drake's sister—my sister—she killed him to protect me and Drake. He shot me, and I—" Rayne sobs out the words and my heart clenches. I knew that Drusilla killed

Rayne's father. I should've expected Rayne to have some conflicting emotions about that, but I am not thinking clearly for some reason.

A rumble flows from my chest without warning. If Valerie so much as thinks about retaliating against Drusilla, she will have to go through me.

Valerie releases her daughter with a gasp, looking over her shoulder to find me in the shadows.

She turns back to Rayne.

"Oh, Rayne. I'm not mad at you. I'm furious at your father. How could he shoot you? I don't blame your friend. I would've killed him myself if I were there."

They hug for a long while, and I stand and watch. I am unsure why I feel the need to be present for this tender moment, but I do.

"I need to know, Mom," Rayne says, stepping back.

The two of them walk a little farther away and sit at the base of a tree, holding hands.

"Your friend was correct. I was—or am—an oracle. The gods choose one oracle for every generation. They give us glimpses of the future so we may steer the world in the right direction."

She pauses to take a shaky breath.

"The day I left...I had a vision on the day I left. The hunters had figured out what I was, and they were coming for both of us. I saw the hunters coming to our home; I saw your dad dying trying to save us; I saw them take us and lock us away. I knew the only way to stop the vision from becoming true was to surrender myself. I knew they would leave you alone as long as you showed no sign of magical abilities, so I put a block on your magic and left."

"Is that why you left me the riddle?" Rayne asks.

"Yes. I knew your mate would be a vampire since the day you were born. I had hoped that once you met him, you would find me. Of course, I didn't know that I would still be in that laboratory. I had expected one of the hunters to take me to one of their personal workshops to live out the rest of my days. Martin was a sick bastard though. He knew your father would do anything to get me back, so he kept me tucked away where he would never find me."

"I don't understand. All my life, Dad said that supernaturals were evil. Why would he risk himself to save you if he truly believed that?"

"I was his mate," she explains simply. "You know the pull you have with Drake. It doesn't matter who or what he is; you will still love him."

"We hated each other when we first met but couldn't fight the pull to be together." I smile at that thought. I had serious doubts that they would work it out after Sebastyn and Sarah's mating ceremony. At the time, I thought I would have to give them a little push in the right direction. It turns out I didn't.

She nods. "It was the same for your father and me. I knew what he was, and I detested every time he left the house on one of his missions, but I loved the man. He may not have known what I was, but it wouldn't have mattered. We each held half of the same soul. There is no way to deny that pull. It doesn't matter what your beliefs are."

"I guess that makes sense," Rayne says.

Suddenly, I feel the need to go to River and Andrea, and I look between the two women sitting at the base of the tree and the horizon. I feel pulled in multiple directions. I want nothing more than to sit and ask this woman why I feel this pull toward her.

At my next glance, I find Valerie smiling at me, and she gestures with her head to go. Oracles just seem to know things. I do not understand it, and I likely never will. I learned a long time ago not to question it, so I trust that she will make time for me later.

I turn away from them, taking off at a run before shifting mid-air and flying back to Parry Sound.

Chapter Twenty-One

Drusilla

Gods above and below, there are so many types of supernaturals filling the triage tent, and more are coming in by the second.

There are shifters of various kinds: bears, wolves, mountain lions, panthers, and even a jaguar. The most interesting is a sea nymph whom I mistakenly called a mermaid when she first arrived.

After being hissed at and corrected, I now know that they do not like being called mermaids. We currently have five in a large tank of water that we had to get Constance to conjure on the spot and then teleport back and forth to fill with seawater. There was no way for us to anticipate what they would need before they got here. If I wasn't so busy rushing around, replacing bandages, and handing out water and food, I would stop and marvel at them. They're beautiful.

My attention is pulled away by River's surprised cry coming from behind me. I turn quickly, ready to defend her, and watch as she runs to the woman who has just teleported in next to Skarlyt. River jumps into her arms and begins sobbing.

Tears prick at my eyes as I watch the two of them fall to the ground, holding tightly onto one another. I don't even know when River got here, but I'm thankful that this moment could happen.

I take a few steps closer to them. I do not want to interrupt their tender moment, but I am unable to stay away while River is crying. The woman looks up at me, and I can recognize River and Andres in her eyes immediately. The color of blue that shines back at me is unique to them. I've never seen it before. Her eyes scrunch up in confusion, and she pulls her daughter closer to her protectively. I raise my hands to show I mean no harm, but a growl slips out of her anyway.

River turns her head, looking directly at me before raising her hand to reach for mine. Her mother quickly pulls the arm back to her, baring her teeth as she growls louder.

"No, Mommy. This is my Aunty Dru. She's Uncle Andres' mate," River explains. Andrea looks from her daughter and back to me before releasing her grip on River.

"I'm sorry. I'm Andrea," she says hoarsely. As she stands, she sticks out her hand for me to shake.

I take her hand, clasping it firmly in mine. "It's okay. I would have done the same. I'm Drusilla, but you can call me Dru."

She sways on her feet for a moment, and I gesture to an open bed along the wall.

"Why don't you take a seat? I'll get you something to eat and drink while you and River catch up."

Reluctantly, she does as I ask. She curls up on the bed with River, holding onto her like she's the only real thing in the world.

I walk to another area of the triage where we have some of the older supernaturals grilling food to feed all the hungry shifters. I pile up a large plate of food and grab a bottle of water. I stop for a minute, enjoying the smile on River's face as she explains everything that has happened to her mother.

From the snippets that I'm able to hear, she pairs every negative experience with a positive one. She was kept as a captive, but Drake and Rayne saved her. She has been so lonely, but she met Riley. She misses her home, but she and Andres created the pocket world.

Smart girl. Right now, if River only told her mother about the negative things she's experienced, we'd have a dragon on a rampage here. Without Andres, I don't think we'd be able to stop her.

I walk up and place the plate of food on the bed.

"I wasn't sure what you like, so I got a little of everything."

"Thank you," she says, tears still shining in her eyes.

"You're very welcome. If you need anything else, let me know," I tell her and turn to walk away.

Each step I take feels horrible and sends a pang of hurt through my chest. Why does it feel like I'm losing River? I should be happy. She has her mother back. That's what we wanted, right? All I wanted was for River to be happy.

"Drusilla?" Andrea calls out when I'm about five steps away.

I abruptly turn back toward them. "Yes?"

"Would you like to sit with us? I know you have others to take care of. Perhaps you could spare a few minutes while we eat."

"Yes!" I exclaim before toning down my enthusiasm. "I mean, yes. I would love to."

Other than a few words here and there, we are quiet as Andrea devours her food and drink. We do not know how long she has been held in captivity, but it is clear she will need plenty of food to rebuild her strength. She is covered in wounds that will take time to heal. The wounds she carries on the inside, however, I know better than anyone just how hard those are to heal.

"River, sweetheart. Can you go ask the nice lady over there for some more water, please?" Andrea asks. River looks unwilling to leave her mother but nods, heading toward Opal.

"Drusilla, I want to thank you for everything you've done for her," Andrea says as soon as River is out of earshot.

I grab one of her hands. "You don't have to thank me. The truth is that River helped me just as much as I helped her. Without her, I wouldn't have been able to find the strength to let the past go and look toward the future."

She nods in understanding. "River told me they held you captive too."

"They did. But one of the hunters—" I begin, but a growl rumbles out of her chest. "I know the feeling. Trust me. Her name was Rayne, and she helped me escape." Her brows crease together, and a confused look flits across her face.

"Is she a beautiful woman—with long brown hair and big brown eyes?" Andrea asks.

I nod. Tears fill my eyes immediately as my mind races to the worst-case scenario.

"Did you see her? Is she—" I choke on the rest of the words.

"She's okay. She was thrown into my cell after her punishment. She was alive when they brought me here," she explains, and I wipe the tears from my eyes.

"Why are you making my mate cry?" Andres growls from behind me, walking over and scooping me up before sitting back down with me on his lap.

"It's okay, Andres. I just got worried about Rayne for a minute. Andrea assured me that she's fine," I whisper as I cling to him. This morning, I wasn't sure that he would make it back to me, but he's here.

The emotions I've been keeping at bay break free, and I sob in relief. Andrea's here. If what they're telling me is true, Drake and Rayne are okay. My family is alive, and our mission was a success.

Reluctantly, I release Andres. I stand so that he and his sister can embrace.

"I missed you, big brother," Andrea whispers.

"And I you," he responds. "Before River gets back, I must ask. Where is Michael?"

"I don't know. When we awoke, we went our separate ways to search for River. He's weak but not dead. I would have known if he was in that place with me."

Before she can say more, River comes skipping back with another plate of food, some water, and a blood pack for me.

Andres releases his sister with a nod before sitting back down and pulling me onto his lap once more. The four of us sit and eat— or drink—for a while before I feel compelled to get up and get back to work.

When the last captives are brought in, I search everyone for any sign of Drake and Rayne. Skarlyt sees me studying the most recent group as they arrive and realizes what I am doing.

"They're driving," she explains. "Rayne's mother was in there."

"Rayne's *what?*"

Skarlyt, seeing the questions on my face, places her hands on my shoulders to calm me down.

"She was being held there in a cell. She was in pretty bad shape when they brought her to me. Drake is also bringing you a present."

"A present?" I question. I don't really want a souvenir from that place.

"Price," she whispers in my ear, and my fangs drop at the name.

"Really?" I ask, my mood steadily improving by the second. Soon—very soon—I'll be able to close the door on that part of my life forever.

The next few hours fly by as I busy myself with my assigned tasks. Before I know it, my favorite brunette is walking inside.

"Dru!" she yells, and we launch ourselves at each other.

"Glad to see you were worried about me too, sis," Drake snarls from behind her. I open my eyes, narrowing them at him. I reach my hand out for him to join our embrace.

The three of us stand there embracing, my hands rubbing Rayne's back. Feeling a roughness there, I pull my hand back and look at it. I see flakes of dried blood and I push them both away before spinning her around and investigating her back.

She spins back around as a red haze begins to overtake my vision.

"I'm okay," she says, grabbing my face. "Dru, I'm okay. I promise."

It takes a few breaths of me looking into her eyes before I finally calm down enough to talk.

"Who?" I ask. Okay—so I'm not quite able to talk.

Drake nudges Rayne aside and takes her place. He places his hands on my face.

"Price," he says plainly, and I growl. "I have him locked up in the trunk if you want."

I nod my head and step toward the door, ready to exact my revenge. Before I can, strong arms grip me around the waist and lift me up off the ground.

"Drusilla, let the haze go before you head out there," Andres whispers in my ear. "Take deep breaths. Breathe with me."

I feel his chest expand and contract, and I try to match his pace. After a few moments, he puts me back on my feet but keeps me secured to him.

"Take him to the cells on the pack's land, Drake. Tempers are too high right now to deal with him," Andres says.

At the mention of the cells, I get a wicked idea.

"Put him in the cell with Colleen," I add with a grin.

"Yes! Let's do that. Alaric has cameras in there, right?" Rayne pipes in with a sadistic smile. "We need to record every second of that."

There's my psycho best friend I know and love.

"Wait? Colleen's still down there?" Phoebe asks, walking up to us.

"Yup," Rayne says, popping her lips for emphasis. "We couldn't decide what to do with her. I wanted to torture her, but Drake thought that was 'uncouth.' So, we're at a stalemate."

"For the record, I side with Rayne," I say with a shrug of my shoulders.

"Of course, you do," Drake says with a roll of his eyes before giving Rayne a quick kiss and heading off to put Price in with Colleen.

"Are we due for a movie night?" I ask her, thrilled to have my friend by my side.

"Abso-fucking-lutely!" Rayne responds. "Oh, by the way. Drusilla, meet my mother."

She gestures to the woman beside her.

I go to take a step forward and am stopped by something heavy around my waist.

"Uh, Andres, think you can let me go?"

He lets off a little growl but releases my waist.

"It's very nice to meet you." I place my hand out as I take the two steps toward her.

She slaps my hand away and wraps her arms around me. I stiffen briefly before I return her hug.

"Thank you for everything you've done for my daughter," she whispers. She's the second person today who has said that to me.

"Your daughter saved me first," I whisper back. It is the second time today that has been true as well.

She steps back and looks at me in disbelief.

"I mean it," I explain. "Her dad held me prisoner for years before she freed me. She saved my life. I owe her everything."

She looks from me to Rayne. "How old were you?"

"Old enough to know it was wrong, but too young to make a real difference," Rayne responds.

Her mom grabs us both into a hug.

"Okay. Enough with the mushy stuff," Rayne says, stepping back and rubbing her hands together. "Time to go watch a movie!"

I give Andres a quick kiss, and Rayne helps her mom get settled with some food and a comfortable place to wait. Using our vampiric speed, we run back to the house and head straight for the basement to watch the monitors.

Rayne growls loudly as we watch Drake open Colleen's cell. She is disheveled and immediately begins trying to rub herself against him seductively. Rayne smiles proudly when her mate shoves the other woman away before throwing a terrified Price in with her.

It takes seconds—literally seconds—before Colleen pounces and drains him dry.

"Well, that was anticlimactic," Rayne says with a pout.

"It was. I thought there would be more back and forth than that," I respond. "We can always use this as an excuse to get Drake to let us torture her."

"No. That won't work. It was our idea, remember?" she says with a sigh.

She goes to stand up, but there is movement on the screen.

"Look!" I point to the monitor.

Together, we watch as Colleen scratches wildly at her own throat. It looks like she is choking, but she begins throwing up instead. There is blood everywhere. She turns, spewing more across the camera lens and distorting the picture.

"How can she have that much blood to vomit?" Rayne asks in awe.

"I don't know. That can't be possible, right?"

As soon as the words are out of my mouth, we watch as Colleen collapses lifelessly on the floor.

"What the fuck did we just see?" Rayne asks, looking over at me.

"I'm not sure. I don't think Colleen's going to be an issue anymore."

"No, I don't think she will," Rayne agrees. We both sit there, still stunned by what we saw before heading back to the clearing.

"There's something you two need to see," Alaric gets our attention as we approach. The alpha's tone is serious and pulls me from my wonder about what we just witnessed between Price and Colleen. He gestures for us to follow him into one of the temporary buildings. Inside, there is a plastic pop-up table covered in papers and blueprints.

"What are we looking at?" Rayne asks.

The room is crowded with others. Drake and Andres make their way to our side. Sebastyn, Darren, Lennox, Alaric, and their mates give us sullen looks from across the table. Alaric takes a deep breath and releases it in a sigh.

"These are the blueprints for at least five other facilities," Alaric says.

"Five?" I question, my eyes drawn immediately to the bustling triage behind us. We rescued over a hundred supernaturals from just one. How many will we find in five more?

"These are just the ones we know about," Darren adds.

Well, shit.

I guess I know what we're going to be doing for the foreseeable future.

Chapter Twenty-Two

Drusilla

After our initial shock at finding out there are five other facilities, we start planning our next raid.

The next one will be harder because they will know that we're coming.

"What if we place some people in the Orillia facility to keep up pretenses?" Darren asks.

"You don't think they already know we've cleared out that facility?" Andres asks from his place at my side.

"Hunters are shit at communication," Rayne adds, a little hope creeping into her tone. "I'm sure they know about the attack and the rescue, but they probably don't realize there are no hunters left in the building."

Darren nods as if he had expected this.

"Everyone agrees?" he asks, looking around the room. "We can leave a small number of people at that facility to keep up appearances and gather as much information as possible."

"Keep up appearances?" I ask skeptically. I would be happier if no one had to step into that place ever again.

"Keep the lights on," Darren explains. "Make it look like someone is home."

"If the other facilities think there are still hunters there, repairing the building and trying to recuperate their losses, they won't try to come and repair it themselves." Alaric nods his head thoughtfully as he reasons through his brother's plan.

"Drake and I need to be part of that team," Rayne says as she steps forward. "I know the ins and outs of being a hunter. If anyone is going to be able to fake it, it's me. We all know that Drake goes where I go, so he and I can lead that team."

I want to object, but I know she's right.

"Do we have someone who can reprogram the locks?" I ask. We don't want any surprises if real hunters decide to drop in for a visit.

"Yes," Sebastyn answers my question. "We have Matt. He's better with electronics than anyone. It's almost like magic."

We all chuckle lamely at his joke.

"Do you think he can hack into their system to retrieve updated information?" I ask. I can feel Rayne's scowl boring into the side of my face, so I meet her eyes with a wince. "You've been out of the game for a while, Rayne. You don't know what all has changed, and they may have some safeguards in place you don't know about."

She nods in aggrieved acceptance, and I turn back to the group.

We are interrupted by a loud roar from outside. A bear's wild growl shifts into a human's voice yelling, "Where is he?"

We all rush outside, but Alaric quickly moves to the front of our group.

"Axel," he says, trying to calm the burly man now standing before us.

"Alaric, I swear to all the gods that if you do not give me my brother right now, I'll slaughter each and every one of you," Axel growls out, sounding more animal than man.

"Your brother?" Alaric asks, shock and concern mingled on his face. "Axel, he's been missing for years."

"I know he's here. I can feel him," Axel grabs Alaric by the shirt.

His sudden and violent movement has Phoebe stepping forward, her hands already lit with flames.

"Axel, I don't care who you are looking for. If you touch my mate again, I swear on all the gods that you won't live long enough to find them."

Axel's eyes flick to her briefly, and he releases Alaric.

"If we had your brother, we would have called you," Darren steps in. "You know that."

"He's here. I know he is."

"Maybe he's one of the shifters we rescued?" I offer as an explanation, and Axel's rage-filled gaze lands on me. Seeing the threat, Andres swiftly positions himself in front of me.

"Rescued?" Axel turns his question back to Alaric and Darren.

"Yes," Darren confirms with a snarky tone that is uncommon for him. "You may remember the rescue mission that you had no interest in joining?"

This time Axel grabs Darren by the shirt and wrenches him forward menacingly. The bear shifter seems to have forgotten that Darren, like Alaric, has an extremely hot mate watching—and I don't just mean her looks.

Sophia steps up to him, her arms already entirely alight and reaching. She doesn't say a word. She doesn't need to.

Axel lets go of Darren and takes a step back with his hands raised. Smart man.

"If your brother is here, we can find him." Alaric begins, calm and censure equally present in his concerned brow. "But you need to put some pants on and control your temper. The people in that tent have been held captive and tortured for years. They do not need to see you throwing a fit out here."

Axel has the sense to look ashamed for his actions and slips on a pair of shorts someone locates for him.

Curious and wary, we accompany him to the triage tent to look for his brother. We stop short when we hear an altercation in there as well.

"Get him the fuck out of here now!"

It takes me a moment to recognize Opal's voice through the fury and pain.

I turn to gauge Rayne's reaction before taking off at a run. The girls and I enter with the men right behind us, ready to defend our friend.

Opal has collapsed onto the ground, and all eyes are directed toward her.

"What is it?" I ask, searching her for evidence of the problem. She is sobbing. She is no longer the fuming mad Opal we heard moments before. As one, the six girls huddle to surround her, protecting her from prying eyes.

"He's..." she hiccups the words and searches our faces, finally landing on Sarah. "It's him."

Sarah's eyes flash, and I hear thunder roll in as she stands. I want to stay with Opal, but Skarlyt waves me away.

"I'll stay," she says. "Go help her."

By the time I turn around, Sarah is levitating and covered in a purple glow. She is studying each of the beds against the wall across from us.

"Which one of you rejected Opal?" She is speaking, and I can see her lips moving. The voice coming out of her mouth is not her own.

I follow her forbidding gaze around the room. I hope whoever it is isn't stupid enough to—nope—he is that stupid.

A large man who is identical to Axel is levering himself up from one of the beds with obvious difficulty. He is clearly injured, and he doesn't meet Sarah's eyes when he admits his guilt.

"Me."

I take a few steps through the building crowd, placing myself between Andres and Alaric and Darren.

"You!" Sarah points at him. "I banish you from these lands. Until Opal finds it in her heart to forgive you, you will not step foot on any land belonging to the Westwood pack or coven."

He hangs his head in shame. "I understand. For what it's worth, I'm sorry—" he begins, but Sarah cuts him off.

"Don't. Just don't. Leave and don't ever return," Sarah growls.

As he makes his way through the tent, all eyes glued to him, I hear Darren and Alaric whispering to each other.

"I guess we found Axel's brother," Alaric sighs.

"Can she exile people?" Darren asks, nodding toward Sarah. There is no malice in his tone—just curiosity and surprise.

The alpha shrugs his shoulders.

"She just did, and I don't think any of us are going to go against anything she says right now."

"If you two can manage this," Darren says, placing a hand on my shoulder, "I think we have some damage control to do outside."

I look back at Andres before I nod in agreement.

"We can handle it," I say before the brothers leave.

Sebastyn and Sarah teleport Opal somewhere safe and quiet. With the excitement gone, the rest of us try to get things back under control in the triage tent. Each of us take over the care of a few supernaturals and focus on them. It's a lot easier with so many people helping.

Luckily, Rayne's mom is one of my charges.

"So, Drusilla. Sit down. Tell me about how you met my daughter," she says, patting the side of her bed. I glance around the room one last time. I keep searching the faces here for Breanne, but there is no sign of her yet. As the last of our forces return, I worry that I may never find her.

"Well, Rayne's dad took me captive when I was sixteen and kept me in a shed behind their house," I begin. "Your house—I guess."

I stumble over what I should tell her and how to say it. It was her mate who held me captive, but she already knows he was a monster.

"It's okay," she says. "Tell me everything. I want to know. No matter how hard it is for me to hear."

She asks me to tell her the truth, so that's exactly what I do. I tell her how Price tricked me, how they punished me, how Rayne would give me extra blood, and how she ultimately saved me. I tell her about how I struggled in the years after my escape. I tell her about how lost I was until her daughter and I found each other again.

"I'm so sorry," she says, wiping tears from her eyes.

"You didn't do any of those things," I assure her. "You were suffering too."

"I didn't do this, but my mate did. I thought leaving was the right thing to do. Now I realize all I did was twist him into an evil man."

I grip her arms lightly. "That's on him. You didn't make his soul turn black, he did."

"Still. Things may have turned out differently if I had been there."

"Maybe," I agree. "Maybe not. Either way, I'm pretty happy with the way my life has turned out. I wouldn't change meeting your daughter for anything."

"I hope she can forgive me," she admits in a pitiful whisper. I hold her hand as she tells me her own story from the beginning. She knew the hunters would take her and Rayne away because of what they are; she knew that her mate would die trying to protect them; she knew she and her daughter would be tortured by the hunters for years; and she knew the only alternative future began with her giving herself up instead.

She blocked Rayne's magic before turning herself over to Martin. Her fate had been sealed like that laboratory until she was rescued by her own daughter.

"Listen to me..." I pause, realizing I don't know her name.

"Valerie."

I give her a grateful smile. "Listen, Valerie. If I know Rayne—which I do—there is nothing to forgive. You left to protect her. If you told her what you just told me, I already know what she is going to say."

"What's that?" Valerie smiles at me.

"She's going to say that you are a victim—not a villain. She's going to say that—like the rest of us—you have already suffered enough. If I were a betting woman, I'd say she's going to blame herself."

"But..."

I shake my head. "Your daughter has a thing about sacrificing herself and blaming herself for things beyond her control. She thinks she needs to save everyone, and it's her fault if she can't manage it. I've been working on it. Maybe between the two of us, we can help her kick that habit?"

"I'm just happy to have my daughter back," Valerie admits, tears springing to her eyes. "I didn't think I'd ever see her again."

I squeeze her hand in response.

We look around the room at all the battered, bruised, and emotionally drained supernaturals trying to recuperate.

"I have to ask," she begins, drawing my attention back to her. "Who was that woman who was crying earlier?"

"Do you mean Opal? She has blonde hair and was carried out by the guy with the tattoos and the glowing purple woman." I clarify.

She nods. "Yes. Opal."

"She's a witch with the local coven. Years ago, her mate rejected her. That was the guy who was told to leave." She nods without a hint of surprise. I narrow my eyes, feeling protective of Opal. "Why?"

"Because she's the next Oracle," Valerie says simply, and I feel my mouth drop open.

"She's—what?"

"She doesn't know yet, and her gift is underdeveloped. She should have started training with me by age twelve, so we are behind. I will need an introduction to her soon."

I nod, not knowing what else to say.

"Excuse me," a voice from behind me calls, saving me from spilling all of Opal's secrets.

I turn to find one of the mermaids—or not mermaids—standing behind me wearing a large t-shirt that falls almost to her knees. Her blue and green tail has shifted into a pair of long, pale legs that match the rest of her milky skin. Her eyes are round and almost too large for her thin face. Instead of looking awkward, the contrast just adds to her beauty.

"Yes?" I ask once I shake myself out of being awe-struck by how drop-dead gorgeous this woman is in front of me.

"I would like to help," she says. Her voice sounds hoarse—like she hasn't used it in a long time.

"Okay. I'm Drusilla," I tell her, reaching out my hand for her to shake. She looks at my hand and then back up to my face in confusion. I gently reach over and grab her hand, sliding it into mine and giving it a little shake. Once again, she looks down at her hand and then back up at me. "It's a way of greeting each other."

"You are telling me hello?" she asks, tilting her head to the side like a curious puppy.

I chuckle. "Yes."

She nods her head, storing away the information I have just given her.

"I am called Pearl."

"Well, Pearl. What would you like to help with?" I ask, mentally running through the things I could have her do. She's clearly not from here, so I wouldn't ask her to do anything too strenuous or confusing. She could always bring food or water to the patients who are too weak to stand.

"I have healing magic."

"Healing magic?" I question. Although I have quickly become accustomed to the power of phoenix tears and the potions the witches create, I know healing magic is rare. Perhaps this woman can brew potions as well.

"Yes, like this." She steps closer to Valerie, and I tense up. Valerie is unconcerned and gives Pearl a nod. The younger woman reaches out, placing a hand on Valerie's leg.

I watch in awe as a blue-green glow builds under Pearl's pale hand and spreads across Valerie's entire body. The cuts and scrapes peppered across her exposed skin knit themselves together as the light passes under them.

Valerie's mouth drops open.

"Goddess. I haven't felt this good in..." She stretches experimentally and stands up quickly before reaching down to touch her toes.

"That's amazing, Pearl," I say. Pearl looks drained, and I gently help her sit until the color comes back to her face.

"I'm okay," she rasps.

"I don't think you are," I tell her, tilting her chin up so her eyes meet mine.

"I am," she insists. "I just haven't used my magic in so long. I'll be ready to heal again in a few moments."

I glance at Valerie. The oracle is also now watching Pearl with concern.

"Pearl, you need to take it easy. Here, lay down." She pushes Pearl into the bed that she herself recently vacated.

"I will just close my eyes for a moment. After I rest, I can help more."

I shake my head. "You need to heal too."

"I have a debt to pay," she says seriously. "I need to show gratitude. You saved my people from those monsters."

"You don't need to do anything. We didn't save you because we expected something," I explain, and Valerie nods in agreement.

"They didn't even know I was in there, and my daughter was one of the ones leading the charge."

"Truly?" Pearl asks, looking between us.

I nod sullenly. I wish we had known Valerie was in there. If we had known where Rayne's mother was years ago, my friend could have left the hunters earlier. We may have been able to rescue all these people before any real damage was done.

Pearl's eyes slip closed, and I pull the blankets up over her.

"Sleep. I'll wake you soon," I tell her and then gesture for Valerie to follow me outside.

"Did you see that?" she whispers.

"I did. It was incredible," I agree. "But it clearly takes a lot out of her."

"Imagine what she could do when she's back to full strength. If you're going after the other facilities—" I give her a pointed look. She's not supposed to know that. She waves her hand at me dismissively. "Please. I was married to a hunter; I'm an oracle. You think I didn't know about the other facilities?"

"Why didn't you tell us?" The question slips out before I know what's happening. It sounds more accusatory than I intend.

"When? When Rayne first found me? When we arrived here, and others needed aid? When everyone was in an uproar?"

"All right," I relent. "I get it. There wasn't a great time."

"I have been away a long time, but I know enough to see that this pack and coven would feel required to storm another of the hunter's strongholds before they are ready," she explains without apology. "And I know my daughter will go with them."

When she puts it like that, I guess I can't be upset.

"The mermaids—" she begins, and I cut her off.

"Sea nymphs."

"The sea nymphs," she corrects, "could be powerful allies."

I look out at the forest surrounding the area.

"Of course, they would be," I agree. "But they are far from home here. We won't force them to do anything. If they want to go home, heal, find their families, live their lives—who are we to stop them?"

"Do you really mean that?" Pearl's voice comes from behind me, and I spin in surprise.

"Of course, I do. I know that all our leaders here will feel the same," I tell her with conviction.

"You say this even though you know the oracle is correct?" Pearl asks, gesturing to Valerie. "My people could turn the tide of this war."

"That would be amazing, but we would all understand if you chose your own safety instead."

She cocks her head to the side in confusion.

"I don't understand."

Valerie steps up closer. "What Dru is trying to say is that you and your people need to heal. Everyone in that room needs to heal. Fighting this evil will cost us—our peace, safety, and maybe even our lives—and we cannot force your people to pay that price."

Pearl nods, clearly deep in thought.

"I would like to take some of my people home to the ocean. If we can rest for a week, we will happily return to repay our debt." She says the words like a vow and doesn't wait for an answer before returning to the bed inside.

"Congratulations on securing some new allies," Valerie says, clapping me on the back with a laugh.

"I guess—" I begin, trying to sort out how I just accidentally became the liaison between the pack and the sea nymphs. "I guess I should probably tell Alaric."

Chapter Twenty-Three

Andres

I sit with Andrea and River for a while, watching while Drusilla flits busily from person to person before finally taking a break to sit beside Rayne's mom. It is only then that the idea comes to me.

"Do you two want to go home and rest for a few days?"

Andrea looks at me like I'm a crazy person. She watches me warily, wondering if she'll have to be the one to explain that our home is long gone, but River just grins from ear to ear and cheers in agreement.

"What are you two talking about? Our home has been gone for an exceptionally long time."

"We created a pocket world," River explains excitedly.

"You said that earlier, but you didn't say you created our home." Andrea sounds justifiably proud.

River nods. "It has the house, the glen, and everything. It's just like home. Uncle Andres, Aunty Dru, and I stayed there for a few days already."

"Well, then. I would love to," Andrea says, wrapping River in a hug.

There are tears shining in my sister's eyes, and I know it's because she wasn't sure she would get a chance to hold her daughter ever again. I reach over and squeeze her hand, feeling those same emotions for her. I wasn't sure what I would find in that laboratory. Despite the physical wounds, she seems to be handling most of this pretty well.

I reach down and scoop Andrea up, carrying her out of the makeshift building.

"I can walk, Andres," she growls.

"I know you can, but you don't have to. Maybe I want you to need your big brother for a little while longer," I tell her honestly. She hasn't needed me in hundreds of years. By the time she was River's age, she thought she could do everything on her own. I can admit now that it hurt a bit to feel like she didn't need me anymore.

"Oh, Andres. I'm always going to need my big brother," she says, leaning her head into my chest.

"I know. Once we get Michael back—" I begin.

"*If* we get Michael back," she corrects.

I shake my head. "No. I said it right the first time. When we get Michael back, you won't need me again."

She sighs, tears shining in her eyes as she nods. I know that she feels hopeless, like we're not going to find him. Maybe she's right, but I won't give up hope. There's still a chance until she feels their bond break.

It doesn't take long for us to reach the clearing.

"Are you ready, sugar?" I ask, looking down at River.

"By myself?" she asks, her large eyes going wide.

"I can't move my hands because I'm holding your mama. Besides, we already created the world; all you need to do is open the door," I say encouragingly.

She nods and turns toward the doorway, closing her eyes and waving her hands. Her eyebrows scrunch up in concentration as she pulls on her magic. I know it's going to take more than she's accustomed to using, but I also know that she can do it. She has more power humming in her little finger than most adults do in their whole body; she just needs to remember that.

Andrea is watching the open space where the doorway flickers in and out of existence, but I turn my attention back to River. Her blue eyes pop open as the doorway opens, and she begins jumping up and down. When she looks up at me with a smile, my heart swells with pride.

"I knew you could do it."

She doesn't respond. Instead, she pulls on my shirt and leads me through the doorway to our home. The glen is quiet and perfect—just like we left it. River leads us to the house and up the porch steps. She opens the door with a proud flourish.

I gently set Andrea down on the threshold, and she looks around with a deep sigh.

"Welcome home," I say.

"Thank you," she whispers and then turns to River. "Do you want to go see if you can gather up some wood for the fire?"

"But we have—" River begins, looking at the pile of wood I have already chopped and then back at her mom. She must see something there because she nods and rushes outside.

"Andres..." my sister begins, turning to me.

"You don't have to thank me for saving you," I stop her. I know that's where she's headed with this conversation.

"Yes, I do," she says, and I shake my head. She places her hands—shockingly cold and thin—on my face. "You're the best big brother and uncle in the entire world. You didn't need to come for me. You could've left me there. You didn't need to protect River." I go to protest, but she shakes her head. "I know what you're going to say. You're going to say that it's your job, but it's not. There are many people who would've looked the other way or given up hope. Hell, given the number of people you rescued from that place, I'm sure many of their loved ones did give up. I will never be able to thank you enough for keeping my daughter safe when I couldn't."

Tears line her eyes and my own.

Unable to say anything, I pull her into a hug.

We're still embracing when a little body squeezes between us to join our hug. We are almost there. There's only one more member of our family to find before we can be whole once more.

I clear my throat and step back.

"I would like to take you both to the academy tomorrow."

River gets an excited look on her face while Andrea looks confused. "Academy?"

I nod. "The leaders in the area have created a supernatural academy for the children so that they can learn in peace without worrying about being discovered by humans. River was going to start classes there next week. If you don't mind, I would still like her to."

"Please, Mama? Can I? Riley is going, and we're going to be in the same class and everything. Please?" River pleads with her mom, but I don't think it is necessary. The smile on Andrea's face makes it clear she is pleased with this development.

"Of course," she says, smiling down at her daughter.

"That's settled. We'll head over there tomorrow afternoon." I lead Andrea into the house and look down at River. "Why don't you go get the bed ready for your mama?" She rushes through the doorway to the bedroom, and I watch as she pulls back the covers and fluffs the pillows.

"All set," she exclaims and watches as I guide Andrea into the room and get her settled on the bed. After a second, River climbs up, wraps her arms around Andrea, and closes her little eyes.

I begin to hum the lullaby our mother used to sing to us when she wanted us to fall into a deep sleep. Andrea looks at me in confusion before joining in.

Soon enough, River's chest begins to rise and fall in slow, easy breaths. She's in a deep sleep and won't be waking up anytime soon.

"I need to know, Andrea," I whisper, still watching my beautiful niece as she sleeps.

Andrea lets out a deep sigh, turning her bright blue eyes to mine.

"I know," she whispers. "Just please let me finish before you say anything."

I nod and try to hide my pain at the obvious shaking in her voice. What she's about to tell me isn't going to be easy for me to hear, but it's probably going to be even harder for her to say. I grab the small chair in the corner of the room, bring it close to the side of the bed, and clasp her small hand in my own while she keeps the other wrapped snugly around her sleeping daughter.

"After you left, Michael and I stayed at home for two more days, trying to figure out where to go. We knew we needed to go somewhere far away or the temptation to find River would be too strong. Ultimately, we decided to fly across the ocean. We found a large cavern in a land called Greece. The waters there were a beautiful aquamarine that reminded us of River's scales. Even though we were so far away, it made us feel closer to her." I reach up and wipe a stray tear off her cheek. It was hard enough for me to slumber so far away from our little River, but at least I knew where she was.

"We slumbered for a long while. We didn't know exactly how long, but we woke to machines boring into the rock around us. When we surfaced, things were vastly different from the world we left. We had hidden ourselves near an empty seaside cliff, but it had become a large, busy town. Houses had been built into the rock. They were full of humans, and the humans had machines that they took everywhere. Everywhere we looked, there were people. It was both enchanting and terrifying. Michael wanted to leave instantly to search for River, but I argued that we needed to learn to navigate this new world."

I nod my head as more tears slip from her eyes. I can only imagine what she is thinking. If they had left immediately, would things have turned out differently?

I give her hand a squeeze, trying to show support while staying silent as she requested. After a couple of steady breaths, she continues.

"After three days of wandering around, we learned that much had changed in our world. The supernaturals were still in hiding. Beyond that, most believed them to be nothing but a myth. There had been wars, famine, and plague. The humans were slowly killing our earth, and our hearts broke at the sight. Finally, we set off in the dead of night. We started our search at our old home. We knew you and River had headed north, so that's what we planned to do as well. We flew high in the clouds to conceal ourselves from the humans." She pauses and squeezes my hand, and I know what comes next is going to be the hardest part. "When we got home—where our home used to be—there was nothing left. Our quiet home—an island in the sea of its green glen—was just a concrete building surrounded by a metal fence."

I nod my head in understanding. I remember the pain I felt at seeing the same scene.

"They call it a prison," I explain, and she nods sadly. "It is where they keep those who they believe to be dangerous."

"Michael and I landed on the roof, shifting into our human forms as we did. The building had confused us, but we thought we would be left alone. That wasn't the case. The second our feet touched the roof, lights flared, sirens sounded, and we were surrounded by humans with guns pointed directly at us. Michael roared and began to shift, but they shot him. I now know it was a tranquilizer that they used on him. His movements slowed, but it wasn't powerful enough to incapacitate him. He kept moving, so they shot him again."

Tears flow out of her eyes, and I move to the bed, putting my arm around her and pulling her close. I rub her arm as she sobs into my chest.

"It's okay," I whisper, trying to comfort her, but she leans back abruptly.

"But it's not," she says, wiping her eyes. "I just stood there. I didn't know what to do or say. I just stood there and watched them shoot my mate over and over again. It wasn't until they were dragging him away that my mind finally caught up to what was happening, and I began to shift. Then they did the same to me. When I woke up, it felt like days later. I was in a cage next to Michael. That was the last time I saw him. The next time I woke up, I was in the cell you found me in. The things they did to me there—"

"You don't need to tell me," I tell her, and she nods. I learned my lesson after going into River's memories. If Andrea's are worse —which I suspect they are—I'm not sure if I can handle it.

"I can still feel the bond," she whispers. "He's still alive, but he's weak." She sinks into me, and her sobs slowly turn to snores. I gently roll her over, tucking her in next to her daughter.

I give them both a quick kiss on the head before striding out the door to find my mate.

The walk out of the pocket world hardly even registers as I think about everything that Andrea just told me. I focus on Michael and the need to find him. Andrea and River need him, but he deserves to be saved regardless. If his time in captivity is anything like either of theirs, I'm not sure if he will be the same man when we find him.

I find Drusilla standing just outside the doorway with Valerie.

"Everything okay, love?" I ask as I bring my arm around her shoulders and pull her close.

"Even better now that you're here," she says, wrapping her arms around my middle.

"Did something happen?" I ask, looking over her head at Valerie.

"Nothing bad," Valerie smiles. "Drusilla is just excited because she met Pearl."

"Pearl? Who's Pearl?" I ask, looking down at Drusilla. Instantly, she gets a huge smile on her face.

"She's a sea nymph!" she whisper-shouts. "They prefer to be called sea nymphs."

"Okay?" I ask, looking up at Valerie and then back at Drusilla.

"She has this amazing healing magic. Did you know that they can heal someone just by touching them?" I nod because I did, in fact, know that. Before we agreed to go into hiding, I served on the supernatural council with two sea nymphs.

"You knew?"

"Yes. I knew a few sea nymphs many years ago."

She waves her hand at me with a laugh. "I keep forgetting that you're really old."

I don't know if I should be offended by that or not. She places a soft kiss on my cheek, and I decide to let it slide.

"Are you done here?" I ask. "You need to get some rest before we take Andrea and River to the academy tomorrow."

"You two go on. I can take over Drusilla's patients," Valerie says.

"Are you sure?" I ask, and she nods.

"I feel shockingly well-rested after a round of nymph healing," the older woman laughs as she heads back toward the tent.

"I'll be right back. I want to run over and see Rayne and Drake quickly before we leave," Drusilla says and begins to walk over to one of the smaller structures. I already know that they have been there studying the blueprints of the other facilities.

"I'll come with you," I growl, snagging her by the waist and pulling her back into me.

Together, we approach the temporary building and the group inside.

"Hey, guys." Rayne is the first one to notice our approach.

"Any news?" I ask gruffly, wanting nothing more than to retire somewhere with my mate. Now that I'm thinking of it, I'm not sure where we will go since Andrea and River are currently using the only bedroom in our pocket world.

"We've settled on some general search areas for at least five facilities in Canada, but we know there are more worldwide," Alaric says with a grim look. Despite this somber news, hope bubbles up from within me at the possibility that Michael could be held in one of those facilities.

"You two are heading back to Orillia tonight?" Drusilla asks, ignoring everyone else and zoning in on Rayne and Drake. They both nod.

Even though she has never seen that horrible place herself, I can feel the anxiety thrumming beneath the surface at the thought of her loved ones heading back.

She steps up to them, wrapping her arms around the two of them in a somber hug.

"Alaric, Phoebe?" I say, pulling my eyes away from my emotional mate.

"What's up?" Phoebe asks, taking the hint and looking away to give them some privacy.

"Would you allow Drusilla and I to use Skarlyt's old room in your basement for the night? My sister and River are sleeping in our cabin."

"I could come with you," Skarlyt interrupts. I turn to find her already standing. "I mean—if you'd rather stay close to them, I could come with you and expand your cabin."

Behind her, Sebastyn is nodding excitedly.

"That would be much appreciated," I agree quickly. I did not enjoy the idea of leaving my niece and sister so far away after having just found them. I also feel certain my mate will feel safer and happier in our pocket world as well.

Drusilla steps back from her quiet conversation with her best friend and brother and back to my side. I reach out and shake each of their hands, wishing them luck.

"Darren, can I talk to you for a minute?" I ask, gesturing just outside.

"Uh, sure," he responds, obviously confused.

"I was hoping to bring Andrea and River to the academy tomorrow. I wanted to make sure that's okay."

His confusion quickly morphs into excitement. "Absolutely. We can meet you there in the morning." He shares a look with Sophia and then with Sarah. "Around noon?"

When each of them nods, he turns back to me.

"That's perfect," I respond, turning back to my mate. She is nearly asleep on her feet. "Thank you for everything, everyone. I think my mate needs to get some sleep."

A round of goodbyes rings out, and I scoop up Drusilla to carry her back toward our pocket world. Sebastyn and Skarlyt follow closely behind. I can see the shimmering opening of the doorway ahead of us.

Surprisingly, both Sebastyn and Skarlyt stay quiet while we walk. It may be because of the sleeping woman in my arms, but I see both their eyes sparkle with interest as we near the portal and walk through. They quickly get to work. They triple the size of the cabin, creating both a bedroom and a separate bathroom for us.

I gently lay my mate on the bed, pulling up the covers and tucking her in gently before leading the witches back outside.

"Thank you," I say warmly.

"You can thank us by letting us come back tomorrow to look around," Sebastyn says.

Skarlyt slaps him in the stomach.

"Of course, we are happy to help," she says. "We are also always happy to learn about interplanar travel as well."

"I'm pretty sure I can arrange another visit," I agree with a chuckle. I show them the way out and close the door behind them once they exit.

With the portal closed, the world is quiet and peaceful again. I head back inside the cabin, slip silently into bed with my mate, and fall asleep quickly.

Chapter Twenty-Four

Drusilla

I don't remember going to bed or falling asleep, but I wake to a giggling bundle of fun jumping up and down on the bed.

"Aunty Dru," River sings with each bounce. I keep my eyes closed, feigning sleep until she moves closer. When she's near enough, I spring up and tickle her sides.

She cries out in surprise before collapsing into giggles.

"What's that you were saying?"

She tries and fails to get words out between her laughs.

"I know exactly what you were doing," I tease. "Do you give up?"

"Yes," she exclaims, and I stop tickling her.

"Are you excited?" I ask, looking into her aquamarine eyes. They look so much brighter now that we've rescued her mother. It's like the weight she was carrying has been lifted.

"Yes! I hope they let me start school with Riley next month."

"I'm sure they will," I tell her honestly. After everything that has happened over the past few months, I imagine everyone will agree to allow younger children to begin attending the school.

"Drusilla? River? Breakfast." Andrea's voice carries in from another room.

"Coming," River calls back, rushing out the door to meet her mother.

I slowly sit up, taking in the room around me for the first time. Unlike the rest of the cabin—which had been modeled after my mate's ancient household—this room is luxurious and ornate. The bed is a luxury, four-poster bed. The floors are a beautiful hardwood and covered with plush, cream-colored rugs. There is a fireplace surrounded by beautiful, black granite tiles in the corner. I only know I'm in the cabin because River is here with me.

I slowly slip out of bed, placing my bare feet on the cold floor, and look down at myself. I am in a cotton nightgown that Andres must've changed me into last night. I pad my way toward another door set into the wall and open it to find a beautiful en suite bathroom. It's simple: a toilet, sink, and shower created out of a mixture of black and white tiles that sparkle in the light.

I quickly brush my teeth and hair with the tools I find on the counter before heading back out and opening another set of doors that leads to a closet. Inside, I find a few of my own clothes that Andres must've unpacked from the bag we brought when we first came to the pocket world.

After dressing, I make my way into the kitchen to find an excited River being scolded by her mother for talking with her mouth full. I can tell Andrea is not angry in earnest because her lips tip up in the corners.

"Morning," I greet her, and she turns to me with a huge smile on her face. She already looks so much better than she did last night. A night of rest and a nice, hot shower have made her look years younger.

"Good morning," she responds, passing me a silver travel mug. I take it from her and cautiously raise it to my nose. I do not want to be rude, but one sniff fills my nose with the metallic scent of blood, and I give her a smile of thanks before raising it to my lips.

"Where is Andres?" I ask.

"He went to get Skarlyt. She's going to teleport us to the academy, but apparently she wanted to explore the pocket world a little before."

"That sounds like Skar. Are you going to show her around little one?" I ask, turning my attention to River.

She begins to respond with a mouth full of pancakes, but she smartly swallows the bite before responding.

"Yup. The sooner I show her around, the sooner we get to go to the academy."

I chuckle. "That's one way to look at it."

Before she can respond, I hear Skarlyt speaking animatedly just outside.

"You better go get started then," I whisper, and she jumps to run out the door, leaving Andrea and me to clean up the kitchen.

By the time we're done cleaning, River returns with Skarlyt pouting behind her.

"Don't worry, Skarlyt. You can come back later and explore more," I call out, knowing that Skarlyt's curious mind is desperate for more time to explore.

"Promise?" she asks, and I laugh.

"Okay, then. I can't teleport us from inside here, so let's head out." She abruptly spins on her heel, heading back out the door. That's where I find my mate, looking sexy as hell and leaning up against the cabin. My eyes roam up and down his body as I approach. When my eyes flit up to meet his, I find him doing the same and I lick my lips.

I run the rest of the way and jump into his waiting arms. I wrap my legs around his waist at the same time our lips meet, and a moan escapes from deep within my chest. I lick at the seam of his mouth, and he opens readily, thrusting his own tongue out to tangle with mine.

"Ahem..." A feminine voice interrupts us, and it is followed by a girlish giggle. I remove my lips from my mate's regretfully before dropping back to the ground.

Andres gives me one last kiss.

"To be continued," he whispers against my lips before we both turn to the others.

Andrea is smiling at us fondly while River giggles. Skarlyt looks sympathetic but annoyed.

"We're ready," I announce, grasping Andres' hand and pulling him to the doorway.

We barely even step through the doorway before Skarlyt is teleporting away with River and Andrea before coming back for Andres and me.

When we finally land in front of the academy, I find both Andrea and River standing there in awe. Their mouths are gaping open as they study the large building before them. Their obvious excitement makes my heart swell. They both deserve to feel like this every second of every day.

Darren and Sophia walk toward us with Riley, and I watch as River breaks away from our group to sprint toward him.

"Their bond is extremely strong," Andrea says in disbelief.

"It is," I admit, not wanting to say anything further about the prophecy and ruin her happy mood.

The tour of the campus goes better than I expected. I had wondered if Andrea would be ready to part with River after being away from her for so long, but I don't think that's something I will need to worry about. It is clear that she's excited for her daughter to have this future ahead of her.

I snag her arm and pull her to the back of the group with me.

"Everything okay, love?" Andres asks when he sees me do this.

"Yup. I just want to talk to your sister for a moment," I explain, blowing him a kiss and linking my arm with Andrea's.

"You wanted to talk to me?" she asks, seeming nervous.

I nod. "You know, they're always looking for teachers."

Her eyes light up, and I know that I'm on the right track. "Specifically, right now they need teachers who would be willing to live on campus."

"Really?" she asks, looking around in awe.

"Really," I confirm. "The school is developing some housing for students to stay in, and they need some adults to stay with them. I thought you might be interested."

Her steps falter, and she spins to look at me.

"I'd live here?"

"You and River would both live here. We'd probably build you your own house unless you wanted to share with others," I explain. I watch as her eyes begin to mist up.

"I hadn't given much thought to where we would live," Andrea admits. "The pocket world is not a permanent solution—it is dangerous to keep it open too long."

"I am not part of the school," I confess. "But I do know everyone who is. I have a feeling they would be happy to have you here if you were interested in staying." I turn and spot our group just up ahead stopped before the gymnasium. Andres is looking back toward us with a smile on his face that proves he has been eavesdropping.

"Are you sure?" she asks, wringing her hands.

"I am," I respond, linking our arms and leading her toward Darren, Sophia, Riley, River. and Skarlyt.

"Hey, guys. How would you feel about Andrea being a faculty member and living here on campus?" I ask simply—nonchalantly solving several problems at once. "You needed some faculty on campus, didn't you?"

Both Darren and Skarlyt immediately beam as they turn to us.

"Gods, yes," Darren admits.

"Oh, my Mother," Skarlyt's relief is evident. "I thought I was going to have to live here with a bunch of teenagers by myself."

The conversation quickly evolves beyond my purview. In a rush of excitement, Darren and Skarlyt pull Andrea forward, taking her around the school once again with a new perspective. They discuss logistics like where they should build her house and which classes she'd be comfortable leading.

"I think you're a mind reader," Andres says, snaking his arms around my middle as I watch his sister speak excitedly with our friends.

"Why's that?" I ask, tipping my head back to look up at him.

"That's exactly what I had hoped to happen," he says, and I smile. I should've known. I knew it felt like he was rushing our visit to the academy.

"You don't think she'll need more time and space to heal?" I ask, voicing my only concern.

He shakes his head. "No. I think it's going to give her the motivation she needs to get better. She's always loved teaching. She used to have a following of younger kids, and she would go around teaching them anything and everything she could. If she figured out how to do it, she was teaching others to as well. I think this will be exactly the normalcy she needs to heal."

"Okay," I concede and melt into his embrace before I remember my next concern. "Andrea told me that it's dangerous to keep the pocket world open for long periods of time. Do we need to find a new house for ourselves?"

He lets go, spinning me around before placing a kiss on my lips. He almost makes me forget my question. He tilts my chin up with his finger as he pulls his lips back.

"First, I would never have left it open long enough for anything bad to happen," he says, and I nod. "It's true that it can distort the space it occupies if left too long. If that happened, there would be a merging of the two planes in the clearing. That could be disastrous."

My brows furrow with worry that it's already been open too long, but Andres continues. "It would take at least a month for that to begin happening, so we don't need to worry about that just yet."

After being reassured, I take his hand in mine and pull him to catch up with everyone else.

The next few days are surreal. Now that we have some time to breathe, we try to sort out why I can now walk in the sun. It's a mystery that started with Rayne and Drake, but I am another chapter that makes even less sense.

Andres and his sister spend a surprising amount of time with Rayne and Valerie. The older oracle possesses some measure of their mother's power, and being together seems to make them all feel some peace.

River invites Riley and Ryker into our pocket world for a sleepover. We share popcorn and watch the stars together. They love it, and we do too.

It makes me long for the day when Andres and I will have our own children running around. As I press my hand to my stomach and feel the little flutter of a heartbeat, I know that I can't wait much longer to tell Andres—that is, if he doesn't already know.

"Are you okay, love?"

Think of the devil. The man in question comes walking over to me and places a kiss on my head.

"Of course. Why wouldn't I be?" I ask.

"I just wondered if the stress of deciding to tell me you're pregnant was finally getting to you," he responds seriously—no smirk to be found.

"You knew?" I ask and slap his chest.

Now he laughs.

"I knew the second the egg took hold. I'm an empath. He or she is another being."

"So, you knew before me?"

"I didn't want to ruin the surprise," he says. I let my anger simmer for a moment. I want to be angry that he didn't tell me the second he found out. I can understand, though, that he wanted me to believe I was the first to know. Haven't we told River to do the exact same thing about Riley being her mate?

"Thank you," I tell him seconds before I place my mouth on his.

As we come up for breath, he steps back.

"The future's going to be a little rough from now on, my love."

"As long as we're together, we can get through anything," I respond, moving both our hands to rest on my stomach. The last month—hell, the last decade—of my life's been rough. Searching through my memories now, I realize just how much I've overcome.

The future is full of uncertainties, but I have faith that everything will turn out all right. As long as I have my mate and the little peanut growing inside me, things will be even better than just all right.

Epilogue

Zeke

Even after eleven years of imprisonment, not a day goes by when the memory of my angel hasn't consumed my thoughts, plagued my dreams, and urged me toward death. If I were a better man, I would have begged to be reunited with her instead, but that is impossible. I'd rather be dead than live with the pain I caused her.

Imagine my surprise when I am finally—finally—rescued only to find my angel among those who have saved me. She is the one person in this world who I am supposed to love and protect above any other, and I now have no claim to her.

I will never be able to forget the pain on her face as I spat the words of rejection at her. She crumpled to the ground, her hair still wild from our lovemaking and my seed still dripping down her thigh.

It took everything I had to say those words. It broke me just as much as it broke her, but I was unable to show it. I wanted to keep her safe, and being near me was not safe for her. My only comfort was the fact that I knew she wouldn't be truly alone when I left her. She couldn't have known that I was not her only mate, but I knew he would be able to put the pieces back together and make her whole again.

My brother is the better man anyway. When I ran away from my responsibilities, Axel stepped into them with honor. I didn't want to feel the restrictions of staying within our sleuth, but he was strong enough to be what they needed.

I know it hurt him deeply when I left. After all, we share the same half of a soul. We are identical twins. We shared the same womb, the same mind, and the same everything. Feeling his pain had me struggling to take the steps away from him, but he must have known my pain too.

I sneak small looks at my angel from across the room. I wish that I could grab her and tell her it was all a mistake. I know I won't get the chance if she sees me here.

My mate is a strong woman. I can see how the years after my rejection have hardened her. Where she was soft, caring, and loving, she now has a slight slump in her shoulders when she thinks no one is looking. It kills me knowing that I am the one who put that exhaustion there. Why hasn't my brother found her yet?

Did I make a mistake? Was I really her only mate? No, that's impossible. As rare as it is for identical twins to be born, it's even more rare for those twins to have separate mates.

She glances my way but looks past me. Perhaps she feels me watching her, but she doesn't truly see my face. Her eyes sparkle with the evidence of unshed tears.

I try to look away and hide my face. After all, the last thing I want to do is cause her more pain, but I am unable to hide.

As her eyes return to mine, I see the recognition dawning on her face. I have only a moment's notice before she begins screaming.

"Get him the fuck out of here!" She raises her finger to point at me. "Get him out of here! Now!" I watch as she loses all strength and crumples to the ground, her body wracked by hard sobs. I want nothing more than to rush over and comfort her, but eleven years of torture has left me unable to move.

There's a shocked silence around her, but she is quickly surrounded by other women. They gather around her a flurry of support, and I am thankful. If I can't comfort her, at least she won't be alone.

One of the women stands and turns to study the patients in the beds around me. There is fire in her eyes and a purple glow surrounding her.

"Which one of you rejected Opal?" she asks, her voice sounding more like a rumble of the thunder above than a woman's voice.

It takes me longer than I would like it to, but I throw off the blanket and stand on shaky legs. It is stupid of me to admit to it, but I take a few weak steps forward anyway. The least I can do is be honest.

"Me."

"You!" She points at me, venom in her voice. "I banish you from these lands. Until Opal finds it in her heart to forgive you, you will not step foot on any land belonging to the Westwood pack or coven."

I hang my head in shame. I know it is what I deserve, but I am exhausted from my constant regret, my recent rescue, and now this banishment. I know there is nothing that I can say to fix this, but I have to try.

"I understand," I begin. "For what it's worth, I'm sorry—"

"Don't," she cuts me off. "Just don't. Leave and don't ever return."

With that, I make my walk of shame past the large group. I can barely keep my legs under me, but there is no way to avoid the eyes all around me. Each person watches my trek with a mixture of hate and pity.

As I pass Darren and Alaric, I give them a small nod of my head as they whisper to each other.

I pray to the gods above for death. I lived with my actions for eleven years knowing that I would never see her again. I had made a kind of peace with the fact that I would never have the chance to change anything. I was trapped in that laboratory, so I had no choice.

The pain almost killed me then. How will I be able to live in a world where she is so close, but I am still unable to see or touch her? I won't.

I also know that the man waiting just outside for me won't let me die either. I wish I could return my brother's embrace as he rushes toward me, but I can't.

I long for the peace only death can give me now.

Somehow, I'll find a way to put an end to this misery.

* * *

Want more from the Westwood Pack?
Of course, you do!
Information on Book 7, Bound by Fate here:
https://fdfairauthor.wixsite.com/website

About the Author

F.D. Fair is the author of the Westwood Pack Series. As an avid reader of Paranormal Romance Novels for the past 20 years, she turned her love of everything paranormal into steamy True Mate novels with a twist.

F.D. Fair lives and works in southern Ontario, Canada and

spends her time when she is not working or writing with the loves of her life—Her husband and 3 boys.

She is as weird as they come but is proud of it. Embracing her weirdness makes for some great stories.

Sign up for FD Fair's Newsletter:
https://dashboard.mailerlite.com/forms/76323/
5809623843156931o/share

Make sure to stalk her...

Instagram:
https://www.instagram.com/f.d.fairauthor
Facebook:
https://www.facebook.com/profile.php?id=1000716886485 16
Goodreads:
https://www.goodreads.com/author/show/21734156.F_D_Fair
Twitter:
https://twitter.com/FdFair
Bookbub:
https://www.bookbub.com/authors/f-d-fair

More from Foundations

Max Cherry

~Supernatural Thriller~

GET IT HERE: https://www.foundationsbooks.net/library/
supernatural/

Max Cherry was born in Thorn, Mississippi on what he believes is a hotbed of psychic activity.

Sherman Lancaster has lived 1 1 9 years. The only thing he fears is living 1 1 9 more.Sherman wields a divine sword named DeeDee and delivers God's justice to those who cross the line.Sherman's two great-grandsons are coming to stay with him. The boys believe it's because their mother can't afford daycare. Sherman knows the truth—one of the boys will become his apprentice.Sherman has sent legions of demons back to hell. He's killed enough men to decimate a small country—but the odds are stacked against him this time. Before an apprentice can be named, Sherman must confront an enemy who threatens to unravel everything and doom him to another 1 1 9 years behind the sword. He's old and he's tired.Sherman Lancaster lives by a simple code to which there are no exceptions:The Guilty must pay.

Foundations Book Publishing

Our mission is to exceed the expectations of our authors and the reading community with an uncompromising commitment to quality, individualism and personal pride. We measure our success one book at a time.

You can find more great works in multiple genres including Romance, Literary Fictions, Thrillers, Suspense, Young Adult, and more!

Visit us at FoundationsBooks.net

www.ingramcontent.com/pod-product-compliance
Lightning Source LLC
Chambersburg PA
CBHW050407260626
47156CB00003B/910